Consenting
Behavior

P. S. BAILEY

PROLOGUE

"Jason let me in," Ronnie pounded her impatience on his condominium door. "Damn it! You know I still have a key, don't make me use it."

"What are you doing here?" Jason opened the door half-way, placing his body across the opening. "I thought we were on a break. And keep your voice down. You know how nosy they are." He pointed at the adjoining condo. "I can feel them listening through the walls."

"Screw 'em," Ronnie said as she brushed Jason aside and entered his apartment. "And just because you've decided we need a break doesn't mean we can't have a little fun does it?" Ronnie asked, making a beeline for the wet bar.

"Yeah, it kinda does." He followed her into the living room, not in the least surprised by her boldness. He watched as she poured a healthy measure of Scotch in a glass and splashed ice cubes in after it. Taking a small sip as she walked from behind the bar, Ronnie stopped in front of him. Tipping her head slightly to meet his eyes, she gave him a sly grin and offered him the glass.

"Thanks," Jason said. Accepting the drink, and the fact that she wasn't leaving anytime soon, he sat down on the couch and patted the seat beside him. "We have to talk."

Forty-five minutes later, the pair decided upon a reconciliation and Ronnie led Jason to his exercise room, which also served as a bondage chamber, where she strapped him naked to the St Andrew's cross standing in the middle of the room. Picking a deerskin flogger from the assortment she found in the closet, she twirled the supple fabric against his genitals. A short time later, despite the alcohol in his system, Jason rewarded her efforts. Releasing him from the straps and handing him the flogger, she mounted the cross, her anticipation palpable as Jason tightened the wrist and ankle restraints. His ministrations quickly had her wanting more than the whip and as Jason entered her, he placed his hands on her shoulders.

"Higher!" Ronnie pleaded, wanting Jason to put his hands around her neck. "Please," she whispered, urgently.

Her desperate pleadings for strangulation brought him to his senses. He released the restraints, backed away from the cross and left the room.

Jason staggered into his bedroom, the alcohol and sex beginning to take their toll. He flopped down on the bed, head-first.

"If you're so committed to being done with the scene, why do you still have all that bondage stuff here?" Ronnie asked, following Jason into the bedroom.

"I didn't say I was dead," Jason replied, hearing the bed squeak as she sat down on the other side. "Most of it is yours anyway," Jason mumbled into the pillow. "I thought you might want it back."

"You keep it. I can always get more." Ronnie snuggled next to his prone body. "I'm sorry, Jason, I know you're serious about not wanting to do bondage anymore." She began massaging his back. "I've missed you so much."

Truthfully, he'd missed her too. He turned to his side, she spooned him, running her hand slowly up and down his side. Tall and blonde, Ronnie was a successful, smart businesswoman, and Jason could easily see himself spending the rest of his life with her. Surprisingly, it was the sex that was the wedge between them. Her appetite for kink, while stimulating at first, was too extreme for Jason's more reserved desires. Her predilection for breath play was alarming and was what had driven him to the breakup. Jason had been clear then, or so he thought, that if they had a future together, there wouldn't be any more of that particular activity, but as Ronnie's hand slid between his legs and her slow rubbing became faster stroking, Jason's concerns were pushed aside.

Getting up twenty minutes later, Ronnie headed into the bathroom as Jason snuggled deeper into the pillows. "Sorry about your new girlfriend being dead," she said as she turned the shower on.

"What girlfriend?" he muffled.

"Don't deny it. I saw you with her at the bar the other night." Ronnie leaned on the bathroom door frame waiting for the water to warm up. "That's how

I recognized her in the paper."

"Her name's Lindsay and she's not my girlfriend...and what do you mean she's dead?" Suddenly Jason was wide awake.

"I thought you knew," Ronnie said, surprised at his reaction. "She died last night." Ronnie turned back into the bathroom. "It's in today's paper."

Jason's bare feet hit the floor and he was halfway down the hall before she'd finished her sentence. Downstairs on the entryway table, Jason spotted the unrolled paper next to the unopened mail. Thumbing through the pages, he found the write-up on Lindsay and confirmed her death for himself. He threw the paper back on the table and took the steps back upstairs two at a time, he called to Ronnie, "You have to get out of here, now!"

Realizing she couldn't hear him over the running water of the shower, Jason barged into the bathroom. Screeching the curtain along the rod, he reached past her into the stall and cut the water off.

"Jason, what the hell?" Ronnie sputtered.

"You have to get out of here." Jason grabbed a towel from the rack and threw it around her.

"Why? What's going on?" Ronnie followed Jason into the bedroom, patting herself mostly dry. "What's going on?" she asked again as he gathered her clothes from the other room and brought them to her. "Jason! Stop! You're scaring me."

"I'm sorry." He stopped long enough to help her finish dressing. "I can't get into it right now," Jason said harsher than he intended. "But you have to leave, and I have to find my sister."

"Damn it, Maddy, pick up the phone." Jason ended the call and punched the numbers again. Once again, it went straight to voicemail. Not that he blamed her for that. For a long time, his calls had meant nothing but trouble for his big sister. Maddy was five years his senior, and she had been everything to him growing up. While having children seemed like a good idea to their parents, raising them wasn't something either one of them had the time for. Jason had spent most of his childhood following Maddy around, and to her credit, she never made him feel unwanted. Maddy taught him how to ride a bike, taught him how to play baseball, gave him tips on how to treat women and helped him through his first relationship when it ultimately crashed and burned.

The trouble for Jason really began when Maddy left for college. She wasn't there to act as mediator between him and his parents. Their constant criticism, while motivating for Maddy, had only made Jason angry and rebellious. The more they pushed him to achieve, the more he failed. By the time he graduated high school, his relationship with his parents was extremely strained and he was ecstatic when his father got him into a school halfway across the country.

Going into his office after packing an overnight bag, Jason picked up a flash drive and a pad of paper from the desk, his thoughts returning to Lindsay. Meeting four years earlier, when his website business was still in its start-up stages, he'd set up her website. The two immediately hit it off and began dating. Their fire had blazed hot and heavy for a couple of months before it sizzled out, but uncharacteristically for Jason and he suspected for Lindsay as well, they remained friends. She did his taxes every year, helped him to streamline his business accounts and he kept her website updated. They had sex occasionally: when they were unattached, before he met Ronnie, and before Lindsay started dating someone she didn't discuss on their monthly meet-ups. Twirling the drive in his free hand as he wrote on the pad, Jason hoped Lindsay's death had nothing to do with what was on it.

Lindsay had messaged him yesterday afternoon, knowing she was more likely to reach him through his computer than his phone. She asked him to meet her at the Tumbledown Bar later in the evening.

Arriving early, Jason ordered himself a drink and waited. And waited. His texts went unanswered and as the early evening diners shifted to a heavier drinking crowd, he was beginning to think she'd stood him up. Finally, tired of the waitress giving him the evil eye for taking up a high dollar tipping table that was currently netting her nothing, he got up to leave only to see Lindsay searching the crowd for him. Spotting him, Lindsay smiled and waved. Moments later as she sat down across from him, Jason couldn't help but notice her disheveled and flushed appearance.

"Sorry, I'm late," she apologized, trying unsuccessfully to withhold a grin which belied what she'd said.

"Wow!" Jason said, recognizing the look. "New boyfriend? I think someone, meaning you just got laid." He waved their waitress over to get Lindsay a drink.

She smiled mischievously at him. "That obvious?"

"Only to me, and anyone else who has had sex with you." Jason laughed. "I knew you had a new fish on the line, but why didn't you answer my texts earlier. We could've rescheduled. But now that you're here, why don't you tell me all the gory details."

"Because I'm not ready to share him yet," Lindsay said, pulling the flash drive Jason now held from her purse. "I wanted to give this back to you and put your mind at ease about Nick."

Picking up on her use of his first name, Jason said, "I'm not as good as you with accounting, but as you know, I do my own books and I saw two sets of ledgers there, one from his accounting firm, the same one you work for, and one set Nick made up showing the Hollowell Clinic is making a profit. Why would he do that?" Jason asked.

"I don't know but doing so doesn't mean he's doing anything illegal. How did you get this anyway?"

"I was updating the website at the clinic and he was acting weird, like he didn't want me to find something. I've never trusted that asshole, so I copied what I could and got out of there."

"He's not an asshole," Lindsay hissed, then realizing she'd overreacted, she added, "I've talked to him a few times at the office. He seems nice."

"I'm getting the impression you've done more than talk," Jason said. "Am I right?"

"Yes," Lindsay said, hoping to leave the extent of their relationship unclear and aware Jason would know if she was lying.

"You were with him before you got here," Jason said, putting the clues together.

"Yes," Lindsay admitted.

"You're aware that he's married to my sister, right?" Jason asked, sarcastically.

"I wasn't when we first started seeing each other, but he's going to leave her. That should make you happy, I know how much you hate him."

"What is it about this guy?" Jason asked, shaking his head. "He's lying to you, Lindsay. But I guess, you'll have to find that out on your own. Did you tell him that I have a copy of his files?"

"No, but I asked him why he made the false ledgers and he told me they were for budgeting purposes, and I believe him. I also told him if I find out he's publishing false documents, I'll have to tell my boss."

"He didn't ask you how you found out about them?"

"No, he said the ledgers didn't matter anymore," Lindsay said.

"What did he mean by that?" Jason asked.

"I don't know," Lindsay answered, exasperated. "All I know is we love each other, and he wouldn't do anything illegal."

"Only immoral."

"What are you going to do?" Lindsay asked, concern in her voice.

"I'm going to protect my sister in whatever way I can," Jason responded.

Now, less than twenty-four hours later, Lindsey was dead. There had to be a connection to Nick.

Finishing the note, Jason ripped it from the pad, then sealed it in an envelope. He grabbed his lockbox from the shelf above his desk and placed the envelope and the flash drive into it, locking it securely. Dialing Maddy again, he headed into his exercise room, the smell of Ronnie's perfume still hanging in the air. Kneeling in front of the closet, Jason pushed a couple of boxes to the side, lifted the plank from the floor and slipped the box into the hole underneath. He slid the board back into place, running his hand over the seams and scooted the boxes back over the plank. He dialed Maddy's number again, expecting and getting voicemail. He left a short message after the beep. Satisfied there was nothing more he could do, Jason reached to grab his overnight bag. He felt an electrical charge passing through his body and then his world turned black.

CHAPTER 1

S pewing gravel as he pulled into the parking lot of Hidden Lake Forest Preserve, Sam Bartell spotted his former police partner Andy Miller stretching against a nearby oak tree. He parked alongside his Toyota SUV and joined him as he warmed up for their bi-weekly run.

"You're late," Andy grunted, as he lunged on his left than his right leg. "Reminds me of the good 'ole days when you were still on the force," he laughed.

"I was never late for work," Sam said, stretching his own legs. "And my memory of those days isn't clouded by age." Notwithstanding how his career ended, the five years he'd spent on the Chicago Police Force were unforgettable.

"Just for that, rookie, you're going to suffer," Andy promised, taking off his jacket to reveal a sweat wicking tee he'd received from one of the many Chicagoland half marathons he'd ran over the years.

"I've known you for ten years, Andy," Sam declared, following him back to their cars. "When are you going to stop calling me a rookie?"

"When you stop acting like one." Andy chuckled at Sam's irritation and threw the jacket in the Toyota's trunk. Slamming it shut, he said, "Come on, we're burning daylight and unlike you, I can't show up to work whenever I feel like it." Andy took off toward the trail head.

"I can't either if I want to pay the bills," Sam shouted to his back.

The sun was slightly over the horizon and the two men saw their breath as they ran side by side along the lake. The brisk wind swirled fallen leaves around their feet and Sam knew the days of running in winter sleet and snow were coming soon. Andy had been running these trails for years, dragging Sam along when his relationship with Maddy went to hell and his career with the force ended. His first time out with Andy had been an eyeopener. Keeping himself in shape had been a part of his job as an officer and Sam was certain he could match anything Andy could throw at him. Reality hit around mile two when Sam had to quit, huffing and puffing and Andy left him in his dust. As the months of running passed and the miles added up, Sam's endurance built along with his appreciation of the sport. Now he found his runs rejuvenating and mentally healing.

"It's called Hidden Lake Forest Preserve," Andy said, cutting into Sam's thoughts, "but that's a misnomer."

"Really?" Sam inquired, half listening. Andy loved Chicago history almost too much and shared it whenever he had the chance.

"There's actually two lakes, Round Lake, which is what we're running around and Eagle Lake which is deeper in the Preserve and isn't accessible. As the name suggests, the area is a nesting ground for endangered eagles. I've seen them a couple of times. I'm sure I've told you this before."

"Maybe once, or twice."

Finishing their first circuit of the three-mile trail, they stopped by their cars to get a drink. "How's work?" Andy asked, inquiring about the private investigating agency Sam had opened after quitting the force. "You haven't said much about it lately."

"The usual, bail-jumpers, missing people, an occasional adultery case," Sam replied. "But it's steady. I don't worry about paying the bills so much anymore."

"Good to know," Andy confided. "I was concerned about you for a while."

"I was too but having Elyse has made all the difference." "

This from the man who never wanted an assistant," Andy teased.

When Elyse Fowler had first appeared at his office three years ago asking for a job Sam had openly laughed in her face. "I can't afford a secretary," he told her flat out and aimed her towards the door.

"Assistant," Elyse corrected him. "And you can't afford not to hire me. My computer savvy will help you solve cases quicker and it will allow you to offer services that you alone don't have the time to provide-electronic background checks, cyber investigations, just to name a few. But the biggest asset I can be is protecting your ass. You shouldn't work alone in your profession."

Looking at her golden blonde shoulder length hair encircling her pale face,

Sam could believe Elyse spent a lot of time behind a computer screen. But it was her eyes that caught his attention, the deepest of aqua blue, they sparkled as she pled her case, but he also recognized those eyes.

"I know you from somewhere...don't I?" he asked, searching his memory.

"I have one of those faces," she brushed him off, lowered her eyes.

"No, you don't," Sam countered, then the needle dropped, Sam remembered her. Elyse was the loan officer at his bank. He didn't see her frequently, he did most of his banking through the little cylinder of the drive through. The only time he'd seen her this close was when she'd denied his application for a loan to start his agency five years ago. She'd said he was too much of a risk. Even as she denied him, he could tell she was going places. Barely twenty-five, by his estimation, she was First American's chief loan officer with CFO and several other letters within sight. Why she was standing in front of him almost begging for a job mystified him and as with all mysteries that crossed his path, he needed an answer. He invited Elyse to take a seat in his inner office.

"Tell me why you're really here," Sam said. "And believe me, I'll know if you're lying."

"I won't lie to you, Sam. Do you mind me calling you Sam?" her blue eyes questioned.

"Not yet," Sam answered.

"Good. First off, I know you remember me from the bank. I quit."

"Get tired of shooting down people's dreams?" Sam asked, more bitterly than he'd intended.

"I approved a lot more loans than I denied, and I wanted to give you one, but I couldn't get it past my boss. I'm sorry, but you would have done the same thing."

"Why did you leave?"

"Do you remember about a year ago when the bank got robbed?"

"Vaguely, but I don't know the details."

"A man went up to one of the tellers and gave her a note, demanding money. He said he had a gun and if she touched her alarm, he'd kill her. Her name was Anna..." she paused.

"She was shot, if my memory is correct," Sam said. "Were you there at the time?"

"I saw the whole thing from my office. You probably don't remember, but there were glass panels on either side of the door to my office and I could see Anna's station from my desk. I knew something was wrong, I could tell by her face."

"What did you do?"

"What I was trained to do. A.D.D. Avoid, Deny, Defend. I pushed the silent alarm, turned off the lights in my office and locked the door. By that time, Anna was shoving cash from her drawer into a bag the robber handed her, and she was terrified. I had to do something, but I didn't know what, so I just stood there, frozen in the dark."

"What happened?" Sam asked.

"Something spooked him. I don't know what it was, but the gun went off and he sprinted out of the bank with the bag of money. He was never caught."

"What about Anna?" Asking but sure he knew the answer.

"The bullet hit her in the heart. I got to her in time to hold her as she bled out."

"I'm sorry, but I hope you aren't blaming yourself for Anna's death. There wasn't anything you could do."

"After nine months of therapy, I know that, but I don't want to work in the public sector anymore."

"I can understand that, but why here?"

"Because I can use my computer skills to help people and I'm truly sorry I couldn't get you that loan."

"I believe the first part, but not the last."

"I *am* sorry I couldn't get you a loan," Elyse asserted.

"Yes, but that's not why you're here. You want me to find the robber."

"I'm impressed, but no, I want you to help *me* find the robber."

"Why would I do that? This is an active case, the police could take my license or worse if I interfere."

"Now who's lying. If we solve this case, I know there's nothing more you'd like to do than throw it in the faces of the people who fired you." She stared at him with those piercing blue eyes and dared him to deny it.

"Let's be clear, I wasn't fired. I quit. I'll hire you for a probationary period. You work on my cases first and your vigilante case second. Got it?"

"Got it. When do you want me to start?"

Coming out of his reverie, Sam agreed with Andy "It's true, I thought I didn't need an assistant, but her computer skills are amazing. We have companies calling from all over the state asking for background checks now. The money they're willing to pay is absurd."

"Not too absurd to take, though," Andy laughed.

"We charge an hourly rate, Andy. That doesn't change because of the client. But if they offer Elyse a bonus, I see no problem with that."

"Most people would take what they could get," Andy scoffed. "When are you going to stop being a boy scout?"

They ran on in silence for a while, stopping at their cars again when they finished six miles.

"What happened to that fancy belt you usually wear that holds your water bottles?" Sam asked as they rehydrated.

"Couldn't find it this morning. I thought I'd left it here in my trunk, but I guess not."

Sam poked around in the packed trunk, saw the buckle of the belt sticking out of a pile of newspapers and pulled it out. "Maybe if you didn't have all this crap in here you could find something."

"Don't start on me…" Andy was interrupted by Sam's phone, the volume turned to the maximum. "No phones allowed on the trails," Andy scolded.

"It's Elyse," Sam said, reading the name on the screen. "I'm guessing she went to the office early. And it must be important, she knows we're running this morning." He stepped away from Andy and accepted the call.

"I'm sorry to bother you, Sam, but there were several messages left on the machine late yesterday afternoon by the same woman asking you to call her back."

"Who was it?"

"Madeline Maxwell. She sounded so desperate I thought you might want to call her first thing this morning." Sam asked for the number, ended the call and dialed it, moving further away from Andy and turning his back to him.

"Maddy, Sam here," he didn't know what else to say.

"Sam…I thought you weren't going to return my calls. I'd given up."

Her voice hadn't changed since the last time he'd heard it six years ago, and it still bore through his soul. Swallowing the lump in his throat, he replied, "I was in court yesterday afternoon and didn't get this message until this morning. What can I do for you?"

"I need your help." Sam could hear the tremor in her voice and knew she was close to tears. "My brother was murdered--and I want you to find his killer."

A few minutes later, Sam ended the call and walked toward Andy who was standing next to his car.

"Who was that?" Andy got a look at Sam's bloodless face. "Did someone die?" he asked half-jokingly.

"No, but I have to grab a shower and get to the office." Hoping he would let that be the end of it, Sam headed around Andy toward his car.

"Wait a minute." Andy stepped in front of him effectively cutting him off from the driver's side door. "Tell me what's going on. Is it Elyse? Is she alright?"

"She's fine," Sam said, letting silence fall between them as he deliberated on whether or not to tell him it had been Maddy on the phone. Concluding that Andy was going to find out anyway and that the sooner this particular confrontation was over with the better, he spilled. "It was Maddy. Her brother died a few weeks ago and she wants me to look into it."

"Are you out of your mind?" Andy asked in disbelief.

"I'm meeting her at Jason's apartment later on this morning. I want to stop by the office on the way to see what I can find out about his death."

"His death was an accidental suicide," Andy said. "Simple as that."

"You knew about Jason's death and didn't think to tell me?"

"I didn't realize he was Maddy's brother until now."

"What have you heard?"

"Not much really," Andy said, averting his eyes. Sam knew what that meant, he was lying.

"Maddy thinks he was murdered."

"Of course, she does," Andy said, rolling his eyes.

"Was murder considered?" Sam asked.

"All I know is the scuttlebutt that goes around the station. I heard he hung himself nude from a closet pole. I assume foul play was ruled out because the case was closed within a day or two."

"There's more you're not telling."

"I'm telling you that you should stay out of this. The last thing you need right now is Maddy Richards coming back into your life."

"Don't worry about me. I know what I'm doing."

"Famous last words, but ask yourself this...why is she calling you and not any other private investigator out there?"

CHAPTER 2

C alling Sam was a decision Maddy hadn't come to easily. As she paced in front of the toaster, she was still uncertain their meeting at Jason's apartment was a good idea. Jason's death was still an open wound and she didn't need the torrent of emotions seeing Sam would inevitably bring to the forefront. Sam had been distant and to the point on the phone, but she knew him well enough to recognize the same apprehension in his voice. She also knew he was the only one who would help her, even though he was having second thoughts. Contacting Sam at all wouldn't have been necessary if the police had done their job. Their incompetent handling of the investigation of her brother's death had her fuming as she ate her bagel. But thinking of the police also brought back the memory of how she'd met Sam. The memory of how young and naive he'd been when they first met always brought a smile to her face. How he loved her so unconditionally and, in the end, how their breakup had been messy and prolonged, nothing like the beginning had been...

She'd met Sam early in the school year eight years ago, her second-grade students spent part of their morning cutting and pasting fall leaves to decorate the wall of windows on the east side of their classroom. After knocking on the door, two policemen approached the front of the room, their progress met by oohs and aahs from the kids and then silence when they reached the front. She had a brief conversation with the elder officer and then turning to her students, she announced, "This is Officer Andy, and this is Officer...I'm sorry, I didn't catch your name." She turned to Andy's much younger partner, for the first time focusing her full attention on him.

She was momentarily stunned and not sure why. He was attractive, but she'd dated plenty of handsome men. His demeanor suggested shyness, but she suspected there was a fire behind his hazel eyes. Most of all, he looked lost and the impulse to hug him came suddenly. It took all her willpower to suppress it as he spoke to her for the first time.

"Sam," he responded, his voice a whisper, louder as he continued, "but I'm only here as an observer. Andy does all the talking."

"Officer Sam," Maddy said to the class. "They're here today to discuss stranger danger. Does anyone know what that is?" Half of the hands in the classroom went up. "Good. Now I want all of you to listen closely to what Officer Andy is going to tell you," Maddy said, giving the floor to Andy. Turning to Sam, she took his hand as if he was one of her students and led him to the back of the room. They sat at second-grade-sized desks and listened as Andy began his presentation.

Sensing Sam's unease, Maddy leaned toward him and whispered, "You look too young to be a policeman. How long have you been on the force?"

"Two years now, believe it or not, all partnered with Andy up there."

"Well, thanks for coming today. I'm sure this isn't all that exciting for you guys."

"Not true, Andy's been talking about this all week. He loves doing these presentations. His own children are grown and live out of state. He doesn't get to see them or his grandchildren very often."

"How about you?"

"Not so much," Sam admitted.

"Not into kids? I can see how uncomfortable you are sitting there." She brushed the sleeve of his uniform and felt an electric current travel up her arm. Now she was the uncomfortable one. She blushed and looking into his eyes, saw that he felt it too. Caught in his stare, she felt like she'd been awakened from a deep sleep.

"Yeah...no," Sam answered, reluctantly breaking eye contact. "I like kids, but I think our time would be better spent catching bad guys."

"This is important too," Maddy said, somberly, her demeanor changing instantly. "You don't realize how seriously these kids will take stranger danger coming from a police officer as opposed to me or the principal." Her reproach was met with a broad grin. "You find this amusing?"

"No ma'am," Sam denied. "I find you amusing."

Finished for the day, Maddy walked to her car in the school's nearly empty parking lot, thankful she'd brought her sweater as the fall wind stirred the real leaves around her feet. Still pumped from her students' enthusiastic feedback from Officer Andy's presentation, her spirits were quickly squelchèd when she flooded her car for the second time in a week. Grabbing her purse and paper stuffed valise, Maddy exited the car slamming the door and kicking it for good measure, stubbing her toe in the process.

"I'm going to let you sit for a while," Maddy reprimanded. "But you'd better start when I get back or I'll have you hauled away as junk." Maddy began walking the half mile to her apartment, her mind quickly turning from her car to the stack of grading that awaited her when she got there. Deep in thought, she didn't notice when a patrol car slowed and pulled alongside her, matching her pace.

"Need a ride?" She heard a voice ask through the open passenger side window.

"No, thanks," she said waving over her shoulder and quickening her pace. "I'm right up the street here."

"You shouldn't be walking alone. Haven't you heard of stranger danger?"

Maddy stopped and turned to peer inside the now stopped car. She went to the window and leaned in, giving Sam a mischievous grin. "Do you know that only ten percent of abductions are from strangers. Most are done by people you know."

"I've heard that before," Sam returned her smile in kind. "Good thing you don't know me at all."

"Why are you here? School's out," Maddy asked, hopping into the passenger seat.

"Forgot this in a classroom," Sam said, picking up his cap. "I've already lost two of these. Sarge says I have to pay for the next one I lose."

"Rookie mistakes," Maddy teased, wondering if it was a mistake or a well thought out plan to see her again. "Where's Andy?" she asked.

"We were almost back at the station before I realized I'd left it, so I dropped him off," Sam said, pulling back into traffic.

"I can tell you admire him a lot."

"He's the best. He's been on the force twenty-five years. Could've been a Captain by now, but Andy says real cops are on the street every day, out there putting their lives on the line."

"He's right about that, especially in Chicago," Maddy said. "I admire his dedication--and yours."

"Working the streets every day is great for Andy, but I intend to be a detective," Sam said confidently. "I hope to be promoted within the next couple of years," he paused. "Where do you live, by the way?"

"I was wondering if you were going to ask or if you had already looked it up, which would be kinda creepy," Maddy said, laughing. "My apartment is right up there," she pointed at a brownstone building among a row of similar brownstones. "My car should be ready shortly."

"At the shop?" Sam asked.

"No, I keep flooding the stupid thing. It'll start if I let it sit for a while."

"How about I take you to dinner while we wait?" Sam didn't wait for her answer as he drove past her apartment.

"Where are you from?" Maddy asked, after they'd placed their dinner order and gotten their drinks from a spirited waitress with an abundance of restaurant flare.

"Is it that easy to tell I'm not from around here?" Sam asked, disappointed.

"The way you pronounce some words is definitely Southern, but not Deep South. I would guess southern Missouri?"

"Northern Arkansas, but close," Sam laughed. "And I've worked very hard at losing my colloquialisms. I guess I haven't worked hard enough."

"Why would you do that? Aren't they a part of who you are?" Maddy asked.

"I hadn't thought of it that way," Sam said, as the waitress checked on their drinks and brought a blooming onion. "How long have you been a teacher?" he asked, after the waitress had left.

"This is my third year. Teaching second graders is so much fun," smiling at the thought of her kids. "They want to learn, and they are like little sponges, they learn so fast."

"By middle school, they think they know everything," Sam added.

"So true," Maddy agreed. "Now it's my turn to ask the questions. Why did you become a police officer?"

"My father is a sheriff back home. Dalton is a very small town, the occasional drunk on Saturday night, kids getting into mischief, that kind of stuff. I knew early on I wanted to go into police work, but I couldn't stay there."

"So, you came to the big city," Maddy said.

"Yes ma'am, I did," Sam grinned, causing his dimples to deepen.

"I bet you left a lot of broken hearts back in Dalton," Maddy teased.

"If I did, it's news to me," Sam blushed, and Maddy realized what a rookie he truly was. "But I did leave my mom and dad disappointed and more than a little worried about my moving to Chicago."

"I know about disappointed parents. My dad wanted me to become a doctor. He's a cardiologist at Northwestern. I went through a year of pre-med before I worked up the courage to tell him I wanted to be a teacher."

"Is he still disappointed?" Sam asked.

"Resigned, but hopeful I'll change my mind when I get teaching out of my system."

"Siblings?"

"A younger brother, Jason who starts college at UCLA in a couple of months."

"Medical school?" Sam asked.

"No, another disappointment, I'm afraid. He's into computers."

"Why California? Tired of the cold winters?"

"He needed a change and to get away from our parents truthfully. They were much harder on him growing up. I still remember when my mom let me hold him for the first time. I was thrilled to have a baby brother. Even with the five-year age gap, we were close. He went everywhere with me."

The waitress interrupted with their dinner and asked, "Anything else I can get you folks?" as she placed their food on the table.

"No, thanks," they said in unison. Maddy continued their conversation between bites of steak and potatoes, waving her utensils as she talked.

"I spent my teen years getting good grades and staying out of trouble. Not to say there weren't a few close calls," she smiled wickedly at Sam, assuring him there were. "I advised Jason to do the same, but he couldn't--I blame all that testosterone you men have pumping through your system." She waved her fork in a circle in front of him. "He started rebelling shortly before I left for college, fights at school, bad grades. After I left, things got worse and he was expelled from a couple of schools before he finally graduated from a private school. When I did come home for the summer breaks and holidays, he was rarely there, hanging with his own crowd and arguing with my dad when he was home," Maddy paused. "I don't want you to get the wrong idea. My dad can be overbearing, but he loves us very much, he's just not the best at showing it. Kids aren't like surgery, where the patients are anesthetized and can't talk back."

"You haven't said much about your mother. Why's that?"

"Not much to talk about really." Maddy frowned. "She loves being a doctor's wife and spends most of her time doing charity work. American Cancer Society, Children's Miracle Network, Red Cross and every heart charity there is. She thinks there isn't any reason I can't spend my life doing the same thing."

"Someone has to do it and it sounds like she's good at it."

"Charity starts at home and spreads abroad," Maddy said, bitterly. "Maybe if she'd spent more time at home, things would've been different with Jason...but enough about me, it's your turn to talk."

And talk he did, through the rest of dinner and dessert. Maddy thought she had opened a dam, the words spilling out as if they had been held back for a long time. Sitting across from him, listening to his soft, yet strong voice, Maddy fell in love. Afterwards, he drove her back to her car, which started on the first try. Resisting an overpowering desire to invite him into her apartment, Maddy reached into her purse, pulled out a sharpie marker and writing her phone number on the palm of his hand she said, "I know you could look it up, but this way you won't forget."

◆◆◆

She did invite him into her apartment the next day when he called. Sam came over for dinner and they'd barely finished the spaghetti she'd made for him before they were in bed together, garlic breath unnoticed.

That was the way it was with Sam. She wanted him all the time, missed him desperately when he went to Arkansas to visit his family or attended training sessions away from home. Sometimes it scared her the way she needed him, depended on him, but those fears didn't stop her from asking him to move in with her five months after they'd started dating. The lease on his apartment was up and he was paying outrageous rent for a one-bedroom basement apartment that flooded every time it rained. They were together three years before she broke up with him, certain it was her only option.

Sam had become frustrated with his job and with her. Two junior officers were promoted to detective over him. Sam was convinced, rightly so, that the promotions were based on the number of asses you kissed. His frustration with her stemmed from her refusal to marry him. She couldn't even give him a reason why.

Then Sam started getting death threats after arresting a man for the attempted murder of his estranged wife. Sam wouldn't go into much detail about what had happened, leaving Maddy no choice but to go to Andy, who reluctantly filled her in. The two had answered a call about a domestic disturbance several weeks earlier. When they arrived, they could hear the couple shouting inside the house and entered the home to find the estranged husband beating his wife. After pulling them apart, Andy handcuffed the husband while Sam attended to the wife.

When the ambulance arrived, Andy told Sam to go with her to get a statement and he would take the husband down to the station for booking. Turned out she had several broken ribs and was in no condition to give a statement that night, so they went back the next day. Halfway through her statement, the husband showed up, already out on bail, carrying a bouquet of flowers and a box of candy.

"Sam just lost it," Andy said, "I'd never seen him so angry. Sam threw him against the wall and would've hit him if I hadn't pulled him off. I sent the jerk on his way, we got our statement, wrote up our report and I thought that was the end of it."

"It wasn't," Maddy said.

"No. The wife started calling Sam, giving him her sob story, telling him she didn't know what to do. Crying that she was scared of what her husband would do if she left and she needed his help to get away from him."

"Sam being Sam fell for it," Maddy uttered.

"No, he didn't," Andy rejected. "He told her there were places that could help her get away from her husband. He gave her several numbers and offered to call a social worker for her. He did everything by the book."

"Then why is he getting death threats?"

"Because the husband found out she was calling Sam and claims he's the reason she won't reconcile. He filled a complaint against him at the station and threatened to file a suit for harassment."

"And then he sent death threats to our home," Maddy

Sam didn't take Maddy's concerns about the threats seriously until a week before he was to testify against the husband when a brick was thrown through their front window into their living room. Wrapped around the brick was a note stating that if Sam testified against him, that he would kill Sam and his pretty girlfriend. That was when she'd snapped and told Sam she needed a break.

"Maddy," Sam said, sweeping up broken glass. "I know we've been going through a rough patch, but this will all blow over. Things will get back to normal."

"There's never going to be a normal with you, Sam. You're a cop. Not only do I have to worry about you getting shot and killed, now this," she said as she looked out through the broken window and the tears started streaming down her face.

"Those death threats are only meant to scare me." Sam dropped the broom, took Maddy in his arms. "Once I testify, it'll be over."

"Until the next time you arrest some psychopath they let out on bail." Maddy pushed him away. "I want you to leave, Sam, at least until this trial is over. I need to think clearly, and I can't do it with you here. You take all the air out of the room."

"Where is this coming from? Your father? That bastard has never thought I was good enough for you. Good enough to protect his sorry ass though."

"He's worried about me." Maddy defended him. "You can't deny that your job is dangerous. He's afraid I'm going to be collateral damage."

"More likely, he's embarrassed by the publicity this case is causing. Is that it Maddy? Are you embarrassed by me?"

"That's not what he said," Maddy said, crying. "Or what I meant."

"What did he say?" Sam pressed. "That he was disappointed in you? We both know how you can't stand disappointing dear 'ole dad."

"Listen to me, Sam. It's your job. It makes you angry. Angry at a system that doesn't work, and you can't fix. Angry at putting your life on the line every day to arrest criminals that will be back on the street before you can get the paperwork done. Angry at protecting people who don't appreciate what you do for them but are the first to judge every decision you make in the line of duty. Every time I get under that bad-ass exterior you put on with the rest of your uniform, something like this happens and I'm back at square one. I know there is a wonderful, caring, funny man underneath, that's the man I fell in love with. Being a cop is drowning you and it's getting harder and harder to pull you back to the surface."

"I can change," he begged. "Go to the shrink the force pays for. I'm going to be promoted soon. Things will be a lot better then."

"You can't change who you are. I wouldn't want you to. But I have to save myself."

Then two days after their blow-up, the accident happened. Stopping by the apartment to get some clothes, Sam had impulsively asked Maddy to dinner. She accepted his offer, but on the way to the restaurant, their car was broadsided. Though the proof would never be found, everyone knew the psycho husband was responsible. Sam sustained a broken leg and head injuries that put him in a coma lasting for three days. Maddy's injuries were emotional and irreparable. Standing over his bed, praying he would wake up, she decided to end the relationship, a decision she had no other choice in making and a decision she would stand by relentlessly as Sam pleaded from his hospital bed for another chance

A few weeks later Sam moved out of the apartment. Maddy intended to make the break-up as painless for the both of them as possible. She knew about the road to hell. She called, wanted him to pick up his mail, wanted him, if she was being honest. He stopped by, they ended up in bed, no surprise there. They talked a few times a week until one day Sam didn't answer his phone, didn't answer for the next two days. He'd moved into a one-bedroom efficiency near Matteson. She stopped by to check on him, hoping she had guessed correctly the schedule rotation he was on. She knocked on the door a few times, calling his name. No answer. She turned the knob, it was unlocked.

His apartment was small, the living, dining and kitchen all one room, barely bigger than the bedroom she'd grown up in. He hadn't unpacked. Moving boxes were stacked against the wall. He had dug into a few of them to get what he needed at the time, silverware, a few pots and pans. The TV and the cheap stand it was resting on were the only furniture in the room except for the rocking chair Sam was sitting in. She could see into the bedroom, his suitcase lay on one side of the unmade bed, underwear, socks and t-shirts scattered inside. His uniforms were hanging inside the open closet.

Maddy was shocked. Sam had his bouts of depression, but she had never seen him like this. Almost catatonic, she marveled that he made it to work every day. She knelt in front of him, put her hands above his knees. His eyes registered her, and she saw the love there. She also saw the pain, the hurt, the betrayal. She started to cry, put her head in his lap. His hand covered the back of her head, petting her. They stayed that way for a long while, then she took him by the hand and led him into the bedroom. She undressed them both, wincing at the weight he had lost. Once they were in bed, Maddy waited for him. Sam couldn't touch her. She knew he wanted to, that was obvious, but he had gone somewhere even she couldn't reach.

That was the last time she saw Sam. Certain he was heading for a nervous breakdown, she called Andy, desperate to know what she should do and begging Andy to get Sam psychiatric help. Andy told her to stay away from Sam, she was making things worse. Knowing he was right, no matter how much the words hurt,

Maddy moved on.

Standing in her walk-in closet, her thoughts slowing her progress, Maddy dressed in an old pair of jeans and a well-worn blouse. Turning off the light to the closet, she glanced at her husband's clothes, stored neatly on his side. Instead of Sam, she was the one who had hightailed it to the psychiatrist, and then married him.

Maddy was grateful Nick had already left for the clinic by the time she'd gotten up this morning. He would've followed her around, asking her where she was going and how long she was going to be gone. Nick had changed over their three-year marriage. At first, she thought he was being overprotective, but now it felt controlling. She wondered if he'd always been that way and why she hadn't seen the signs.

Maddy would deal with Nick later, no doubt he'd be furious with her for bringing Sam back into their lives, that was his problem. She was confident Sam would find evidence the police had overlooked in what she considered a haphazard investigation. She grabbed her phone along with her keys and headed for the garage.

Redwood Estates, a tony newly built condominium complex in Downers Grove, was thirty-five minutes from Sam's office. Jason's condo was one of several cookie cutter duplexes lining the avenue. Parking in one of the four slanted visitor parking slots in front and assuming Jason had parked in a garage at the back of the building, he settled in to wait for Maddy. But not for long. His nervousness at seeing Maddy again getting the better of him, he exited his car and began scoping out the perimeter of the building. A small, well-manicured lawn surrounded the condo, with low maintenance shrubbery accentuating the front. Jason's name was lettered on the mailbox of the condo to the right of the entryway. Sam stepped to the left side and snapped a picture of the mailbox showing the owner of the adjoining condo. Heading around to the backside of the building, he found single car garages and dumpsters. A Ford Taurus beater was parked in front of Jason's garage. Inside, the passenger seat and floorboard were littered with an array of take out bags, soda cups, and cast-off clothing. After writing the make and model of the car on the notepad he kept in his pocket, Sam checked the doors, not expecting them to be unlocked. Confirming they weren't, he walked to the back to get the plate number.

As he sighted the plate on his camera, Sam was reminded of the car Jason had when he knew him--a silver Corolla that belonged to Maddy which she gifted to her little brother when he left for California and college.

Sam's phone vibrated. "What's up?" he asked into it.

"Ms Maxwell called about twenty minutes ago to let you know she's running late," Elyse's voice came over the phone.

"Did she say how late? We can reschedule," Sam said, both disappointed and relieved.

"No such luck," Elyse said. "She should be there any minute. I've been on the phone with a couple of potential clients. I took their names and numbers, but what should I tell them?"

"I should know more after Maddy gets here," Sam replied. "In the meantime, would you see what you can get on Stan and Judith Erickson? They're Jason's neighbors." Sam ended the call, his thoughts returning to his conversation with Andy and how indispensable Elyse had become.

Sam returned to his car to wait. He saw Maddy before she saw him. She parked and got out, looking for him at Jason's door, not realizing he was still sitting in his car. He tapped his horn, she turned and smiled, a familiar smile that said he was the most important person in the world to her. When they were together, that smile was the sexiest thing in the world to him.

Maddy met him at his car, grabbing his hands and squeezing them, then pulled him in close for a hug. Sam hugged her back, hesitantly. The embrace was both pleasure and pain.

"I'm sorry about Jason," he said. "How are you doing?"

"I'm okay." She pulled back, scrutinizing his face. "You look tired."

Maddy, even casually dressed in jeans and a blue top looked beautiful. Her curly black hair had gotten a few strands of grey in it. She'd pulled it back, but tendrils had escaped and were flying around her face. She could pass for twenty-five although she was ten years older.

"Thank you for coming," she said, taking his hand as they walked to the condo. Maddy had always been a toucher, holding his hand when they sat together, touching his arm while she talked, rubbing his back while they waited at the checkout line.

As they approached the front of the condo, Sam noticed the door was slightly ajar, new scrape marks along the jamb. Drawing his gun, he waved Maddy behind him.

"Stay here," Sam ordered.

"Sam...?"

"There's someone in there. Stay here." He pushed the door open with his foot and went in. Quickly moving through the empty rooms and checking the closets, Sam ascertained the bottom floor was empty. He returned to the foyer, motioned for Maddy who'd stepped inside to get back, and silently climbed the stairs.

Reaching the top riser, he noted five doors along the hallway. Three bedrooms, a bath and a small closet, closest to him. He was two feet from the door when it suddenly flew open and the intruder barreled into him, throwing him back and almost headfirst over the bannister. Regaining his balance, Sam chased after him, throwing himself airborne down the stairs. Sam landed on the man halfway down, the two crashing in a heap, the intruder on the bottom, taking the brunt of the fall. Pressing his advantage, Sam moved in.

Sensing, his imminent capture, the assailant charged Sam from his knees, throwing them both to the floor at Maddy's feet. Maddy grabbed a lamp from the entryway table, waving it above her head. Presented with a clear shot, Maddy struck. Sam crumpled to the floor, the lamp in shards around him. Stunned, Maddy could only stare at Sam's unmoving body as the man fled past her through the open door.

CHAPTER 3

"I'm sorry, Sam," Maddy apologized, handing him a cold compress. "I had a clear shot, but you moved."

"You hitting me on the head is my fault?" He asked, gingerly placing the compress against his swelling temple.

"Don't be a baby. There isn't any blood and we both know you have a very hard head," Maddy said, a smile spreading across her face.

"Your bedside manner still leaves much to be desired." He swiped lamp fragments from his clothes. "And what's so funny?"

"Even you have to admit it's a little bit funny me hitting the wrong man," she replied, helping him to his feet.

"Yeah, it's hilarious. Did you get a look at him before he got away?"

"No. Everything happened so fast and I was worried I'd killed you."

"Is Jason's car here?" Sam asked, trying to keep his balance.

"No, I had it taken to my house. Why?"

"There was a car parked in back earlier," Sam said. "I'm going to see if it's still there."

"No, you are not," Maddy said, firmly putting an arm around his waist and leading him to the couch. "You sit here, I'll go check for the car."

After confirming the car was gone, Maddy wasn't surprised to discover that Sam had moved from the couch. She went upstairs where she found him in the midst of Jason's devastated office.

"My God!" Maddy exclaimed from the doorway.

"It appears our intruder was looking for something," Sam said.

"What?" Maddy asked. "The only thing of value is his laptop and he left it."

"I don't know, but whatever it is, they think someone will find it."

"Why now? Jason died three weeks ago."

"Who else knows you called me?" Sam asked.

"No one, I haven't even told Nick yet," Maddy said, looking around the room at the savage ransacking. Her lips began to tremble as the strain of her brother's death overcame her, tears flowing unheeded down her cheeks.

Sam picked up the overturned leather office chair, placing it in front of the desk. He helped Maddy into it, handing her a box of Kleenex he found among the debris on the floor. Resisting the sudden, but not unfamiliar urge to take her in his arms and comfort her, he began picking up the clutter from the floor giving her time to regain her composure.

"I don't know where that came from," Maddy said, wiping her eyes. "I thought I was handling things pretty well." She shrugged. "Guess not."

"No one handles these things well. You get through every day the best way you know how and eventually the pain isn't as bad as it was the day before." Understanding that he didn't only mean Jason's death, Maddy moved over to him, halting him in his cleanup and embracing him. "I'm sorry. I know what I did hurt you and I wouldn't blame you if you hated me..."

"I don't hate you," Sam said, slipping from Maddy's arms and moving to a safer distance. "Let's get back to Jason. I did a search online after you called. The paper stated that he was a web designer. I'm assuming he worked from his office here?"

"Yes."

"And the cause of death was ruled an accidental suicide?"

"That's the conclusion the police came to."

"Was he found in this room?"

"No," shaking her head. "In the room across from his bedroom. It was his exercise room." Maddy looked up at him. "Don't ask me to go back in there," she entreated. "I haven't been in there since I found him."

"You don't have to," Sam assured her, engulfing her hands with his own and rubbing them. "Tell me what happened and then you can stay here while I go take a look."

"Okay," Maddy said, letting out a slow breath as she collected her thoughts. "It was three weeks ago today. I'd finished some shopping and I was early for an eleven o'clock hair appointment, so I stopped by to check in on him. We hadn't talked for a couple of days, which wasn't unusual, if you're going to ask, but the last time I'd spoken to him, he seemed upset about something."

"Do you know what was bothering him?" Sam stopped her.

"No," she replied, shaking her head and continuing. "He didn't answer when I rang the doorbell. I thought he couldn't hear me over the headphones he wore while he worked so I let myself in with Jason's spare key," Maddy paused.

"You're doing fine," Sam said, encouraging her to continue. "What did you do after you came into the apartment?"

"I checked downstairs, then went to the garage to see if he was working on his car. When I didn't find him, I came upstairs. He wasn't in here and I was beginning to think he was sick and still in bed. I went down the hallway, calling for him. When I got to his bedroom, I noticed his exercise room door was open. I went to the doorway and looked in…" Recalling the scene brought fresh tears to her eyes, but she quickly wiped them away and continued.

"He was kneeling…leaning on the frame of the closet," Maddy whispered. "I knew right away there was something wrong, he wasn't moving… and he was naked. When I got up a little closer, I saw the noose around his neck tied to the closet bar. He wasn't breathing. He was already gone but I checked for a pulse, he was so cold." She rubbed the palms of her hands on her jeans, getting them warm. "I don't remember much after that. I know I called the police because the next thing I remember is an officer taking me from the room to get my statement."

"That's enough for now." Sam patted her shoulder. "I'm going to take a look in the room, but first, I'm going to get you something to drink."

"Jason has some scotch downstairs."

Sam opened the door to Jason's exercise room. It was dark. He searched for the light switch with his hand, caught movement out of the corner of his eye and reached for his gun. The man in the room did the same, Sam's heart skipped a beat. Then he realized that he was the other man, his image reflected in a floor to ceiling wall to wall mirror. Embarrassed, he holstered his gun. "Now that's what I call a mirror," he muttered.

In front of the mirror, was a three tiered weight rack filled with dumbbells. In the corner nearest the door was a NordicTrack treadmill. On the wall opposite the treadmill, hung a flat screen tv and a poster demonstrating several dumbbell exercises. In the center of the room stood a St Andrew's cross.

"Interesting," Sam mused.

The closet was to the left of the treadmill, the nearest bi-pass door open. Sam noted the tape the police had placed to designate where the body laid, as near as they could get it to the head. The tautness of the rope would have allowed Jason's body to slump into the doorframe as Maddy had described, but not to fall entirely to the floor. The rope, Sam assumed, was at the police station, gathered as evidence. The floor was hardwood, scuffed by use.

Inside the closet were several rows of white comic book boxes stacked neatly along the back wall. Sam recognized them from the small collection he too had stashed away in what for him was an unused closet. Opening the nearest box, he rifled through the plastic-bagged comics inside.

"Find anything?" Maddy asked from the doorway.

"The Spectre," Sam said, startled by her unexpected appearance.
"The what?" "The Spectre," pulling a comic from the box. "It's about a detective. A dead one."

After sending Maddy downstairs on a mission to make them some tea, Sam walked over to the St Andrew's cross. Made of solid walnut, it was sturdy, no fear of tip overs. It stood on wheels and could easily be rolled against the wall or into a corner when not in use. There were hinged rings with reversible leather restraints attached on the top and bottom. He estimated the price tag to be approximately two thousand dollars. "I bet you could tell some stories," he said, fingering the wrist cuffs and recalling the first time he'd tried restraints...
"C'mon, it'll be fun," Maddy said, a gleam in her eye. She'd surprised him earlier, naked in his bed when he came home to his apartment after work. In short order he joined her, his uniform thrown on the nearest chair. Twenty minutes later, their initial desire spent, Maddy got up from the bed, spying the case for his handcuffs on his belt. She pulled them out, spinning them on her finger.
"Those things pinch," Sam said.
"How would you know?" she teased.
"We had to practice putting them on at the academy."
"Likely story. But don't worry. It'll be worth a little discomfort. I promise."
They'd been dating for two months, Sam thought he would never get enough of her. He'd never felt that kind of desire, didn't believe it existed, at least not for him. He was twenty-six years old, his sexual encounters could be counted on one hand--his left-- most of them after drinking too much at a frat party. For all intents and purposes, Maddy was his first. She was the experienced one. After the first few sessions of his unsure pawing and quickdraws, she taught him how to take his time, guiding his hand, directing his fingers. He was a quick study, feeling her whole-body tense as he brought her to the very edge, brought her back and there again until she couldn't wait any longer. She took him inside, her hands clawing down his back, grabbing his ass, helping him pump himself empty inside her. Afterwards, they would lay together for hours listening to music and talking about anything and everything. Sam felt like he'd been bottled up for years and the floodgates were suddenly open.
Sam would've kept her all to himself, content to stay at his apartment or hers, watch movies and eat popcorn, but Maddy insisted he needed culture and where better to get it than Chicago. They spent hours at the Field Museum of Natural History, The Discovery of King Tut, the first visiting exhibit they explored. The Museum of Science and Industry presented 'Titanic the Artifacts'. Sam and Maddy were each given the names of actual passengers

on that doomed voyage, his didn't make it, Maddy's did. They touched a piece of an iceberg, Maddy awed at the size, Sam at the logistics of getting it from city to city without it melting. Titanic history became a fascination for a while, Sam's collection of ship memorabilia was now stored in the same closet his comics were in. When they wanted a change, they would ride the American Eagle at Six Flags or attend Maddy's favorite, Bristol Renaissance Faire, where she loved the improv and he refused to eat the roasted turkey legs. Sometimes, with no destination in mind they'd start down the interstate, pick a deserted exit and drive until it seemed they were the only ones in the world. Have a picnic under a tree, sex afterwards, or before, or both.

Shaking his head to clear it of his memories, Sam moved from the cross back to the closet. The twelve comic boxes took up the left side, the right side was clear: room for the bondage related activities. No clothes, not even a hanger on the pole. On the board running above the pole were shoe boxes, stacked neatly, four high, three across, once again on the left side. The right side held two boxes, unmarked. Sam could guess what was inside them, but he pulled them down to check them anyway.

During the time Sam and Maddy were together, Sam didn't see much of Jason. He was in college, didn't come home for holidays and worked over the summers. The first time he'd had a conversation with Jason was the day Maddy gave him her car. Maddy explained to Sam that she needed a new car anyway, even though it was only three years old and he'd taught her by now how to avoid flooding it. Sam knew the real reason she wanted her brother to have it. At the time Jason had a barely breathing Chevy Cavalier, he was leaving for college and needed something he could depend on. Why she felt the need to make other excuses for giving it to him, Sam didn't know and didn't ask. Why their parents didn't step in and provide him safe transportation, when they clearly could have easily done so, Sam didn't question either.

Jason was six inches taller than his sister, but with the same black, unruly hair, and luminous blue eyes. Sam had followed Maddy to Jason's apartment to take her to the Toyota dealership to pick up her new car. Maddy had invited Jason along and the three of them went out to dinner. That the siblings were close was obvious, but beyond the physical resemblance, Sam saw no similarities in their personalities. Maddy was the typical extrovert while Jason was withdrawn, almost sullen. Crediting his age, and the fact that he was barely out of high school, Sam chided himself to give the kid a break, remembering his own teen years of sullen, silent revolt.

By the end of dinner, Maddy had worked her magic and gotten Jason to open up. They talked about college and how it was going to be a fresh start for him. She told him how much fun she had while she was away at school while Sam remembered his four years mostly as a blur of studying and working to pay his tuition. Jason wanted to become a webmaster, Sam wasn't sure what that was, but it sounded cool. Jason was sure he was going to be the next Steve Jobs.

When the subject got around to what Sam did for a living, Sam was surprised by the concern Jason expressed for his sister.

"I know my sister," Jason said. "She's serious about you."

"We haven't been dating long enough for either of us to be serious," Maddy scoffed.

"You could get shot and killed tomorrow," Jason continued, ignoring Maddy's protests to stop. "Don't you think you should get into a line of work that's less dangerous?"

"I plan on becoming a detective. That'll take me out of harm's way, for the most part."

"How long will that take?" Jason asked.

"Couple of years, if I play my cards right," Sam said.

"See that you do. I'm not going to be around to keep her out of trouble, and you seem like a nice guy."

"Keep me out of trouble?" Maddy laughed.

CHAPTER 4

"The iced tea you requested," Maddy said, placing a glass on the kitchen table in front of Sam. "Which I know was your not so subtle way of getting me out of underfoot." She picked a loaf of bread off the counter, saw the mold through the plastic wrap. "I can probably find some stale crackers in one of these cabinets if you're hungry," she said, walking over to the trashcan and throwing it in.

"Sounds good, but no thanks."

"How's your head?" She moved to his side gently running her fingers over the knot above his temple.

He caught her hand, felt the wedding ring on her finger, released it. "Hell of a headache."

She stepped over to the cabinets and returned with three Advil tablets, then sat down in the chair opposite him.

"Before we get started on Jason, let's talk about Nick," Maddy said.

"What's there to talk about?" Sam replied, bitterly. "Unless you think he's involved in Jason's death. I find it interesting that his clinic specializes in sexual issues and Jason's death appears to be sexually motivated."

She wasn't surprised Sam had done research on Nick. "I don't think Nick had anything to do with Jason's death and I suspect you knew about Nick way before I called you."

"I investigated Nick the minute I found out you married him. I wanted to know what he has that I don't."

"And?"

"The only thing I don't have is the doctor in front of my name. Or the money that comes with it."

"I don't need to justify my decision to you," Maddy rankled. "But believe me when I say I didn't marry Nick for his money." Sam recognized the look of irritation that briefly crossed Maddy's face, leading him to suspect there may be some trouble in the Maxwell paradise. Getting away from Sam's scrutiny, Maddy moved from her chair, pulled the garbage can closer to the kitchen cabinets and began throwing away the contents that couldn't be donated to the nearest homeless shelter.

"How did Jason and Nick get along?"

"They didn't for the most part. Jason was against our marriage and made it clear to me he thought Nick was marrying me because of our dad's status at the hospital they both worked at and the help he would provide in Nick's career. Earlier I told you that the last time I talked to Jason, he was upset. He was working on updating the clinic's website and the two of them had gotten into an argument over it. Neither one of them would tell me the details."

Sam watched as she emptied a cabinet full of powdered protein drinks and vitamins into the can. "Why was Jason working for Nick if he didn't like him?"

"I asked him to. I thought if they worked together, they might straighten out some of the issues they had. Clearly a bad idea."

"What issues did Nick have with Jason?" Sam asked.

"He thought Jason was lazy and too dependent on me. Honestly, I think Jason didn't want to like Nick simply because he wasn't you."

"Smart kid. I had no idea he felt that way."

"Before your head gets any bigger, let me tell you why that smart kid went to California in the first place. A month or so before I met you, a girl Jason had been dating accused him of rape. Jason swore it was consensual; the girl was fifteen, didn't want daddy to think his little girl gave it up on her own. Her parents knew we were wealthy and promised not to press charges for hush money. How much my parents paid, I never found out. After that, dad called a friend he knew at UCLA and got Jason accepted. That's when you met him."

"Why didn't you tell me this at the time?"

"Because, I didn't and still don't believe Jason raped her. I wanted you to meet him with an open mind."

"Thanks for the vote of confidence, but we were together for three years, you never mentioned it in all that time." The doorbell rang.

"It's probably the locksmith I called to fix the front door. I wasn't expecting him so soon," she said, leaving the kitchen.

Opening the front door, she was greeted instead by the owner of the adjoining condo. "Mr. Erickson, how surprising to see you," Maddy said, not surprised at all and trying unsuccessfully to hide the annoyance in her voice.

"I saw your car outside and I wanted to tell you how sorry I am about your brother," he said, easing his way over the threshold.

"Thank you," Maddy replied, blocking his entry. "You stop by and tell me that every time I come here. I've someone coming to fix the door, as you can see, it's broken. So, if you don't mind…"

"Mr. Erickson?" Sam asked, coming down the hallway. "I'm a private investigator looking into Jason's death and I was hoping you'd answer a few questions for me."

"Oh, really? I'd be happy to do whatever I can do to help," Erickson stepped around Maddy to shake Sam's hand.

"I wanted to keep this investigation quiet," Maddy hissed, between clenched teeth, glaring at Sam.

"Investigation?" Erickson asked, the gleam of fresh gossip in his eyes.

"Yes, sir, but I'm sure I can trust you not to tell anyone, right Mr. Erickson?" Sam asked, putting his arm around the man's shoulders and leading him to the leather sofa in the living room.

"Not a soul--except for my wife Judy, of course."

"Of course. We' were just having a glass of iced tea and I'm sure Maddy wouldn't mind getting you one." Rolling her eyes at Sam, Maddy left for the kitchen.

Quickly appraising the man as he sat down across from him in a matching leather armchair, early sixties, thinning gray hair, a few inches shy of six feet and more than a few inches hanging over the belt in his Khakis, Sam asked, "Mr. Erickson, did you happen to see or hear anything unusual this morning?"

"No, but I left early, and I've just gotten home. Had a doctor's appointment, my heart isn't so good." He tapped his chest. "I had a couple of stents put in a few years back. Haven't had any trouble since then, thank God." He crossed himself and pointed to the ceiling. "You never think about how fragile life is until you stare death in the face. Here one day gone the next. Like Jason, such a shock, him being so young and all. What do you think happened?"

"I just started the investigation today," Sam replied.

"Right, right. The police didn't investigate at all. Had it all wrapped up in less than two hours. Do you think he was murdered?" He leaned closer to Sam and lowered his voice. "Is she going to be alright?" He asked, pointing toward the kitchen. "She's over here all the time. Judy and I are worried about her."

Feeling the same annoyance Maddy couldn't hide earlier, Sam attempted to get Erickson focusing on Jason. "Mr. Erickson, I'm sure Maddy appreciates your concern, but let's talk about this morning. What time was your appointment?"

"Nine, I left around eight. There wasn't anything wrong with the front door then."

"How can you be sure of that?"

"I've been checking it on my way out and when I return every day since the apartment's been empty. You can never be too safe I always say. Not that this area is…"

"Is your wife at home?" Sam interrupted. "Maybe she heard something," hoping she was the less talkative one.

"No, she left shortly after I did for the Humane Society. She volunteers there some mornings, loves the animals. Good thing we can only have two pets, otherwise she'd bring them all home with her."

Taking a deep breath, Sam let it out slowly. Noticing his impatience, Erickson said, "To answer your question, I'm sure she would've called me if she'd heard anything unusual or if the door was broken open." Having himself arrived at nine-thirty, Sam estimated the intruder was in the apartment for roughly forty-five minutes before Sam flushed him out of the closet.

Returning with Erickson's tea, Maddy handed it to him. He tasted it, grimaced, "Unsweetened. Do you have any Splenda?" She glared at him, then headed back to the kitchen, muttering something Sam couldn't and didn't want to hear.

"How long have you lived next door, Mr. Erickson?"

"Please call me Stan, everyone does. We've been here ten years, long before Jason moved in. The Andersons lived here before him. They were a disgrace. Judy and I were both happy to see them go. I think he worked at a repair shop, always working on cars, revving engines. The noise drove me absolutely crazy. I work the night shift at Ford, I never got any sleep. They owned motorcycles too, coming and going at all hours of the day and night. He even parked a boat out front, left it there for days. That's blatantly against the HOA regulations."

"Getting back to Jason..."

"Right, right, Jason. When he moved in, I told Judy he was going to be as bad as the Andersons, nothing but trouble."

"Was he?" Sam asked.

"No, quiet as a mouse. We wouldn't see him for days, which I thought was strange, him working at home like he did." Sam didn't think it was strange at all. "Judy was always bringing food over to him--she makes too much now that our kids are out of the house. She always said he seemed lonely, but he didn't to me."

"What do you mean?"

"He had 'company'." Erickson said. "I'd see women coming in the evening or leaving in next morning and they weren't clients, at least not for his business."

"Did he introduce you to any of these women?"

"No," disappointment in his voice.

"Were you home on the evening of Jason's death, Stan?"

"Yes, I was home in the evening, but I worked that night. I told the police when they finally got around to questioning me, that a woman came out of his apartment about nine-thirty. She was in a big hurry, she ran right into me."

"How can you be sure it was nine-thirty?"

"My shift starts at eleven. I have to leave here by nine-thirty to get to work on time."

"Had you seen this woman before?"

"Oh, several times. Real looker and the clothes she wore didn't leave much to the imagination." Returning to the living room, Maddy handed Stan his Splenda and sat down on the arm of Sam's chair.

"Did you see what kind of car she was driving?" Sam asked.

"Black Monte Carlo, license plates RACK and may I say she had a mighty fine one."

"What did the police say when you told them about her?"

"They said she wasn't important to the case," Erickson said. "Told me Jason offed himself, laughed about it." He looked at Maddy. "Sorry, you didn't need to know that."

"Back to the woman you saw, Stan." Sam said. "Would you be able to identify her?"

"Sure, like I said, she's a real looker. Do you think she killed him? She looked like she wouldn't take any nonsense and Judy said they'd get loud sometimes after I'd left for work."

"Arguments?" Sam asked, his interest peaked.

"Uh, more like sex getting a little rough, according to Judy. Personally, I didn't hear any of that." Sam was positive he'd tried. "The interior walls aren't that thick, if you know what I mean."

"Did Judy mention anything else about Jason's dates?"

"We've heard enough from Mr. Erickson," Maddy said, rising from her perch and taking Erickson's tea. "Sam, why don't you give him one of your business cards and I'm sure Stan will give you a call if he or Judy remember anything pertinent to the investigation."

Handing him a card, Sam walked Erickson to the door, asking him to continue keeping an eye on the apartment.

"Why in the hell did you encourage that nosy old bastard?" Maddy asked as soon as Sam shut the door.

"He's going to snoop anyway, might as well use him in case whoever broke in here this morning comes back."

"I couldn't take any more of his innuendos. He doesn't know anything that'll help us anyway."

"Not entirely true, he gave us a license plate. I'll call Andy later and ask him to run it."

"Didn't he leave the force when you did?" Maddy asked, surprised. "

You mean when I was asked to leave," Sam corrected. "And no--Andy keeping his job was part of the agreement I made when I left."

After the accident that left him in a coma, the wife recanted her story, accusing Sam of stalking her and insisting her husband wasn't responsible for the accident. The newspapers had a field day with the story culminating with Sam's suspension and an internal affairs investigation. Feeling pressure from his superiors, his sergeant called him into his office three weeks after the accident, confronting him with an ultimatum.

"The way I see it, I can fire you right now for improper conduct, or you can give me your resignation today and save yourself a lot of hassle," Sergeant Billings said.

"I did nothing wrong and you know it. She's lying because she's afraid her bastard husband will kill her."

"It doesn't matter what I know. Internal affairs isn't going to let this go with a slap on the wrist. They need a head on a platter and there's no question it's going to be yours. The question is... do you want Andy to lose his job too, because if you fight this, that's what going to happen, and he'll leave without his pension. Are you willing to take the chance that I.A. will see your side of this?" Sam was willing to risk his career, but not Andy's and Billings knew it. Sam tendered his resignation. That was the day Maddy showed up at his apartment in Matteson. The last time he'd seen her until today.

They returned to the kitchen where Maddy refreshed their now watery iced teas before she continued with her cabinet work. "For the record, I never believed what the papers wrote about you," Maddy said.

"A phone call would've been nice," Sam responded.

"Andy told me in no uncertain terms to leave you alone. I thought it was for the best."

"Debating the issue isn't why we're here," Sam said, bitingly. "Do you have any idea who this girlfriend could be?" Pulling his notebook and pen from his shirt, Sam turned to a clean page.

"Jason was private about his social life, at least to me. He didn't have any close male friends as far as I know. He dated periodically, not the revolving door, Erickson made it out to be. I thought he was getting serious about a woman he started dating six months ago, but they broke up. That may be who Erickson saw, but I never met her. When I asked what happened, he said they just wouldn't work and didn't go into details. I didn't push."

"Did he say who broke off the relationship?"

"He did, I think," Maddy said. "That makes her a suspect, right?"

"I'll definitely have to look into this rack," he grinned. "Let's talk about the day you found Jason." Maddy stopped working and sat down at the table.

"What did you do while you were waiting for the police to arrive?" Sam asked.

"Nothing," Maddy said, shaking her head. "All I remember is sitting down next to him and crying."

"I know you better than that, Maddy. Your brother was naked. I'm willing to bet you covered him before the police arrived."

"Of course, I did. I thought that went without saying. I grabbed a towel from the bathroom and covered the front of him the best I could. Was that wrong?" She looked at him incredulously.

"Completely understandable, but I have to know if there was anything else you did to protect Jason."

"I didn't hide evidence, if that's what you're asking." She took a sip from her tea, wiped the condensation on the glass with her thumb and placed it back on the table. Her hands now empty, Maddy placed them together and rested them on the table, awaiting Sam's next question.

"Was there anything on the floor around Jason's body?"

"No, I looked for his clothes, but I guess he took them off in the bedroom before he went into the exercise room. I found some on the floor next to his bed."

"Did you call Nick before or after you called the police?"

"After. He was on his way to St. Louis and I wanted him to know before he got there."

"Didn't he turn around and come home?" It was Sam's turn to be incredulous.

"Yes, he did. But I wasn't really expecting him to. He was supposed to do a book signing and I didn't know whether he could cancel it."

"What time did he get home?"

"I'm not sure. Maybe around seven that morning."

"Did you drive yourself home?"

"Yes. After they took Jason's body and the police left. I really don't remember the drive home. I was still in shock. When I got home, it was too early to call anyone to make funeral arrangements, so I went to bed. The next thing I remember is Nick getting home."

"Did the police have any suspects?"

"Things never got that far. Once they knew about his past, the case was closed without any further investigation," Maddy said, disgusted.

"The police wouldn't have known about the rape accusation, so what aren't you telling me?"

"It's what happened while he was at college, in his junior year in California. About three months after you and I split, he started dating someone. It got intense for a while, at least for Jason. Then he caught her cheating, they had a big blowout, she dumped him. Jason got drunk, went back to his dorm and tried to commit suicide."

"Hung himself?"

"Yes, from the closet door. Luckily his roommate came back in time to cut him down before any physical damage was done."

36

"So, the police assume his attempted suicide in California was actually an autoerotic episode that went wrong and are saying the same thing happened here."

"The detective who closed the case said as much."

"What makes you so sure that isn't what happened?"

"Because when we flew out to see him while he was still in the hospital, I saw how messed up he was over the bitch who cheated on him. She never even called to check on him. The psychiatrist handling his case, Edward Holloway, was concerned Jason was going to try again and he kept him on suicide watch for a while. We stayed with him until he was better and then we brought him home."

"Who's we?" Sam asked, knowing the answer.

"Nick went with me."

"Quite the house call," Sam said sarcastically.

"He went as my friend and Jason's doctor," Maddy said, ignoring Sam's tone. "It turned out well for him, Holloway's now his partner at the clinic."

"Edward Holloway. I read about him on the clinic's website. How did they become partners?"

"Nick has always wanted to open his own independent clinic and Holloway felt the same way. They discussed it while we stayed with Jason and the idea grew from there. They decided to open one together. They combined their names Holloway and Maxwell, and that's how the Hollowell Clinic was born." Sam was surprised Nick let Holloway take first billing.

"Holloway was willing to give up his practice and start all over in Chicago?"

"He was excited about the move, especially when Nick agreed to come up with seventy-five percent of their start-up capital."

"Did Jason continue his treatment after he moved back here?"

"For a while, but if he was seeing someone recently, he never told me."

"Would Nick tell you if Jason was a patient?"

"No, but I can say with certainty that if Jason was seeing someone at the clinic…" the doorbell rang. "it wasn't Nick. Let's hope it's the locksmith this time." Sam followed her out of the kitchen.

"While you're taking care of that, I'm going to look around Jason's office." Sam said, heading up the stairs.

Sam had picked up most of the clutter from the floor and was on his cell phone when Maddy finished up with the repairman. She waited outside the door as he talked to Elyse.

"Andy called. He's stopping by the office on his way home," Elyse said.

"I asked him to run a couple of license plates for me. Why didn't he call my cell?"

"He said he didn't want to disturb you and your new client. I think it's his passive aggressive way of letting you know he doesn't approve."

"I got that. Did you find anything on the Ericksons?"

"Not so much as a parking ticket."

"I'm not surprised. I shouldn't be here much longer." Ending the call, Sam spotted Maddy in the doorway.

"Find anything?" she asked.

"Nothing that screams motive for murder," Sam replied.

"I know you think there's something in here the intruder didn't want me to find, but how would I know what it was if I'd found it?"

"I think he planned on taking the computer, it's still intact, untouched on the desk. But I've searched everywhere and can't find any external storage devices. If there were any, he pocketed them. Whatever he doesn't want you to find is probably on them. If you don't mind, I'm going to take the laptop back to the office and see what Elyse can find on it."

"Anything you need to get to the bottom of this," Maddy said. "Speaking of Elyse, she seems a little overprotective of you, or maybe it's jealousy. Are the two of you involved?"

"That's a ridiculous question and has nothing to do with Jason," Sam said, picking up Jason's computer and heading towards the stairs, then he stopped and returned to the office, "I know you don't want it to be so, but what makes you think Jason's death wasn't an accident?"

"It doesn't track. Granted he was a mess for a while after the breakup, but he moved back here, finished his degree in computer science and started his own company. He was even getting along with our parents...until..."

"The car accident," Sam finished. He'd read about the seven-car pile-up on I-80 that had taken her parents' lives a few years after their breakup.

"Losing them was a shock for us both."

"I'm truly sorry for your loss and I don't mean to be crass, but how was their estate divided between you two?"

"I received half of their estate at the time, but Jason's half was left in a trust until he turned thirty. Why are you asking about this? It has nothing to do with his death."

"How can you be so sure of that?" Sam questioned.

"Because he hadn't received any money. He was killed two weeks before his thirtieth birthday."

"Does that mean you inherit his half?"

"I assume so, if Jason didn't change his will. I've spoken to his lawyers, but I've been putting off reading his will." One more thing Nick had been nagging her to get done.

"How did Jason afford this condo if he hadn't received any money?"

"He received a stipend out of his trust every month and I co-signed on it." Over vehement objections from Nick.

Sam stood up to leave the room again, but Maddy stopped him. "You haven't said anything about what you found in Jason's exercise room."

"I don't see any reason to."

"You're protecting me Sam and that's not your job anymore, not that it ever was. I'm a big girl and I know Jason had sexual issues that he never discussed with me, but those issues could've gotten him killed."

"Alright, did you know Jason was into kink?"

"What do you mean?"

"Those boxes in the closet...I found whips, floggers, cuffs, blindfolds, bondage straps." Sam continued, "and the St Andrew's cross in the middle of the room is used for..."

"I can imagine what it's used for," she shivered unconsciously.

"This wasn't amateur bondage play. Whether Jason was into it as much as his partner or partners, we won't know, but at the very least he participated. From the wear marks on the closet pole, the night he died wasn't the first time he'd tried that. He may have gotten so weak from the asphyxiation that he couldn't stand or whatever fail safe he had didn't work. It happens, more than you'd think."

"You sound like the police," Maddy said, disgusted. "I don't believe for a minute Jason died from autoerotic asphyxiation, but someone has gone to a lot of trouble to make it look that way."

"Which leads to the question, why this setup? There are several ways to make murder appear to be self-inflicted, why the sexual slant?"

"So, the police would be quicker to close the case, and it worked."

"That would mean the killer knows about Jason's past," Sam said.

"So, you think it was murder, too," Maddy said hopefully.

"I didn't say that," Sam backpedaled. "But I haven't ruled it out. I'll follow-up on the license plates, look into what the coroner found and hack Jason's computer. In the meantime, if you could find Jason's cell phone, it would be helpful to know who he was talking to the days before his death. If you can't find it, I'll get Elyse working on getting his phone records."

"I hadn't thought of that," Maddy replied. "I'll look around and if there's anything else I can do, just ask."

Once again, Sam headed toward the stairs, getting to the front door before he stopped to say his goodbyes. "One more thing. Why haven't you told Nick you've asked me investigate Jason's death?"

"I don't want him in the way. He's already hounding me to get things packed up here. Once he finds out I've asked for your help, he'll be in a bigger hurry."

"Why?"

"To protect me. He thinks I can't handle stress. He's the reason I don't teach anymore. I got tired of arguing with him about it. I don't know why all the men in my life feel I can't take care of myself."

"Not all of them Maddy," Sam replied, opening the door. "Now that you own this place, what are you going to do with it? You could easily rent it out in this area, if you don't mention the next-door neighbors."

"No, too many memories of Jason. Once you've finished your investigation,

I'll put it on the market...eventually. I come over here and try to get his things packed, but I never seem to get started."

"Maybe you should let a moving company do it for you," Sam suggested. " That's exactly what Nick says," Maddy said exasperated. "I don't like the idea of strangers going through his personal things."

"Why don't you work on those and let the movers do the rest? But for right now, leave the upstairs as it is. I'd like to get another look after I see the police report."

"All right, Sam, I guess I can't keep putting it off. I'll contact the company that moved Jason in here and find out when they can start."

CHAPTER 5

Other than Andy, Dale Sanders was the only one from his days on the police force that Sam kept in contact with; he was the man who owned his office building. Dale was a criminal defense attorney who knew police procedure as well as or better than most officers and when those procedures weren't followed, he showed no mercy. For that reason, the majority of Sam's fellow officers loathed him. Sam's encounters with Dale were strictly as a witness for the prosecution, until the incident with the battered wife became the beginning of the end of his career. Seeking advice after the harassment suit was filed against the department and himself personally, Dale had been his first choice in representation, if only to piss the department off. Sitting on the client side of the desk, one strikingly similar to the one he now had upstairs, Sam discovered Dale cared deeply about his clients. They discussed potential outcomes if the case went to court and what Dale's strategy was going to be. For the first time in a long time, Sam felt someone was on his side and always left his office confident they could deal with whatever happened.

Upon leaving the force, the charges were dropped, but their friendship continued. Dale's office was in a two-story brick fronted building in the suburb of Westmont, a ten-minute drive from Sam's home. The bottom floor held Dale's offices and those of another attorney who dealt with family law. At the time Sam gave him a retainer, the upper level was used for storage, but when Sam left the force and subsequently decided to open his detective agency, he proposed the idea of his renting half of it. Dale, whose business acumen was as sharp as his legal finesse, took him up on his offer. Aware of his shortage of funds Dale charged significantly less than what the space was worth.

Parking in his allotted slot, Sam grabbed Jason's laptop from the passenger seat and headed up the stairs, where Elyse was waiting at the door.

"Andy here yet?" Sam asked, handing her the laptop.

Sitting down behind her desk, Elyse opened the laptop and began typing on the keyboard. "I'm assuming this is Jason's?" She gave him a quick glance for confirmation, then went back to work.

"Can you hack it?"

"Please. This'll be a piece of cake," Elyse said, her hands fluttering over the keyboard.

"I'm glad to see those computers classes I paid for are being put to good use."

"You'll get a nice deduction on your taxes when I file them next year. But you should know it isn't the stuff I'm learning in school that's going to get me into this computer," Elyse said, her hands paused. "It's my Garcia, Criminal Minds mad skills." she smiled wickedly.

"I've told you, I don't want to know when you're doing something illegal."

"As her employer in the eyes of the law you're just as guilty," Andy said from the doorway.

"Hey, Andy," Elyse said, snapping the computer closed.

"Don't bother. If I arrested everyone who illegally hacked a computer, half of the people I work with would be locked up. I'm just glad you work for the good guys. Mostly," Andy said, giving Sam a quick glance. "Jason's?" He asked, pointing at the laptop.

"Yes, somebody was ransacking Jason's office when I got there this morning. I was hoping to find out what they were looking for."

"Did you call it in? That's called breaking and entering. Something we cops like to know about."

"No, I didn't but the license plate number I gave you earlier should shed some light on the perp."

Andy grunted his disapproval and said, "Doesn't it seem like an odd coincidence this break-in happens the same day you start investigating? Jason has been dead for three weeks. Why now?"

"Good question," Sam said. "And one I've asked myself. I don't believe in coincidences any more than you do."

"Did you consider the possibility that the whole thing was a set up?" Andy wasn't tall, about three inches shorter than Sam's six feet, but his workouts at Planet Fitness and his twice weekly runs with Sam kept him impressively fit for a man in his late fifties. Now, riled up over Maddy's sudden appearance and his concern over Sam, he was a force to be reckoned with.

"Never even crossed my mind," Sam countered, his disgust with the question apparent in his voice. "Come on, Andy, Maddy wouldn't do that."

"Bullshit, she wouldn't! I don't believe there's anything your old girlfriend wouldn't do. Especially if it meant getting back in that head of yours." The two men glared at each other.

"I knew it!" Elyse interjected, hoping to diffuse the moment. "I knew there was something between you two from the phone calls. I'm actually going to meet this heartbreaker."

"Not if I have anything to say about it," Sam said, turning his attention away from Andy, he said to Elyse, "I thought you were trying to get into Jason's computer."

"I did that five minutes ago. I was just watching the two of you posturing over a woman."

"More like duck and cover," Andy said, half in jest as he simmered down and his humor returned.

Elyse shook her head at the two of them. "You're only making this Maddy sound more intriguing."

"Enough about Maddy," Sam said, terminating the conversation and grabbing the laptop off of Elyse's desk, he went into his office, leaving the two of them to stare after him.

"Touchy, isn't he?" Elyse said as they followed.

"The majority of these files are devoted to Jason's business," Elyse said, clicking quickly from file to file. She was sitting at Sam's desk after replacing him at the keyboard when she became impatient with his sluggish peckings. Now the two men flanked her as she opened Jason's business accounts. "He was very organized, updated QuickBooks program, some innovative unique add-ons he installed himself. This guy knew his stuff. Not as good as me...but come on, who is?"

"You're impressed with his programming skills," Andy said. "Then he must've been very good."

"He has over four hundred accounts here. Alphabetically organized but also sorted by the products they sell and the services they provide. If you think his death was sexually motivated, maybe we should start with services, see what kind of services he was writing web pages for."

"Are you thinking one of his clients murdered him?" Andy asked. "I can't see anyone getting upset enough over a website to commit murder."

"We've all seen murder committed over much less. People be crazy," Elyse said.

"I am going to start by going through his emails," Sam said, checking the number on the inbox. He whistled under his breath. "Damn, there are over five hundred here, this may take a while." He shooed Elyse from his desk chair and sat down. Sam began deleting obvious spam messages, soon so engrossed in his task he didn't notice when Elyse and Andy left to get a drink from the soda machine outside the lawyer's offices downstairs. Returning ten minutes later, Elyse put a Coke on the desk for Sam and took a seat on the short filing cabinet against the wall to the side of Sam. Sitting down in the empty chair in front of the desk Andy wondered for the hundredth time why Sam kept two chairs when one of them was always full of paperwork.

"Wouldn't it make more sense to put that paperwork on the cabinet and sit in the chair?" Andy asked Elyse.

"That's what I've been telling him since I started. He won't let me file anything, says he has a system," She laughed. "If he does, it's a mystery to me." Sam grunted from behind the computer, acknowledging he'd heard, but not defending his office management. "Speaking of mysteries, Andy," Elyse said. "I have a good one for you." Elyse had an insatiable thirst for the macabre and knowing Andy's love of Chicago history, she was always looking for ghost stories about the places he talked about.

"Okay, shoot."

"You know The Drake hotel downtown? The one you've probably run by on at least one of those insane runs you do?"

"They're called half marathons, but yes I'm familiar with it. It was built in 1920, has five hundred plus rooms and a six-room Presidential Suite that both Queen Elizabeth II and Princess Diana stayed in."

"I bet they didn't know about 'The Lady in Red'."

"She died there, I assume. Lots of people die in hotels."

"Not on Grand Opening night. She found her husband and his lover in what we'll say a compromising position. Jealous, angry and hurt, she takes an elevator to the tenth floor and jumps to her death. She's seen walking the halls of the tenth floor all the time."

"Even if that's true, where's the mystery? She killed herself."

"The mystery is why she didn't kill her cheating husband and the skank he was with first?" Elyse smiled. "That's what I'd have done."

"Noted."

"How's it going?" Elyse asked, turning her attention back to Sam.

"Whittling it down. I have about three hundred to go through yet," Sam said, stopping to take a drink and then returning to his work.

Elyse gestured at Sam. "So, Andy, since this one here won't spill the beans on his great love affair, why don't you fill me in while he's snooping emails?"

"Not much to tell," Andy replied. "They met, they dated, they broke up."

"Details," Elyse snapped back. "How long did they date? How did they meet? Is she pretty? and most importantly, who broke up with whom?"

"Look, Elyse," Sam said, rescuing Andy. "We were together for about three years, we met when I was a cop, and yes she's pretty."

"Why did she dump you?"

"Why do you assume she's the one who dumped me and does that really matter?" Sam asked, exasperated.

"What matters," Andy interjected, "is why she's coming to you. There're plenty of detectives out there."

"I'm a very good detective."

"Agreed, but with Maddy there's always another motive. Something else has brought her back into your life and I for one don't want a repeat of what happened last time."

"What happened?" Elyse said, looking from Sam to Andy, getting no response. "What happened?"

"Maddy's my friend," Sam said, ignoring Elyse. "She's asking me for help and I'm going to give it to her if I can. Our past is ancient history."

"Not too ancient," Maddy said from the doorway. "At least I hope not." All eyes turned to her. "There wasn't anyone at the desk in your waiting room," Maddy said, coming into the room. Andy got up giving her his seat. "You must not have heard me."

Sam introduced the two women. "Elyse, this is Maddy Richards, our newest client. Maddy, this is Elyse, my secretary."

"Maxwell," Maddy said, accepting Elyse's handshake. "Sam forgot I'm married now."

"Assistant, he also tends to forget that without me, he wouldn't solve half of his cases."

"Andy," Maddy said, turning to offer her hand to him. "How nice to see you again. I hope you are well."

Andy said nothing, ignored her hand.

"What are you doing here?" Sam asked. "I thought you were going home after you finished at Jason's."

"I did go home. When I got there, I decided to check Jason's car. I had it driven to my house a few weeks ago, but I never thought to check inside. I found this," Maddy said, pulling a cell phone from her purse.

"This will need charging," Sam said, taking the phone and handing it to Elyse. "Would you see if one of our chargers on your desk will work on this on your way out? I know you have a class to go to."

"Oh, I can miss one class to help you solve a case."

"Oh, I don't think you can," Sam said, mockingly. "I have a lot of emails to go through and I don't need you here for that. Go study or something."

"I can take a hint." Elyse frowned at Sam. "Nice to meet you Ms. Maxwell," Elyse said as she headed out of the door.

"I have somewhere else to be too," Andy said. "Call me at home if you need anything, Sam. Are we still on for our run in a couple days?"

"Sure thing."

"Six sharp, don't be late, Rookie." Andy nodded his head at Maddy and left the office.

◆ ◆ ◆

"He's worried I'm here for nefarious reasons," Maddy said.

"Should he be?"

"No, I heard you tell them you were my friend, no matter what has happened, and I believe you. And I believe you'll do your best to find out the truth about Jason's death no matter what the outcome."

"As I said earlier, the past is ancient history. I'm helping you clear up a questionable death. That's it. When I'm done, I'm sure you'll once again do what you think is for the best."

"You sound so bitter, Sam. I never would've thought that of you."

"I call it realistic. And when it comes to you, a little bit of bitterness is always a good thing. Now, if there's nothing else, I need to get to work on these emails."

"I can help you with those," Maddy said, picking up her chair and placing it next to Sam's behind the desk.

"What about your husband? Won't Nick be wondering where you are?"

"He has a group therapy session at the clinic this evening."

"Great," Sam said sarcastically, moving his chair so Maddy could join him at the computer.

"Wouldn't it make more sense to check his Facebook page instead of these emails?" Maddy asked after ten minutes of sorting through online order confirmations and spam.

"It would, but he didn't have one. I'm surprised you didn't know that."

"I never thought to ask him. I don't think he would have friended me even if he did," Maddy laughed.

"Facebook would have been helpful, but these emails tell me a lot about Jason's frame of mind before his death. He placed several online orders for clothing, shoes and supplies for his business."

"Jason bought everything he could online. He hated going to stores."

"I know the police ruled it accidental, but since you told me about his attempted suicide, I wanted to be sure it wasn't a possibility. You did say he had recently broken up."

"That was over a month ago, he was upset, but he seemed to be handling it well."

"From what I'm seeing here, I would have to agree. What I find interesting is that I don't see any orders for bondage accessories," Sam said. "The best thing about buying online is the anonymity. Only the postman knows."

"He wouldn't have bought all that stuff at once," Maddy said.

"Granted, but look here," Sam brought up Jason's bookmarks page. "He has all his favorite stores marked…" He pointed to Sears, Office Depot and the list that followed. "He would have bookmarked any bondage accessory store he frequented."

"Unless he wasn't buying that stuff anymore."

"True, but it's also possible he bought locally, or someone else bought them for him."

"I still don't see how any of that matters," Maddy said, confused.

"Pieces, I'm gathering pieces. Hopefully what I gather becomes a puzzle. Looks like one of the last emails he received was from someone named Lindsay." Sam said, clicking on the name. They read the message:

I've looked at the flash drive. Let's talk about it over dinner tonight at the Tumbledown. Meet you at 8.

"Do you know this Lindsay?" Sam asked.

"No," Maddy said. "Sam, what if that flash drive is what that guy was after in Jason's office this morning?"

"Possibly, but we have no way of finding Lindsay...unless Jason talked to her on his phone."

Sam left the room, Maddy could hear him shuffling things on Elyse's desk, looking for Jason's charging phone. Finding it, Sam stood staring at the charge indicator light as it glowed a bright green. He came to the doorway to his office and stopped.

"You lied to me Maddy." She saw the anger moving up his face. "This phone is completely charged, and it hasn't been on Elyse's charger long enough for that if it's been in Jason's car for the last three weeks."

"Sam...let me explain."

"What's to explain? You've barely been back in my life for twelve hours asking for my help and you're lying to me. Don't tell me it's because you're protecting Jason."

"No...not Jason." She started crying.

"Tears won't work anymore Maddy." Sam walked to the front of the desk, glaring at her. "Who are you protecting, Nick or yourself? The way I see it, you two are the only ones who would gain by Jason's death. No splitting the inheritance. Either way, I'm done. Find someone else to shed those tears to."

"Sam, please listen. I took the phone, but I honestly don't remember doing it."

"Oh, come on Maddy. Do you really expect me to believe that?"

"I don't care what you believe. It's the truth. I was sitting by Jason, waiting for the police, just like I told you. I saw the phone had fallen into the closet, it was on the floor wedged between the carpet and the wall. I must have picked it up. I don't remember doing it. I found it in my pocket later that day."

"Why didn't you tell me that when I asked you earlier?"

"Because I didn't want you to find out that I was the last person he called."

"Please tell me you didn't erase his calls." Sam checked the recent call history, didn't see Maddy's name, but he did see Lindsay's.

"I deleted his last calls to me. I didn't delete anything else."

"Why?"

"I didn't answer the phone. I knew it was him and I didn't answer. He was in trouble and I ignored him."

"Why didn't you answer the phone?" Sam asked, the anger turning to inquiry.

"Because I'd spent the evening at Northwestern Hospital. The hospital where my dad worked. Nick thought it would be good for the clinic's business if I had a presence there."

"You volunteer?"

"Yes, I visit with the children dealing with mental issues and that's where I was until around eight. When I got home, Nick had already left for his trip to St. Louis and I was mentally exhausted. I went to bed and when the phone woke me up later, I turned it off. I know what you're thinking...that I hated all the time away from Jason and me that my mother spent doing her charity work and I end up ignoring Jason doing the same thing."

"That's why you made it a point to stop in the next day. You felt guilty," Sam said.

"Yes."

"Did he leave you a message?"

"I deleted it too. I'm sorry, but I couldn't listen to it again. He sounded so desperate."

"What did he say?"

"He said he was on his way to my house. That he would explain everything to me when he got there. Then he said if he something happened to him, find you, but to be careful or you would be dead."

"I would be dead? That doesn't make sense. I haven't seen or talked to Jason in years. Are you sure he said I'd be dead and not you?"

"Yes. I don't know what he meant either, but he definitely said you would be dead. That's why I waited so long to call you for help. I don't want anything to happen to you because of me."

"Alright," Sam said, his anger gone. "No more lies, Maddy or I swear to you, I will walk away."

"You know everything now," Maddy said, obviously relieved Sam had forgiven her.

"There's a call to Lindsay here the same day she messaged him. It was later, at eight-thirty. Maybe she didn't show." Sam scrolled down the list of phone calls, stopping at a contact named 'Maven'.

"What did you find?" Maddy asked.

"Calls to 'Maven'. Fairly regular until about a month ago. Then they stopped."

"Maybe Maven was the name of his girlfriend. I told you he had recently broken up, that would explain the cutoff."

"I don't think his girlfriend's name was Maven."

"Why not?"

"Because 'Maven' is a BDSM term used to describe a dominatrix. A maven is a connoisseur of all things bondage."

"I don't know if I should be impressed or worried you know that."

"Either way, it would mean Jason had a serious bondage relationship going until recently."

Sam's phone buzzed, followed close behind by Maddy's. "It's Andy. I'll take this in the outer office." Sam said, leaving Maddy some privacy to answer her own call.

"Checking up on me, Andy? You've been gone ten minutes."

"Cool your jets. I have the results on those license plates you wanted me to run. Interested? Or are you too busy right now?" Andy chided.

"Keep it up, old man. What did you find out?"

"RACK belongs to one Veronica Wells, 1412 Woodland Ave in Woodridge. No priors. She works at an adult bookstore called Playthings. Ever heard of it?"

"I've been inside a few times. Purely on professional business."

"It always is. Do you know what RACK stands for?"

"I know what it means to me."

"Risk aware consensual kink. I googled it when I found out where she works. It basically means she wants all those into bondage to be aware of the risks and to protect themselves by getting informed consent before tying each other up."

"I like my definition better," Sam replied.

"Me too, but at least it sounds like this Veronica is attempting to be a responsible participant, or she's protecting her own ass in case her store gets sued."

"Responsible or not, she may have been the last one to see Jason alive. I think I'll run over to Playthings and see if she's working."

"Lucky you, if you can wait until tomorrow, I'll go with you. Lend the visit a police presence."

"Sorry, that's not likely to be of help in this case," Sam replied. "What about the other license plate? Anything on that?"

"In what I'd call not so much of a coincidence, it belongs to Tracy Fellows who also works at the aforementioned bookstore."

"Even more reason to stop by the store. Were you able to get the coroner's report?"

"I should get it tomorrow," Andy answered.

"Thanks for your help, but I don't want to involve you in this. If the police screwed up Jason's case, I don't want you near any fallout. You're too close to retirement to put yourself in jeopardy."

"Don't worry about me. You on the other hand...do you really think it's smart to get involved with Maddy again, Sam? Like I said before there are plenty of other detectives she could take this to."

"I appreciate the concern, but I'm not the same naive hick anymore who believes it every time someone says that they love me."

"This someone is different. Just be careful," Andy warned.

Returning to his office, Sam immediately recognized Maddy's frustrated-about-to-get-mad face and quietly began backing out of the room. Catching him and motioning him back into the room, she terminated her phone conversation.

"You didn't have to hang up," Sam said.

"Yes, I did. That was Nick and we were getting nowhere."

"OK," Sam replied, not knowing what she meant, and hoping she wouldn't explain.

"He's demanding I empty Jason's apartment by the end of the week." She sat down at his desk, frustrated.

"Why?" Sam asked, immediately sorry he had.

"Closure. God, I hate that word. He says I'll never move forward, get closure," she air pumped quotation marks, "if I don't get Jason's things packed up and his place sold. He's a psychiatrist, he should know better than that."

"Maybe, he thinks it's a start..." Sam began.

"Don't you defend him, Sam," aiming her anger at him. "You don't even like him."

"That's not true," Sam lied, he didn't like him. "I don't know him, but you married him, so he can't be all bad."

She stared at him, silently contemplating Sam's angle for taking Nick's side. "I know what you're doing," she finally said "Reverse psychology won't work on me. I know you don't like him simply because I married him and you think if you prove him a killer, I'll get what I deserve for leaving you."

"If you truly feel that way, you shouldn't have me investigate Jason's death," Sam said. "What I'm doing is trying to find out what happened to Jason. In order to do that, I have to keep an open mind about your husband, and everyone else who's a suspect."

"Including me. You said as much earlier."

"No one is exempt, not even you."

"I didn't kill him for the money," Maddy shot back at him. "Nick wouldn't either."

"Really? How's the Hollowell Clinic doing financially?" Sam asked.

"It's been tough, but Nick thinks they'll make money this year. He says it's not for lack of patients, there're plenty of them. The problem is that the patients don't want to submit psychological claims to their insurance, if they have insurance, and are even more resistant to submit sexual claims. Most are rejected and the ones that are covered, take forever to get paid. It takes a while for any small business to build enough of a cushion to cover the bills while waiting for patients and insurances to pay."

"Where did he get the seventy-five percent startup cash to open the clinic in the first place?"

"A loan from my parents, to be paid back with interest."

"And then your parents died in a car accident…"

"So much for that open mind you're supposed to be keeping. I don't like what you are implying," she protested.

"What did you and Nick decide about the apartment?" Sam asked, changing the subject.

"I told him I was going to Jason's lawyers in the morning to start finalizing his financial affairs. I was actually planning on doing that anyway. It placated him for the moment."

"You'll find out where Jason's money goes then?"

"You sound like Nick!" Maddy fumed. "I hope he left it all to charity! Then Nick won't want it for his clinic, and you won't think I murdered him."

"Calm down. I'm just curious what's in the will. Money is a powerful motive for murder, and so far, I haven't found anything else to go on," Sam said. "Why do you think he was murdered?"

"I don't know," Maddy said. "But I'm telling you, it had nothing to do with money."

"Andy will have the coroner's report sometime tomorrow. After I get that, I'd like to take another look at Jason's exercise room."

"That's fine. I will meet you there. I'm going over to his apartment right after I see the lawyers."

"I probably won't need to go back to his apartment after that."

"Then I'll have no reason to keep the place," Maddy sighed heavily. "Did Andy have anything on the license plates?"

"Yes. RACK belongs to Veronica Wells. She works at an adult bookstore. I'm going there now, hopefully she's working this time of day," Sam said, checking his watch.

"Why don't you call first, make sure she's there?"

"Because if she is, I don't want to tip her off."

"Why are we still sitting here then? Let's go," Maddy said, grabbing her purse.

"Hold on," Sam stopped her. "There's no 'we' in this. Not this time. She'll be more likely to talk to me alone. You go home, do what you need to in the morning, and I'll call you when I'm coming over to Jason's apartment."

"Ok," Maddy said, placing her hand on his arm, "but Sam be careful."

"You're the second one to say that to me in the last hour," Sam said, stepping back out of her reach. "I'm always careful."

"If that were true, the people who know you best wouldn't be telling you to be careful."

CHAPTER 6

Heading south from his office toward Playthings in the early evening traffic, what would normally have been a fifteen-minute drive became an hour-long crawl. As he started and stopped, Sam's thoughts turned to Jason. What had become of the sullen teenager who cared so deeply for his sister? Was his death by his own hand? How deep into kink had his interest gone? His collection of adult paraphernalia was by no means extensive and except for the St Andrew's cross, relatively inexpensive. How harmful could his predilections be if he kept his equipment in boxes along with his collection of comic books?

Remembering *The Spectre* comic he'd found in Jason's closet brought back the second time the two had met. Two weeks after Maddy had given Jason her car, Sam stopped at Graham Crackers Comics of Downers Grove, more intrigued with the name then with the hope of finding *The Spectre* among the racks. Having visited almost every comic shop in the area the elusive number 57 comic book remained unfound. Among the few browsers in the store, Sam saw Jason flipping through a row of comics.

"I would have thought you a Superman fan," Sam commented, easing up next to him.

"He's a boy scout," Jason scoffed. "And I wouldn't take you for a comic book fan at all."

"Is that right? For your information, I've been collecting since I was eight. Nothing much else to do where I come from. Most of my collection is still back in Arkansas and I've been looking for a number 57 *The Spectre* for a while now. Once I have it, I'll have the entire run. It's a very interesting comic. I will let you read it sometime."

"No thanks," Jason said, moving away from Sam to another row of comic books. Not to be dissuaded, Sam moved with him and continued.

"It's about a police detective in the 1940's named Jim Corrigan who crossed

53

paths with the Mob, was locked in a barrel of liquid cement and thrown in the river to drown. God decided to have Corrigan merge with the Spectre entity and become the newest incarnation of The Spirit of Vengeance."

"Because the Spectre must be bound to a human soul to walk the Earth again. How passé."

Surprised and pleased that Jason knew the origin of the comic, Sam countered, "How can you say that? Do you know the Spectre is one of the most powerful beings in the DC Universe?"

"Whatever," Jason replied. "You're such a nerd. You better not let my sister find out. It's bad enough you're from Arkansas." The two carried on their comparison of the DC and Marvel universes, browsing the stiles as they talked.

"What's *Strangers in Paradise* about?" Sam asked, gesturing to the comic in Jason's hand.

"You wouldn't get it," Jason asserted.

"Try me," Sam said.

"It's about two women, Francine and Katchoo..."

"Katchoo? Really, that's her name?"

"Told you."

"Sorry, go on," Sam said.

"Katchoo is in love with Francine, Francine just wants to be friends. Their friend David is in love with Katchoo. Your basic love triangle, right?"

"Not really."

"Anyway," Jason continued, "turns out Katchoo was a lesbian hooker who worked for David's sister and was a Parker Girl who are these badass trained ninja killers. Then you have Big Six. It's a crime syndicate tied into everything--politics, business, the powers that be. Katchoo and Francine get in a lot of trouble."

"But they always find their way out and the bad guys go to jail. Just like the Spectre," Sam concluded.

"Yeah...no," Jason said, shaking his head.

Now, finally just a few miles from meeting presumably the last person Jason saw before his death, Sam thought as he did then, that Jason was a considerably more complicated individual than first appearances would seem.

Arriving at what during the day was a nondescript storefront surrounded on three sides by an eight-foot privacy fence, Sam was met with glaring neon lighting. 'Playthings', the block letters placed disjointed and angled on the roof, was blinking on and off, in red, blue and green. The forty-foot signpost at the entry to the parking lot was similarly illuminated, outlined in chasing neon with 'Playthings' 'Novelties' and 'Toys' blinking on and off. Underneath all the glitter was 'Adult Bookstore' in solid white neon.

Recollections of his first visit to an adult bookstore were nothing like this. He and Maddy had driven fifty miles from home in an effort to ensure they didn't run into someone they knew. That didn't seem to be a concern these days, with adult bookstores popping up like Walgreens. Sam was fascinated, had never seen so much merchandise devoted to sex. It was in that moment, more so than at the museums Maddy had taken him to, he realized how small-town backwards and uneducated in the ways of the world he actually was. His naivete was always a source of amusement to Maddy and one of embarrassment for Sam. As they wandered the aisles, he couldn't help but wonder what Maddy's sexual experiences had been and why she was with him. They spent almost an hour perusing, pausing when something caught their eye or imagination, stopping when they absolutely had no clue how what they were looking at was used. Mostly they just laughed and enjoyed the experience. Reaching the checkout counter empty handed, Maddy urged him to pick something new from the assortment of items stocked in front of the register.

"Lover's dice? That could be interesting." She put them back, pulling something round out of the next jar. "Cock ring?" she asked waving it in the air and smiling.

"Put that down," Sam hissed. "No way I'm getting that." Knowing that gleam in her eye and certain Maddy wouldn't let it go until he'd picked something, Sam grabbed the nearest thing within reach.

"Here," Sam said, handing her the package. "Now let's get out of here."

While the experience was eye opening and had piqued his curiosity, it left him with the realization he didn't understand the need for paraphernalia. What he took away that day, in addition to the studded condoms, was an awakening to the knowledge that many people did and if he wanted to be a detective his worldview had to be expanded.

Sam swept the lot, noting five parked vehicles near the front, none of them with a RACK license plate. The Chevy he'd seen outside Jason's apartment was parked in what Sam presumed to be the employee parking area. Intent on getting some answers from Tracy, he entered the store where he was met by a revolving stile, beyond which stood a perky redhead ready to take the one-dollar cover charge. Assuring him the charge would be taken off his purchase, she stuffed the dollar in her bra and, Sam pushed through. The store was packed with merchandise, every inch of selling space taken. To his left, a few customers wandered the aisles where along the wall and in free-standing racks, the magazines were displayed. Adjoining the magazines, was to Sam an excessive number of DVDs, with a section devoted to employee top ten picks.

Changing out the display for the week was a clerk, his back turned to Sam. Approaching him to ask about Veronica, Sam tapped him on the shoulder. The clerk turned to face him, "How can I help..." he stopped mid-sentence, recognizing Sam and looking around for a means of escape.

"I need to have a word with you," Sam said, stepping in close to Tracy. "Do you want to do it the easy way or the hard way?"

"Break..." Tracy backed away. "I'm on a break." Tracy turned and dashed, as well as he could with a noticeable limp, towards a door at the back of the store which had Employees Only stenciled on the front.

Catching him as he turned the knob, Sam grabbed him by the neck of his shirt and pushed him through the door, slamming it shut behind them.

"You're the punk who broke into Jason's apartment this morning. I'm still getting pieces of lamp out of my hair because of you." Sam forced him against the wall, tightening his grip on his shirt, choking him.

"It... wasn't...my idea," Tracy sputtered between breaths. "It was hers."

"Her who?" Sam eased up on his choke hold so Tracy could answer.

"My boss, Ms. Wells. She told me to do it."

"What exactly did she tell you to do?"

"She said to get any flash drives I could find and mess up the place. I was supposed to get the computer, but you showed up."

"Where are the drives now?" Sam asked, throwing him into one of the chairs in the closet-sized lounge.

"She has them. Don't tell her you know okay? She'll kill me if she finds out."

"Don't worry, I won't, at least not right away. I suggest you grow a pair and don't do everything she tells you to. Breaking and entering is illegal. I could have you arrested."

New panic spread across his face. "I didn't break and enter, I had a key. She told me to bust the door so it would look like a stranger did it."

Sam left the lounge, leaving Tracy to finish his break in peace and finding himself in the middle of the leather section of the store. Harnesses, hoods, puppy mitts, wrist and ankle cuffs, and an assortment of collars and whips graced the shelves. Against his mission-oriented nature, Sam found himself pausing to stare at the merchandise, his reverie broken a few minutes later by the voice of the redhead from the door, who had come up behind him unnoticed. Another unusual occurrence for Sam, he was rarely snuck up on.

"That's a good choice," the clerk said, indicating the riding crop in Sam's hands. "Just the right thickness for a nice spanking. Would you like to try it out?"

"No thanks," Sam said, turning to face Amanda, the name on her badge said and spotting the bondage equipment over her shoulder. He walked past her toward what had attracted his attention. Stepping around displays of suspension equipment, swings and slings, Sam stopped in front of a St Andrew's cross identical to the one in Jason's apartment.

"Keep in mind, we do deliver," Amanda said, mentally calculating her commission on a two-thousand-dollar sale.

"A little out of my price range," Sam said, checking the price tag.

"Can I interest you in a confinement box then?" she continued, determined to make a sale on anything.

"That's a dog crate that I can get at any pet store for seventy-five dollars and you are selling for three times that much. I don't think so."

"I'll let you look around on your own then," Amanda said, deflated.

"Actually, maybe you can help me. I was looking for Veronica Wells."

"She's tied up right now."

"Figuratively or literally?" Sam asked.

"Either way, she won't be available for an hour or so. Do you want me to give her a message for you?"

"Would you ask her to meet me at the Tumbledown Bar at eight o'clock?" Sam asked, checking his watch. "It's just down the street."

"She knows where it is. What should I say this is concerning?"

"Tell her it's about Jason and please give her this," Sam said, handing Amanda one of his cards.

Circling the Tumbledown Bar parking lot several times hunting for an available space, Sam eventually parked in the adjacent lot. As he ambled to the front, he ran his hand through his unruly hair and pulled his jacket against his body. Flashing his identification at the massive bodybuilder bouncers, he passed through a solid wooden door into darkness and deafening music. Stepping out of the flow of entering and exiting traffic until his eyes adjusted, Sam slowly began discerning the interior of the bar. Past the narrow entryway, the room opened onto a hardwood dance floor, surrounded by booths, most of them occupied with early evening revelers. An elevated platform for live entertainment covered the back wall, currently darkened until nine when karaoke started, according to the sandwich board Sam nearly tripped over in an effort to avoid a drunk and his angry girlfriend. Stairs to his left ascended to a second level where a balcony with metal railing surrounded the bar. Suspended from the ceiling hung four metal cages, their occupants, in various forms of undress, all of them nearly nude, gyrating to the reverberating music blasting from the sound system.

To Sam's right was the liquor, behind a bar spanning a third of the way down the wall. He headed towards the nearest barstool with a vantage point of the entry door, knowing if Veronica got past him into the throng, he would never find her.

Expecting a long wait for either of the two bartenders to get to him, Sam swiveled his stool towards the door, hoping his wait for Veronica would be shorter than the hour the store clerk had told him.

"What can I get you?" Sam heard a voice behind him ask.

"Scotch and soda, please," Sam said, turning toward the bar and capturing his first glimpse of Delbert, one of the bartenders. Wearing a skintight muscle shirt displaying hours of devotion in the gym, a golden cross in one ear and his head topped with a do-rag, Delbert wiped the counter in front of Sam. He flashed Sam a mouthful of teeth and said, "Be right back," giving Sam a view of his skinny jeans as he left.

Impressively, Delbert was right back, depositing a napkin down on the bar followed by Sam's drink. "Would you like something to eat? We only serve appetizers, but they're good." he pulled a laminated menu from under the counter and slid it over to Sam.

Realizing he hadn't eaten since breakfast, Sam ordered a plate of chicken fingers and another drink, checking the front door every couple of minutes. Thirty minutes later and halfway through his dinner, Delbert stopped in front of him and shook his head.

"Think she stood you up, stud. But I get off in thirty minutes if you want to try the wilder side."

"What makes you think I haven't already?" Sam questioned.

Delbert burst out laughing. "That's a good one. Let me freshen up your drink, I'll get you a stiff one," giving Sam a wink, he took his glass and returned a few minutes later.

Wincing as he swallowed the mostly Scotch drink, Sam decided to take advantage of the momentary lull in thirsty customers. Leaning over the counter and raising his voice above the din he said, "I'm waiting for Veronica Wells. Do you know her?"

"Ronnie, sure. Who wants to know?" Suspicion crept into his eyes.

"Name's Sam," he replied, "I've never met Ms. Wells and I don't want to miss her in this crowd."

"Honey, you aren't going to miss her. But you're wasting your time. You're definitely not her type," Delbert waved his towel acknowledging a customer further down the bar.

"I'm not looking to date her," Sam said, wondering what her type was and ignoring Delbert's offhanded put down. "I have questions concerning a friend of hers."

"Jason? What a fine specimen and his death such a terrible waste. In my opinion he was too good for her." Delbert left to refill drinks, leaving Sam to finish his cold fries. When he returned, Delbert had some questions of his own.

"I so didn't peg you for a cop...are you? Wasn't Jason's death an accident? You think Ronnie had something to do with it, don't you?"

"Hold on," Sam said, stopping him. "I'm not a cop. I just want to ask her a few questions. I heard they were dating."

"You've been listening to the wrong people. They broke up."

"Why?"

"Why don't you ask me?" Veronica said, placing her clutch purse on the bar and sitting in the stool next to Sam. "Delbert here, always had a hard-on for Jason. Only Jason didn't fly that way. Or at least not in your direction. Now, make me a martini baby, you know how I like them, and leave the adults to talk." She waved Delbert off and swiveled her seat, facing Sam.

"Private investigator, Sam Bartell,'" she read off the card in her hand. "What the hell do you want with me?"

"Veronica Wells, I presume," Sam said, offering her his hand. Delbert was right, he wouldn't have missed her in the crowd. She was tall, not quite six foot, built like a brick shit house to use his father's phrasing. Solidly muscled, but feminine in every aspect as Sam couldn't help staring at her breasts, sitting up and begging through the skin tight lavender sweater she wore with black jeans. Her auburn hair was pulled back in a ponytail, an infinity scarf covering her neck. Sam wondered what else it was covering. Reluctantly he raised his eyes to meet her hazel ones, noting the pixie nose and plump lips.

She shook his hand. "Yes, but I prefer Ronnie," she said, expecting and returning his appraisal.

"I'm investigating Jason's death." Delbert brought her martini and silently slipped away.

"And that has got to do with me?" She asked, taking a long sip of her drink.

"I was told the two of you were dating."

"As Delbert said, we broke up. Case closed."

"That's interesting because I have a witness saying you were with Jason the evening of his death."

"That would be the SOB who lives next door, I assume," Ronnie said fiercely.

"Is he telling the truth?" Sam asked.

"Yes, but when I left, Jason was very alive."

"Why were you there if you weren't seeing each other?"

"It's complicated, and something I don't want to get into here. Let's go someplace a little more private." She raised her glass. "And you can buy me another one of these." She turned and headed off into the crowd, searching for an empty booth.

"What do you want to know?" Ronnie asked, settling into the furthest booth from the dance floor.

"Why don't we start at the beginning. How did you two meet?" Sam asked.

"How I meet most people. He came into Playthings and we started talking. He asked me if I was interested in a website, offered me a discount. He said it would double our business and he was right about that."

"That lead to you two dating?"

"We saw each other for a couple of months--then Jason became jealous about the extracurricular activities I provide to some of our customers."

"I know you're 'Maven' on Jason's phone. Would those activities be bondage related?"

Ronnie smiled at the mention of Jason's phone. "I remember when he listed me in his contacts that way, he thought it was funny." She sighed and Sam sensed a sadness few would have perceived. She straightened in her seat, took another drink and motioned for another one, which Delbert brought to their table in short order. "To answer your question, detective, yes, I give demonstrations on the proper use of the merchandise we sell on an individualized basis to a very select few of our customers."

"Which is a creative way of saying you provide bondage for hire. How realistic are these scenarios?"

"Depends on how much the customer is willing to pay."

"You said Jason became jealous. Did he want you to quit doing them?"

"Yes, and that was part of the reason we split. No man is going to tell me what I can or cannot do."

"I've been to Jason's apartment and I've seen his collection of paraphernalia. I don't think Jason was as into kink as you are."

"No," she smiled. "He wasn't. Those first few sessions were eye opening for him. He toyed with bondage, no pun intended, the basics which I'm sure you're familiar with-- handcuffs, I tied him to the bed once in a while, and you saw the cross in his exercise room. He was intrigued, so I introduced him to some things from the store. For a while things between us were fantastic, but then he wanted me to do things to him and I refused."

"What sort of things?"

"Things a lot rougher than the usual spankings and floggings I do. He wanted pain...really wanted me to hurt him. That's not my thing."

"So, you're ok with whipping and spanking, but pain is where you draw the line?"

"Look, I don't do what I do to hurt people. I spank bare asses, slap them with a whip...doesn't even leave marks, not for long anyway. My clients get off on me telling them what I'm going to do to them if they don't behave. Mommy issues...isn't it always?"

"Except when it's daddy issues. Did he ever hit you?"

"Do I look like someone who would put up with that? The only person Jason would ever hurt was himself."

"Why do you think he craved punishment?"

"He didn't crave it, he asked me to hurt him a couple of times, I said no. That was it. But usually when people want to be punished, it's because they think they deserve it."

"Do you think he deserved it?"

"No, but I think his family does for the years of guilt they laid on him."

"You've met his sister?" Certain Maddy had told him they hadn't.

"Not formally, but he talked about her a lot. Jason didn't think she'd approve of our relationship," she scoffed. "She's the one who hired you, isn't she? I should've known she wouldn't let Jason rest in peace."

"The police say he choked to death, but I think you're the one into that, not Jason," Sam said, indicating her neck scarf. "Did he choke you the night of his death?"

"No," she rubbed the scarf and her neck underneath, "I begged him to, but he wouldn't. That was the real reason we broke up. He told me he loved me, but if we were going to stay together, I'd have to give up my sessions and tame it down at home...no more choking in other words. That's the way we left it until that night."

"You were there to reconcile. Did you?"

"Sorta, we had sex. Then he threw me out."

"Why?"

"He lost it when I joked about his old girlfriend being dead. I saw them together here about four weeks ago and then I saw her picture in the obituary in the paper a couple days later. He didn't know about her death and when I told him, he practically threw me out and said he would be gone for a few days."

"Then he dies later that night. Did he tell you why he was leaving?"

"No, but whatever the reason, it's connected to her."

"Who was the woman?"

"Lindsay Mathers. She was a client and Jason told me they had dated briefly before we met."

"Any idea why she was meeting with Jason?"

"I assumed it was about her website. He had a lot of business meetings here at the bar."

"Did you tell the police about all of this."

"Seriously? They stopped in the store for five minutes after Jason's death, just to confirm that I'd left his place at nine-thirty. They didn't want to hear about Lindsay Mathers."

"Let me see if I got this straight, Jason wanted pain, but you don't like to hurt people. You like to be strangled during sex, but Jason wasn't into kink."

"A match made in heaven," Ronnie said, smiling. "No, Jason wasn't into kink, his favorite position was missionary, if you know what I mean, but he loved me and he'd do anything I asked, dominatrix or not. You may think that'd bore me, but it didn't, not with Jason. After we broke up, I realized the bondage wasn't as important to me as he was. Jason was special."

"Special enough for you to get so worked up about his meeting with Lindsay that you murdered them both?" Sam accused.

"I wasn't jealous," Ronnie denied vehemently. "I told you, she wasn't his girlfriend anymore."

"Why was Tracy in Jason's house today?" Sam asked, changing the subject.

"I don't know what you're talking about." Clearly, she did.

"Don't bother denying it. Tracy recognized me when I stopped by Playthings looking for you. He was at Jason's apartment this morning, ransacking his office, almost got me killed with a lamp. He told me you sent him there. What was he looking for?"

"Pictures I don't want found."

"What kind of pictures?"

"You're a detective, right. You should be able to figure that out on your own."

"Why are you concerned about them now?"

"I loved Jason and started thinking about his sister finding them. I know Jason wouldn't want that, so I asked Tracy to break in and take the computer and any flash drives he could find. I haven't gotten a chance to look at them yet."

"Why all the cloak and dagger? Don't you have a key to his apartment? You could've gotten them anytime on your own."

"Between that nosy neighbor and that bitch sister who's always there, I haven't had the chance. I thought maybe a robbery would scare her away for a while," Ronnie replied.

"I'm sure Maddy would like those back, whatever is on them."

"Any more questions?" Ronnie asked, finishing her drink and picking up her purse.

"No, but my investigation is in the early stages. I'm sure we'll need to talk again."

"I'll look forward to your call," she replied, tossing her business card on the table as she walked away.

CHAPTER 7

"There you lie, tied up and subject to your lover's every whim and desire, knowing she or he can bring you pleasure or pain. Perhaps your playmate will taunt you with a feather, titillate you with a spanking or tease you with a vibrator and if you're the one in control, seeing your partner 'helpless' can be a tremendously erotic feeling. Sensory deprivation and restraint are two of the most basic bondage activities. Sensory deprivation allows a top to take control of a bottom, such as in blindfolding, where the loss of sight compels the bottom to focus on his or her other senses, thereby intensifying all sensation. Securing someone's hands and ankles with restraints is at the heart of bondage and something I'm sure most of you have already experienced to some degree in your young lives."

Stepping into the back of the auditorium-sized classroom, Sam quietly sat in the back row. At the front of the classroom stood Edward Holloway forty minutes into his nine o'clock Sexual Deviancy class. Sam had called the Dr.'s office to set up an appointment earlier and had learned that Holloway was teaching at Roosevelt University in Schaumburg. Hoping to talk to him after his lecture, Sam opened the thin file Elyse had given him on his way out of his office. It contained all she could find on the good doctor's childhood.

Edward Holloway was born to Carla Hicks, no father listed on the birth certificate, on June the fourth, thirty-three years ago, he was five years younger than Nick and not much older than Jason. Carla was an aspiring actress among the thousands in Los Angeles and in her prime a 'B' actress at best. She appeared in several commercials, played the dead girl on several crime shows and probably thought she was on her way to stardom when she got a part in a debuting television sitcom. It was cancelled before its first airing and shortly thereafter, she gave birth to her only child, Edward, named after her grandfather.

Carla and Edward moved frequently during his childhood, all within Los Angeles county, Edward attended seven different schools before the age of ten. Carla supported the both of them doing odd jobs, but they didn't last, she was an alcoholic. She went back to acting; pornos, Elyse had penciled in a few of the titles. Then she was killed in an apartment fire. Edward, now fourteen, had gotten out, in more ways than one. He was fostered and later adopted by the Holloways, a childless couple in their fifties who got him through the rest of his teens and then paid for the next eight years of college it required for him to get his doctorate in psychiatry. With a childhood like that, it wasn't surprising Holloway had chosen psychiatry, Sam mused.

"Friday there will be a quiz on Chapters One through Five. If there are any questions, I'll be in my office for the next hour. You can also reach me at the Hollowell Clinic and remember group counseling sessions are open to the public and count for extra credit."

As the students collected their tablets and exited, Sam wielded his way down the steps toward the raised center of the classroom.

"The lectures I sat through in college weren't near as interesting," Sam said to Holloway as he gathered his things.

"Then maybe you studied the wrong subjects," Holloway answered. "How may I help you?"

"My name is Sam Bartell. I'm looking into the death of Jason Richards."

"If you're from Jason's life insurance company, I've already talked to an agent. I have nothing further to say." Holloway said, dismissing him.

"Insurance?"

"The difference between an accidental death and a suicide can mean a lot of money--to Maddy I assume. Jason's death was ruled accidental and you're here to get me to tell you Jason was suicidal, so your company can reject the claim."

"I'm not with the insurance company. I'm a private investigator and I'm actually here to try to understand autoerotic asphyxiation."

"Self-strangulation for the purpose of sexual arousal. What's not to understand?" Holloway said flippantly.

"Knowing what it is and understanding why it's done in the first place are very different," Sam said.

"Speaking medically," Holloway snapped his briefcase closed and looked at Sam. "The simplest explanation is that the lack of oxygen causes lightheadedness, tingling sensations and reduces inhibitions, which enhances the sexual experience. The problem," Holloway continued, sitting on the edge of his desk, "is that it's easy to go too far. As little as seven pounds of pressure will collapse the carotid artery, producing unconsciousness within seconds. Adding to that, many victims combine bondage with the asphyxiation and their bindings make self-rescue difficult. Most are also impaired by alcohol, which affects their judgement and motor abilities, not to mention dulling the whole experience. It becomes a fine line of consciousness. Lose it and you're dead. The irony, and many of my patients have told me this, is that the harder it is to escape the bondage, the better the fantasy is. But, if you lose consciousness at the right phase of the sinus rhythm, your heart stops and can't be restarted by CPR. This is the cause of many deaths when couples are engaging in BCP or when the police use the choke hold and the suspect dies."

"BCP-Breath Control Play," Sam repeated. "Play meaning more than one person, whereas autoerotic asphyxiation is strangulation of oneself," Sam said.

"That's an oversimplification. The two are similar, but autoerotic asphyxiation has many characteristics that go beyond the euphoria of hypoxia."

"You're talking about psychological aspects now," Sam noted.

"Yes." Holloway, now aware he wasn't talking to a layman, continued in lecturer mode. "A large part of the fantasy is the individual's control over their own death. Not a death wish, rather a fantasy of death. Similar to what a daredevil feels."

"Sometimes the devil wins," Sam uttered.

"Unfortunately. That is what my practice is about and why I teach this class. I believe, as does my partner, that students should be taught the most up-to-date methods of treating this activity."

"Why do you use the word activity as opposed to perversion?"

"What's considered to be perversion varies from society to society, and from year to year. Some behaviors that might be classified as deviant by some members of society may be viewed as harmless eccentricities by others, or entirely normal behavior to others. Use of the terms 'sexual deviancy' and 'sexual perversion' give negative connotations. We prefer activities."

"Some of these 'activities' are illegal."

"Certainly, the more extreme ones are, pedophilia, necrophilia, voyeurism and bestiality, to name a few, but they are easier to understand if you think of those behaviors in less extreme versions, which are quite common, and legal. For instance, having a partner 'talk dirty' may be a turn-on for some people. You would agree this is legal?" Holloway asked, not pausing for an answer. "The problem arises, and the behavior becomes a paraphilia when talking dirty is the only way that sexual arousal or satisfaction can occur. Viewing a nude person or watching adult sexually explicit DVDs can be arousing for most people. Paraphilias are magnified to the point of psychological dependency. This dependency can lead to illegal acts."

"Given what appears to be a fine line between the two, how do you treat your patients?"

"There are several therapies for sexual addictions, but the ones practiced by our clinic are cognitive behavioral therapy and psychodynamic psychotherapy. I prefer the former."

"I took a couple psych classes in college, but can you refresh me on the differences between the two?"

"Cognitive therapy focuses on identifying triggers to sexual behaviors, and reshaping the way the patient excuses these behaviors, such as, 'It's not cheating on my spouse if it's computer sex'. The emphasis is on relapse prevention. With the psychodynamic approach, which is what Dr. Maxwell practices, he attempts to find out the conflicts that drive the sexual activity. Once he has the motive, he works on helping the patient develop the coping skills to minimize urges and less harmful ways of dealing with the issue."

"How successful are these therapies?"

"Unfortunately, there is little data relating to treatment outcomes. We have accomplished extraordinary work at the clinic and have seen very positive results as you can read for yourself in our recently published book comparing our results. Our success rates were about the same."

"Under five percent, if I remember correctly." Sam had skimmed the book after dinner last evening.

"You've been holding out on me." Pleased and surprised Sam had read his book. "As anyone who works in this area will tell you," Holloway said, defending his results, "reprogramming a sexual deviant is one of the hardest to achieve, for obvious reasons. Sexual gratification is one of the strongest human motives and the more extreme the deviation, the stronger the motive. Recent surveys have shown that five percent of the general population meet criteria for a sexual obsession. That means there are more sex addicts out there than compulsive gamblers. If you're truly interested, why don't you come to my one of my counseling sessions? They're open to the public and held every Tuesday and Thursday evening as I mentioned to my class earlier."

"Did Jason attend any of these meetings?"

"You're really asking if he was my patient."

"I know he was your patient when you moved here from California and if you've already talked to his life insurance company, then they thought he still was."

"I hadn't seen Jason on a professional basis for almost two years," Holloway said obviously surprised Sam knew about California. "Then about two months ago he attended a few counseling sessions. I asked if he wanted to set up an individual appointment, but he declined."

"Why was he attending sessions?"

"He didn't go into much detail when I asked, but I got the impression he was in a relationship and trying to decide whether he should end it."

"He started seeing you years ago because of an attempted suicide, recently begins attending sessions again, then turns up dead. Given your training and sessions with Jason, do you think his death could have been self-inflicted?"

"After his experience in California, I was surprised with the way he died. He never showed any indication that choking had become a fetish, to the contrary, Jason was one of the few patients I've treated that didn't have obsessive sexual tendencies. But to answer your question, I would have to say his death was accidental. When I saw him last, he didn't appear to be in emotional distress, or I would've insisted he make an appointment."

"I'm sure you would have Dr. but wouldn't it be just as feasible for someone to kill Jason and make it look like it was an accident?"

"Anything's possible, and I can certainly understand why Maddy would want it to be that. But proving it was murder is going to be almost impossible."

"While we're on the subject, where were you on the evening of Jason's death?"

"I was at the clinic all day and covered for Dr. Maxwell at his therapy session Tuesday evening. It was over by nine. I was home, alone by nine-thirty."

"Where was Dr. Maxwell?" Wanting to confirm Maddy's claim he was on the road.

"He was scheduled to begin a book tour in St. Louis Wednesday morning. He asked me to cover his evening session so he could pack and get on the road." Holloway lifted his briefcase from the desk. "I have office hours now, detective. Anything else?"

Returning to his office, Sam was surprised to hear Elyse laughing with Andy in the outer office. He opened the door to Andy's contribution to Elyse's earlier hotel ghost story.

"The Congress Plaza hotel on Michigan Avenue is by far the most haunted hotel in downtown Chicago," Andy proclaimed.

"Really, I thought you didn't believe in ghost stories."

"I don't, but if you put aside the things Al Capone was known to do there you still have security guards reporting apparitions of a young boy on the twelfth floor and the haunting of room four forty-one."

"How does that beat my Lady in Red at The Drake?"

"Because room four forty-one still gets the most security calls. And this ghost doesn't just appear, it moves objects, turns lights on and off and generally makes a nuisance of itself."

"I think you two should get a room," Sam said. "And, if you keep showing up here," Sam said to Andy. "I'll have to put you on the payroll. Don't you have a regular job?"

"I'm using up all my personal time before I retire," Andy said, smiling at the thought. "Worked a half-day. How did your visit with Veronica Wells go?"

"Turns out she was the woman Erickson saw leaving Jason's apartment the night of his death and she's a dominatrix. She claims Jason was alive and well when she left, doesn't know who or why anyone would want to kill him."

"Did you believe her story?" Andy asked.

"For the most part, but she's not telling everything. She's also responsible for the break-in at Jason's apartment, sent one of her employees."

"Why?" asked Elyse.

"To get some obscene pictures she doesn't want Maddy to find."

"This Veronica sounds like someone I'd like to meet," Andy said.

"That can be arranged. If you need something to do with your time, why don't you tail her for a while, see what she does this afternoon. I don't think she's found what she's looking for at Jason's apartment and now that I'm on the case, she knows her time is limited."

"Why do you think she hasn't found it already?" Elyse asked.

"The feeling I got when I talked to her," Sam said, shaking his head. "She's not looking for nude pictures."

"Speaking of pictures," Andy said, waving a manila file in the air. "The real reason I stopped by was to show you the coroner's results and the pictures taken at the scene of Jason's death."

"You didn't have to get those, Andy. I told you to stay out of this," Sam reprimanded.

"By staking out a dominatrix?" Andy asked.

"That's different than asking for actual case files. You know if we really needed them, Elyse could work her magic."

"The way I see it, the quicker we get this thing solved, the quicker Maddy gets out of our lives," Andy said.

"Have you looked at the results yet?" Sam asked.

"Briefly, and I found a few things odd on the autopsy report," Andy said, leading the way into Sam's office, where he spread the contents of the folder on the desk.

"Such as?" Sam asked, scrutinizing each photo individually and placing them back on the desk.

"For starters, there are these marks on his back," Andy said, pointing to a set of round burn marks among red whip markings on Jason's autopsy picture.

"Those look like taser marks," Sam said.

"That's what I thought too, and the coroner agrees. He said tasers are becoming very popular with the kink scene."

"That was quite a shock by the degree of burned tissue. Did the coroner say whether he thought it was given through clothing or not?" Sam asked.

"There were bits of cloth in the wounds, but he died naked," Andy answered.

"Then why is the coroner saying this is accidental? Clearly Jason couldn't have tasered himself from the position of the wound. Plus, there isn't a taser in these pictures." Sam said, searching in all the photos.

"The coroner says it doesn't matter who tased him, he died from asphyxiation several hours after it happened."

"Well, maybe the one who tased him, strangled him," Elyse said.

"A logical conclusion, but…" Andy stopped.

"No one followed up on it, did they?" Sam said, bitterly.

"There was nothing to follow up on," Andy countered. "Ejaculate found near the St. Andrew's cross indicates he had sex, but at least two hours prior to his death. There was also evidence of sexual intercourse in the bedroom," Andy said.

"Ronnie did say they had sex," Sam said. "She didn't say how much."

"Erickson's statement has her leaving at nine-thirty, the coroner figured she tased him during sex and took the taser when she left. Then Jason decided to get kinky with the rope on his own and things didn't turn out so well," Andy said.

"Ronnie didn't mention anything about a taser, and she says Jason was in a big hurry to leave. He wasn't the one into that anyway, Ronnie has the rope fetish."

"Speaking of the rope," Andy continued, "Jason didn't make the noose he was strangled with."

"How do you know that?' Sam asked.

"I'll show you," Andy said pulling his tie from around his neck and a length of rope he had stuffed in his pocket for his demonstration.

"You make a hangman's noose with that," Andy said, throwing the rope on Sam's desk, "and I'll make one with this."

Sam did what he was told and handed it back to Andy.

"So…?" Elyse asked, stepping up to the desk.

"Sam is righthanded, I'm left. See how the loops are reversed?" Now look at the picture of the noose around Jason's neck." Andy sifted through the photos, finding the one with the best view of the neck area. "Here see…the loops match the direction of the one I made, not Sam's."

"How do you know Jason wasn't lefthanded?" Elyse asked.

"That's what the coroner said when I asked him."

"You think Jason was killed by a lefthanded noose-maker?" Elyse asked.

"Ronnie's lefthanded," Sam said, remembering the way she held her drink at the bar. "But that only proves what I already know--Ronnie made the noose because she's the one who used it. Nothing surprising there."

"I said I found it odd, not conclusive," Andy said.

"So far I haven't found much of anything conclusive about this case," Sam said, his frustration apparent. "I have the on/off again girlfriend/dominatrix, Veronica who prefers to be called Ronnie and Lindsay Mathers who met with him at the Tumbledown Bar and is also now dead."

"Two deaths, any suspects?" Andy asked.

"No, and no motive."

"Now what?" Elyse asked.

"Maddy had a meeting with Jason's lawyers this morning, I'm meeting her at the apartment with these," Sam said, gathering the autopsy report and crime scene photos from his desk. "Hopefully, I can find something the police missed. If not, I'll go through his office again."

"Doesn't sound promising," Andy said. "Accidental suicide may be the only conclusion to be drawn here."

"That isn't going to make Maddy happy at all," Sam replied.

CHAPTER 8

Maddy was furious. She turned the ignition off and got out of her car, slamming the door shut and marching up the driveway. Two moving vans were parked in front of Jason's apartment and as she rounded the back of them, she saw they were both nearly full. Entering the foyer, she spotted two men carrying the desk from Jason's office down the stairs.

"What are you doing? Maddy shouted. "I said nothing was to be taken from the upstairs."

The men, stunned at her outburst, set the desk down mid-stairway. "We were told to clear out the office and to leave the bedrooms alone," the man closest to Maddy said.

"By whom?" Maddy asked, gaining her composure. "And who let you in?" Swearing if Erickson was somehow involved, she was going to sue, after she killed him.

"The guy in the kitchen." Maddy wheeled from the men and stormed toward the kitchen.

Recognizing his voice before she reached the kitchen, Maddy walked into the room. "Nick, what the hell are you doing here?" she cried, interrupting his instructions to a couple of movers boxing up the kitchen.

"I told you this morning I took the day off so I could help you," Nick said, puzzled by her anger.

"And I told you I didn't want your help," Maddy retaliated.

Taking her forearm, Nick led her into the walk-in pantry attempting to keep their conversation private. "Maddy, I'm sorry I upset you," Nick began, placating her. "You aren't thinking straight. This isn't what Jason would want--you stressing over his things. Doing everything yourself isn't going to bring him back and it certainly won't bring you the closure you need."

71

"Stop psychoanalyzing me," Maddy hissed. "You don't care about my closure any more than you cared about Jason. You're happy he's gone."

"How can you say that?" Nick retorted. "I did everything I could to help him."

"Help him? You were nothing but condescending towards him. He thought you were a prick and told me not to marry you. I should've listened."

"I know you're distraught right now and you don't mean these things, so, I'm going to help the movers finish up," Nick said, ever the martyr and moved toward the pantry door.

"Why are they here so early? I told them I wouldn't be here until the afternoon," Maddy asked, stopping him.

"I saw the number on the notepad by the phone. After you left, I called and asked them to come earlier, since I was available. I honestly thought I was helping you, that you'd be glad most of the heavy work was done when you got here. I should've known better."

"Poor Nick, always so misunderstood," Maddy said sarcastically.

Returning to the kitchen, they watched as the final boxes from the downstairs were sealed up and taken to the vans. "I asked them to leave Jason's bedroom and exercise room alone. I didn't think you'd want them in those rooms," Nick said, their argument already a thing of the past for him.

"Thank you," Maddy replied, grateful but not as quick to forget, the thought of the bondage apparatus crossing her mind, as it must have Nick's. She wondered if he was protecting her or himself. A well-known sex therapist with a kinky brother-in-law might not help Nick's reputation.

"I forgot to tell you this morning that I called a realtor yesterday," Nick said, cutting into her thoughts. "I let him know you would be putting this place on the market and he wanted to set up a time to meet."

"Without even asking me?" Maddy asked, her anger quickly returning.

"I called you several times. What were you doing that you couldn't answer?" Sam walked into the kitchen, his shock at seeing the emptied apartment coupled with the unexpected appearance of Nick.

"Or should I say who was you doing?" Nick seethed.

"You're such an asshole, Nick," Maddy retorted. "I called Sam to help me find Jason's killer."

"He's the reason why you've been dragging your feet on this apartment," Nick said, scowling at Sam.

"Maybe I should come back another time." Sam retreated a few steps.

"That won't be necessary," Maddy said, walking over to Sam, she took his arm leading him back through the doorway. "Why don't you go on upstairs, I'll join you in a minute." Returning to Nick, determined not to lose her composure she said, "I only called Sam two days ago and as a last resort."

"I should've known you'd drag him into this. I'm truly surprised you waited so long."

"What does that mean?"

"It means the minute something comes along that you can't accept, you run to the one who will believe your delusions and feed them."

"You mean he actually listens to what I'm saying and doesn't disregard my opinions." She took a deep breath, started again. "The last thing Jason said to me was to call Sam and I'll never forgive myself or get the closure you say I need if I don't give him the chance to investigate his death. Surely you can understand that."

Nick softened. "I understand this is something you've convinced yourself you need to do. Fine, let him investigate, but keep him away from me."

"You won't even consider the possibility that Jason was murdered?"

"No, I won't. Jason died by his own hand, accidentally or on purpose, and the sooner you accept that, the better for everyone."

"You mean the better for you, don't you Nick?"

"I don't know what you mean by that and I don't care, I'm leaving," Nick said. "The movers are almost done and I'm sure I can find work to do at the clinic."

Pulling three photos taken of Jason's body out of the coroner's report, Sam placed them on the floor of the closet. The photos captured Jason from three different angles, back, side and in front, the last one taken by placing the camera on a selfie stick in front of the body and shooting, there wasn't enough room for anyone to squat in front and take a picture. Sam had never gotten promoted to detective on the police force, but he was familiar with the process and by all accounts, the detectives who caught the case dotted their i's and crossed their t's, but that's all they did. One interview with Erickson, a short conversation with Veronica and the coroner's report made up the entire file. Sam read the description of the scene when the body was found, then kneeled where Jason had died, closing his eyes and clearing his mind.

Maddy found Sam in Jason's exercise room thirty minutes later, deep in concentration. She watched him silently as he knelt on the floor. She knew what he was doing, he was putting himself into the pictures that lay in front of him in the closet, into Jason's body and mind, hoping to reason through what had happened. She watched as he put an imagined noose around his neck, pulled it taut and then began straining against the rope, either in Jason's ecstasy or his pain. Minutes pass as Sam's writhings reach a peak and then he slumps into the side of the closet, expending a deep breath and became still in death exactly as Jason had died.

Momentarily, the memory of Jason's naked body replaced Sam's in the closet. Tears welled in her eyes and she stepped back from the threshold quietly so as not to disturb Sam's thoughts.

"Maddy?" She heard Sam's strained voice as if he'd actually been strangling and stepped back into the room.

"Yes, I didn't want to disturb you. I can wait downstairs."

"No need," Sam said, grabbing the photos and sliding them out of sight in the folder.

"Did you learn anything helpful?" Maddy pointed at the folder.

"I know it may seem strange to you, but sometimes it helps putting myself into the crime scene. It helps me focus."

"If it helps you solve cases, I'm all for it, but it's creepy watching you do it." Maddy shivered.

"Are the movers done downstairs?" Sam asked.

"Yes, they left ten minutes ago," Maddy said. "I know you wanted to go through Jason's office again. Nick had no right to let them take everything."

"No worries," Sam said, wanting to dispel her distress. "To be honest, there probably wasn't anything to help us except for his laptop, and we have that. I think you're more upset by Jason's things being taken away right now than you are at Nick."

"I have Nick to psychoanalyze me, Sam."

"Trying to help, here," Sam said, holding his hands up in surrender.

"You don't believe me either," Maddy said her conversation with Nick still stinging. "You think Jason killed himself and you're telling me what you think I want to hear."

"I don't know how Jason died," Sam said, aware he was getting the fallout of Maddy's argument with Nick. "I'm convinced it wasn't intentional suicide and half-way to believing it wasn't accidental. There're a few questions that I need answered before I can say for sure it was murder. And to be honest, I don't know if I'll be able to get those answers. That's where I stand."

"I'm sorry," Maddy said. "I'm taking my anger at Nick out on you, and as much as I hate to admit it, you're right. Seeing those men taking Jason's things away has upset me more than I expected. She moved into his arms and before Sam could resist, her mouth was on his. Then the urge to resist was gone, replaced by emotions he'd buried years ago in a tomb of hopes and dreams he had shared with Maddy. That she had so quickly and effortlessly unearthed them infuriated him and he pulled away.

"Maddy, you can't do this." He turned from her, facing Jason's open closet.

"I know," Maddy said, backing away. "But I've missed you, the way you always knew what I was thinking even before I did, the way you understand me so completely. The way you loved me."

Sam stepped closer to the closet; the kiss forgotten. He turned to face Maddy. "Jason said I would be dead, right?"

"What are you talking about?"

"Jason's last phone call to you. He said to be careful or I would be dead?"

"No…" Maddy said. "Not those exact words."

"What were the exact words?" Sam said, taking her hands in his urgency. "Try to remember, it might be important."

"Ok," Maddy said, for the first time sorry she'd erased the message. "He said. 'Call Sam but tell him to be careful or he'll be dead too'."

"Dead too…dead too. You didn't say that the first time. I'll be dead too, like another dead detective. The Spectre." Moving to the closet door, Sam pulled the comic boxes out and placed them on the floor of the exercise room. As he pulled the bottom box out, something caught his eye on the floorboards of the closet. He knelt on the floor.

"What is it?" Maddy asked, kneeling with him.

Sam ran his hand along the floor several times, circling the spot where the boxes had been. Finding an uneven board, Sam reached into his pocket, retrieving a pocketknife he had received from Elyse for Christmas last year. With the tip of the knife, he lifted the board, revealing a small compartment between the floor joists, a foot wide and across. Sitting on the floor of the compartment was a lockbox. Pulling it up and out of the hole, Sam rested it on the floor of the closet. Sam tried the catch. It was locked.

"Did you know about this?" Sam asked.

"I knew he had a lockbox, but he kept it in his office for important papers-- his passport, birth certificate, bank paperwork. I have no idea what it's doing here."

Sam turned the box over, hoping to find the key taped to the bottom, something he had often done so as not to lose it. No such luck in this case.

"Without a key, I'm going to have to destroy the box." Sam said.

"I don't care about the box. Open it and see what's inside."

"I'll need something more substantial than this pocketknife," Sam said. "I'll have to take it to the office."

"Why would he put it there?" Maddy asked. "If I hadn't called you, it never would've been found."

"He told you to call me, Maddy. He knew you'd do as he asked," Sam said. "Veronica Wells told me Jason was leaving town, I assume after he stopped off to see that you were safe. Maybe he wanted someone to know why if he didn't get to you."

"Doesn't that prove he was murdered? Someone killed him before he got to me."

"Veronica could also be making it up," Sam countered. "By throwing suspicion on a ghost, she's getting herself off the hook. I know she's hiding something and she's the one into BCP….breath control play."

"Why make it up unless she's the one who killed him, either by accident or intent. They could've been doing BC…"

"P…BCP is the term you're looking for."

"If she was strangling him, maybe something went wrong. It's possible isn't it?"

"Yes, but that scenario would be impossible to prove. She'll never admit to that and there's no evidence she was there when he died. Our only witness, your neighbor Erickson, puts her leaving at nine-thirty. The coroner puts the earliest time of death at eleven."

"She could've come back later."

"I haven't ruled her out as a suspect and I'll definitely take another run at her, but on another subject, what did you find out about Jason's estate?"

"It stays in a trust." "For how long?"

"For two years. Then it goes to several charities."

"You thought he left everything to you."

"When we set up our wills after our parents died, I left everything to Nick, Jason left everything to me. His lawyer said Jason came in two weeks before his death and changed his will."

"That's harsh. He disliked Nick so much he wouldn't give his money to you?"

"Apparently."

"Why didn't he tell you?"

"I don't know, maybe he was worried what Nick would do if he found out. We don't need the money Sam, but he wouldn't like the slap in the face, even if it was my face."

"Alright, I'm done here. I'm going to the office. Do you want me to wait for you before I open this?" Sam asked holding up the lock box."

"No," Maddy said, shaking her head.

"Are you sure?" Sam asked, surprised by her disinterest in what he considered the only clue they had to what happened the night Jason died.

"Whatever he put in there, he meant for you to see. I'll finish up here and stop by your office on my way home."

"Take it easy," Sam said, picking up on the strain in her voice. "Today has been rough," he took her in his arms and hugged her close, feeling the tension ease in her body. "But it's going to get better."

CHAPTER 9

"What's that?" Elyse asked, pouncing on Sam as soon as he stepped into the office.

"A lockbox we found at Jason's apartment, and before you ask, I don't know what's in it yet. That's what this is for," Sam said, grabbing a pry bar from the toolbox he kept in the outer office closet. He went into his office, Elyse trailing after.

Setting the box on his desk, Sam leveraged the pry bar under the lid and popped it open. Taking out the contents, he spread them on the desk, putting them back in the box after examining each one. He found an envelope with Maddy's name written on the front and laid it aside, unopened. Ending up with a folded newspaper page, Sam opened it. A flash drive fell to his desk. Handing the flash drive to Elyse so she could open it from Jason's laptop still sitting on his desk, Sam gave up his chair.

"How did he know you'd find this?" Elyse asked, sliding the drive into the slot on the side of the computer.

"He told Maddy to call me in his last phone message to her."

"Sounds risky to me. Why didn't he tell Maddy on the phone where it was?"

"If there's something on it that is condemning to Nick, maybe he didn't want her finding it alone."

"Because she'd bury it to protect him?"

"Or because he wanted someone with her when she discovers the truth about her husband," Sam offered.

"Or it's his grocery list," Elyse said.

"Only one way to find out. How's it going?"

"Still opening," Elyse said, checking the screen. "There's a lot of data on here."

Sam picked up the envelope addressed to Maddy and debated on opening it before finally placing it back on the desk. He began pacing around the room. "It's open," Elyse said, striking the keyboard. "Now let's find out what's in it."

As he was coming around the desk to join Elyse at the computer, Sam's phone buzzed. He put Andy on speaker phone. "How's it going?" Sam asked. "I've followed Ms. Wells to Jason's apartment. Looks like your hunch was right."

"Is Maddy still there?" Sam asked, "She was finishing up when I left about an hour ago."

"Yeah, she's here. They're having a conversation on the doorstep. Wells wants to go in and Maddy isn't letting her. Lot of arm waving and some raised voices."

"I bet the neighbors are getting an earful," Sam smiled.

"She must have some pretty wild pictures to be so hot on getting them back," Elyse chimed from behind the computer.

"Maybe she's afraid Maddy will post them on Facebook if she finds them," Andy replied.

"That might be good for her business," Elyse said.

"I doubt it," Andy said over the phone.

"Never know," Elyse mused, returning to the computer screen.

"Looks like the discussion is over," Andy said. "Maddy's locked the door and heading for her car. I'll continue tailing Wells if you want Sam, but now that she knows the apartment's empty, she won't be back."

"Unless she knows about Jason's secret hidey hole Sam found in the sexercise room," Elyse joked. "See what I did there?"

"Clever, but if Ronnie knew about that, she wouldn't have been looking in the office," Sam said. "Go on home, Andy."

"Sure thing. I think she knew she was being tailed anyway," Andy ended the call.

Sam joined Elyse behind the computer as she scrolled down the files that she'd opened from the flash drive

"Those look to be ledgers," he commented.

"They are, but they aren't for his computer business," Elyse said. "They're from the Hollowell Clinic. There's at least six months of accounts here. Patient accounts showing payments and outstanding balances, balance sheets, income and cash flow statements," Elyse continued scrolling through the files. "I've had a few accounting classes and from what little I know; it looks as though the clinic is running at a very low profit margin. It'll take me some time, but I think I can work through this and get a general idea of the fiscal soundness of the clinic."

"Why would Jason have a copy of this, unless he thought Nick was doing something illegal?" Sam asked aloud as he began his pacing around the desk again. "Would you pull up Lindsay Mather's obit?" Sam asked.

"Sure," Elyse replied. "What are we looking for?"

"I want to see if there's mention of where she worked."

"She worked as an intern at Padgett Business Services in Naperville," Elyse read.

"She has a meeting with Jason to discuss what she's found on a flash drive he'd given her," Sam mused. "Then two days later she's dead and within twenty-four hours Jason is found dead. I don't believe in coincidences. Can you find out her cause of death?"

"Already on it," she said, pulling up the coroner's report. "Heart attack? She was young, but heart attacks can happen to anyone."

"No," Sam said, scanning the report. "Her heart stopped, that's cardiac arrest. It says here she had congenital heart disease, more specifically, abnormal heart rhythms. I think she died from electrostimulation."

"How do you get estim from her heart stopping?" Elyse asked, perplexed.

"Don't worry about that. See if you can get pictures from the scene." Sam paced some more.

"Wow, you're good," Elyse said several minutes later. "There's a picture of an electrostimulation power box taken into evidence." There were two pictures of the box, one of the top with two estim lead jacks, a quick disable button, a pulse rate knob and a frequency knob. The second picture showed the bottom of the box with the label DO NOT USE ABOVE THE WAIST adhered to the bottom.

"Why would she do that to herself if she had heart problems?" Elyse asked.

"Because she liked it and that warning label didn't stop her. That's why it's called an addiction. Let's look at the pictures of the scene." He scrolled down the screen. Lindsay was lying naked splayed on the couch in her living room, the electrostimulation box laying on the floor in front of her. The leads hung from her body unattached to the box as they'd been ripped from their jacks when the box fell to the floor during her death throes. Sam spotted the black electrode clamped to Lindsay's left nipple and a lead coming from the ripple-headed insertable electrode in her vagina.

"Says here that the power box shows indications of being tampered with and when the voltage was tested it'd been amped up higher than the specs. Why wasn't this treated as a murder?" Elyse asked.

"No evidence of foul play. The only fingerprints on the box were Lindsay's." Sam took the mouse, enlarged the manufacturer name stamped on top and opened a new window searching for their website. Scrolling down the pages, Sam found the unit matching the picture. Reading the description Sam said, "There are three different types of this unit, each with a different power level, but they all use the same box style. It's possible whoever put this unit together at the factory put the higher-powered guts of the Apollo into what's supposed to be the much tamer Ares unit. There may be a case of product liability and negligence here, but not murder."

Sam flipped back to the police report. "More likely she rigged the box herself or her boyfriend did and lied when he told the detectives who interviewed him that he'd never seen it. His name is Tim Murphy, he worked with her at Padgett Business Services and they'd been dating for about six months. He admits they both did estim, but claims he wasn't there when she died. He later stated that Lindsay was 'way more into it and liked having control over the entire experience'. There's also a side note saying Mr. Murphy was quite impressed with the electrostimulation box when the detectives showed it to him and didn't know how Lindsay had afforded it. Apparently, these units are very expensive."

"Obsessions usually are," Elyse said. "Maybe someone bought both boxes switched them and then gave it to her."

"I guess that's possible, but what's your motive?" Sam asked, not convinced. "Besides, this wouldn't be the first time someone got killed by tampering with things they shouldn't. If only she'd had the presence of mind to shock herself again. It might've put her back into a normal rhythm."

"Even if she'd thought of that in her panic, the leads weren't attached anymore," Elyse pointed at the unhooked leads on the screen and shook her head. "How can someone so smart...which by everything we know so far Lindsay was very smart, do this to themselves for a thirty second thrill?"

"You already know the answer to that Elyse," Sam said. "She either didn't know or didn't care about the consequences. I wonder if she was getting treatment for her obsession," Sam said. "Do the ledgers Jason copied from the clinic give the names of patients?"

With a few keystrokes, Elyse had the answer. "Lindsay was a patient at the clinic a couple of months ago. She attended group counseling sessions with Dr. Holloway a couple of times and then stopped going. Talk about expensive. One session costs two hundred fifty dollars, one-on-one sessions cost twice as much. Looks like she has an outstanding balance."

"I don't think the clinic will be getting payment anytime soon," Sam said.

"She was a busy girl, she did small accounting jobs and taxes on the side," Elyse said. "Looks like Jason had recently updated her website. The site is nicely done too. I really like this guy's work."

Sam didn't remind her that the guy who's work she was praising was dead. "Ronnie mentioned the two had dated," Sam said. "When he became suspicious of Nick's bookkeeping, seems logical he'd asked her to look over the ledgers."

"Things didn't turn out so well for her," Andy said from the doorway.

"What are you doing here?" Sam asked.

"I thought I'd stop by on my way home. How's it going?"

"We're looking into a flash drive I found at Jason's apartment and working on the possibility that Jason's death is connected to Lindsay Mather's," Sam said, not mentioning the meeting between the two of them at the bar.

"If Jason thought Nick was doing anything wrong with his books, why didn't he go straight to the police?" Elyse asked.

"He wanted to know for sure before he accused his sister's husband. Wouldn't you?" Sam asked."

"And both of them are connected to the clinic?" Andy asked.

"Not strongly," Elyse said. "Jason attended a few sessions in the months before his death and he previously was a patient of Dr. Holloway, but Lindsay only attended a couple group sessions. Either she couldn't afford them, or she didn't find them helpful."

"Maybe there are other victims connected to the clinic," Sam said. "How far back did you say those ledgers go?"

"Six months, but I can try hacking the clinic directly. It'll take some time, but I can do it."

"Start with the ledgers you have first. How many patients have died in the last six months?"

"Give me a sec," Elyse said.

"I think you're reaching here, Sam," Andy said, sitting in the chair in front of the desk.

"We'll see," Sam replied, pacing, as they waited and listened to the tapping of Elyse's manicured nails on the keyboard.

"Where did you find the drive?" Andy asked. "I thought they were all stolen."

"Underneath the floorboards in his exercise room," Sam said.

"I like my word better and I get the feeling more sex was going on it there than exercise," Elyse said."

"Sex is exercise," Sam said, filling Andy in on exactly how he'd found the flash drive as Elyse tapped away.

"There's at least five patients on the clinic's ledgers that are now deceased," Elyse said from behind the computer.

"Doesn't that seem high?" Sam asked.

"Not necessarily," Andy contested. "Addicts of any kind are going to have a higher death rate. What did they die from?"

"First victim, Nicole Lakemore, forty-eight years old, died from a drug overdose."

"Told you," Andy said.

"Who's next?" Sam asked, ignoring him.

"Glenn Arnold of Naperville died three months ago and Philip Hutchins from Westmont died two months ago. I haven't found the cause of death for either of them yet," Elyse said.

"Let me run a check on those names," Andy said, writing them down on his notepad. "You know, Sam this case is beginning to sound as fucked up as the last case you had."

"My brother wasn't fucked up, Andy," Maddy said from the doorway.

"We really should shut this office door," Elyse whispered under her breath.

"Sorry, Maddy," Andy apologized, turning to Sam "I'll see what I can find out about those two men and get back with you tomorrow."

"Andy, I told you not to bring this up at the station," Sam admonished him. "If Jason's case was mishandled or if you do find a connection between Jason and Lindsay's deaths, it becomes a police matter. Don't get yourself arrested for withholding evidence." The two at an impasse, Andy said his goodbyes and left.

"What two men was he talking about?" Maddy asked.

"We've discovered at least four people including Jason who were patients of the clinic and have died in the past six months. These deaths may or may not be connected," Sam said, sliding the envelope with Maddy's name on the front under a pile of paperwork on his desk. "We'll know more tomorrow. Why don't you head on home Maddy, you look exhausted," placing his arm around her shoulders and leading her toward the door.

"Wait," Maddy said. "What was in the lockbox?"

"A flash drive," Sam said, neglecting to mention the letter.

"What was on it?"

"Ledger entries for the past six months at Nick's clinic. That's how we discovered the other deaths."

"Why would he have those?"

"We don't know, and we aren't going to find out tonight, so please go home and get some rest."

"Alright Sam, but it feels like there's something you aren't telling me."

Closing the office door behind Maddy, Sam approached Elyse whose attention was directed to the computer monitor. She felt Sam's gaze on her and looked up at him.

"I know that look, Sam. You want me to do something for you and you think I'm not going to like it. Spill."

"You know how you're always asking to go with me on my investigations?"

"And how you always say no."

"Well, this time I want you to come along. I'm going over to the Hollowell Clinic and I want you to go too," Sam said.

She asked, "Really?" controlling her excitement. "What time are we leaving?"

"I want you to drive separately."

"Why would I do that?"

"Dr. Holloway told me the sessions are open to the public. I'd like you to pretend to be a prospective patient."

"As some sort of pervert. This'll be fun. What do you want me to do?"

"I'm hoping one of the patients attending sessions knew Jason or maybe the other two patients who have died recently. Get the scoop if there is any. I'd like to know what Jason was going to sessions for. Confirm or refute what Holloway told me after his class this morning."

"Where will you be?" Elyse asked, a little concerned.

"I'll be there all the time, but I'll be with Holloway. If we do cross paths, don't let on you know me. I don't want Nick or Holloway finding out you work for me."

"Maddy may have already mentioned me to Nick. Maybe I should use an alias."

"I don't think that'll be necessary, but if it makes you more comfortable...okay," Sam said. "What're you going to say when they ask why you're there? Make sure you pick an addiction you know something about."

"Let's make it easy. I'm a sexaholic. Can't get enough."

"You think you can sell that?" Sam asked doubtfully.

"What's to sell, everyone likes sex."

"I can't argue with that, and hopefully no one will question you too strenuously on your first visit."

"Don't worry, Sam, I got this. I've been to therapy sessions before as you know, dealing with the fallout of Anna's death. If I get stuck all I have to do is start crying. Nobody bothers you if you're crying."

"Sounds like a plan," Sam said, grabbing his jacket. "Meeting starts at seven and lasts for an hour. See you there."

"Where're you going? It's not even four yet."

"I have just enough time to get over to Naperville and find Tim Murphy at the accounting offices where Lindsay worked. Maybe he can tell me more about the meeting she had with Jason."

CHAPTER 10

Tim Murphy's teal blue Ford Focus Hybrid was still parked in the communal lot shared by Padgett Business Services and several insurance companies when Sam pulled into a nearby parking slot. He settled in, periodically checking the picture Elyse had pulled from Murphy's employee file against a steady stream of employees exiting the building. Skimming a book when the stream became a trickle forty-five minutes passed with no sign of Murphy. After 6 o'clock came and went, Sam began to consider the idea he'd missed him, maybe Murphy had decided to walk to one of the nearby bars for a drink.

Then he spotted him exiting the building with two fellow overachieving accountants and waving goodbyes as they separated. Throwing the book into the passenger seat, Sam exited his car, catching Murphy as he reached the driver's side door of his own vehicle. "Mr. Murphy, may I have a word with you?" Sam asked.

"Who are you? And how did you get in here. This is a private parking lot."

Sam quickly flashed his badge and slipped it back into his pocket. "Sam Bartell, I'm a private investigator," he extended his hand to Murphy who shook it apprehensively. "I'm looking into the death of Lindsay Mathers. I was hoping you could answer a few questions."

"I've already told the police everything I know," Murphy said, but his eyes told Sam he was lying. "I wasn't at her apartment when Lindsay died." Murphy opened the car door and tried to get in. Sam pushed it shut, pinning him in place. Murphy started to yell, then looking around at the empty lot, he swallowed it, defeated.

"I know what you told the police," Sam said, increasing his pressure on the door. "I want you to tell me what you didn't tell them."

"Okay! Okay!" Murphy conceded. "Just get this door off of me and let's talk in the car."

"We weren't dating," Murphy said, lighting a cigarette. "Lindsey and I along with six other candidates were hired to fill two positions. After orientation and a three-month probationary period, we were the ones they selected. Lucky us, eighty-hour weeks, low pay and scutwork. We hung out a lot, misery loves company, I guess. Became friends."

"Why did you tell the police you two were dating?" Sam asked from the passenger seat.

"Because Lindsay told everyone she knew that we were."

"Isn't it frowned upon for employees to date each other?"

"We worked in different departments, Lindsay worked in corporate accounting and I work in government auditing," Murphy replied.

"She was dating a client and was using you as cover." Sam pegged Lindsey's motives. "Do you know which client?"

"She never told me, even after I threatened to tell everyone at the office about what she was doing. She knew I wouldn't do it."

"If you weren't dating Lindsay, how did you know she was into estim?"

"We hooked up a couple of times during our probationary period, just to blow off some steam. She showed me some of her stuff and how to use it. But she never mentioned anything about having heart problems and she never used the estim box that killed her when I was with her."

"Why didn't you tell the police you weren't dating Lindsay?"

"It was just easier to say I was, instead of having to explain to everyone why I lied. Then there'd be this big investigation into who she was dating, and we have a strict client privacy clause in our contract."

"Did you consider that whoever she was having the affair with could have been involved in her death?" Sam asked, opening the car door to leave.

"The police said the estim box caused her death."

"Hold on a minute," Sam said, running to his car and grabbing the book he'd been reading while he waited for Murphy to leave the office. Murphy lowered his window and Sam turned the backside of the book to him where pictures of both Holloway and Nick were printed on the back. "Do either one of these men look familiar to you?"

"I don't know the one on the right, but the one on the left is Nick Maxwell, and he's here all the time."

◆ ◆ ◆

Nick had lost interest ten minutes into the session. Returning to the clinic after leaving Maddy with the movers, he'd asked his assistant to call back patients he'd cancelled on this morning. Two of them had accepted late afternoon appointments and Nick was now half listening to his last patient of the day.

He was only trying to help this morning at Jason's apartment, but Maddy didn't see it that way and her repeated dismissals were frustrating. With Jason gone, Nick had hoped their relationship would improve, stop the skid it had been on for a while. Not that he hadn't helped put it on that road. Maddy calling Bartell for help infuriated him. The timer on his desk went off, session over. Nick sent his patient on his way, made a few notes in his chart and went in search of Edward.

Finding Edward at his desk, Nick walked over to his bookcase, a wall to wall, floor to ceiling oaken monstrosity and perused the books, waiting for Edward to finish the clinical report on his last patient.

"Surprised to see you here, Nick," Edward said, not looking up from his paperwork. "Your assistant told me this morning you took the day off for personal business. By personal, I hope you meant that bitch of yours."

"Watch your mouth, that bitch is my wife, and I'm working on it," Nick said, sauntering over to the cabinets on other side of the room where he knew Edward kept his liquor. He pulled out the bourbon and poured himself a drink, waving it at Edward to see if he wanted a glass. "At least I've gotten Jason's apartment emptied for the most part."

"We have another problem," Edward said, declining the drink.

"Sam Bartell, I already know about him--he showed up at Jason's apartment earlier."

"What are you going to do about him?"

"Nothing. The man's an idiot." Nick leaned against the cabinet, sipping his drink.

"I won't cover for you if he starts asking about..."

"He won't," Nick stopped him. "He'll poke around for a few days, hold Maddy's hand and come to the same conclusion the police did."

"I caution you to be a little more concerned about this detective. He stopped by my classroom this morning and I didn't get the impression he's the idiot you make him out to be," Edward warned.

"I think you're the one who should be concerned about Bartell asking questions--you were Jason's doctor."

Clenching his hands into fists under the desktop, Edward held his quick temper in check. "I didn't ask you. He'd only been to a few sessions and he probably wouldn't have gone to those if he wasn't working on our website. There's no way I could've known what was going to happen."

"A mistake, none the less--and one I'll remind you that could cost your job, and the reputation of this clinic if this so-called investigation gets out of hand," Nick retorted, noting Edward's attempt to control his anger. "Maybe the detective would be interested in knowing the real reason you were so willing to move from California and join me in this clinic." Nick was goading him now.

"You wouldn't dare!" Edward came from behind the desk, murder in his eyes.

"Careful, Edward," Nick placed his now empty glass out of harm's way and stepped away from Edward, laughing. "You'd better get that temper in check. You wouldn't want Bartell thinking it got the better of you when Jason was on the wrong end of a noose." Nick opened the door to leave finding Sam on the other side.

"Detective," Nick said. "Speak of the devil and he appears. What are you doing here?"

"I decided to take Dr. Holloway up on his offer to watch a counseling session this evening."

"How nice of him to do so and not tell anyone," Nick said turning to glare at Edward and wondering how much of the conversation Sam had overheard, then returned to Sam. "Now that Maddy has dragged you into this, I'd like you to do something for me. Don't worry, it's easy."

"What would that be?" Sam asked warily.

"I'd like you to do what you're getting paid for and confirm that Jason's death was the result of an accident as quickly as possible."

"Maddy asked me to investigate Jason's death and I intend to do so. What conclusions I draw will be based on the facts and I won't be taking any money."

"How honorable," Nick replied. "But I don't believe your intentions are purely professional or that you have considered what a long, drawn-out investigation that reaches the same conclusion will do to Maddy's fragile mental state."

"I think Maddy's much stronger than you give her credit for. She wants to know the truth about Jason's death, and I think she can handle whatever that truth may be."

"You're willing to risk causing Maddy harm to prove that point?" Nick asked.

"I believe more harm is caused by not knowing the truth than facing it."

"I've asked you nicely and I know you'll disregard that request, so I'm warning you to get this investigation over with quickly, or I'll make it my mission to see you don't continue working in the State of Illinois."

Now it was Sam's turn to control his temper, stepping into the room, his fists clenched, his desire to hit Nick apparent.

"Gentlemen," Edward said, quickly placing himself between the two men. "Let's calm down. We're all after the same thing here. Nick, why don't you start the group therapy session and I'll take Mr. Bartell to the observation room."

◆ ◆ ◆

"We use this room for several reasons," Edward said, ushering Sam into a small room adjacent to the much larger meeting room visible through the two-way mirror. "My students use it for educational purposes, some patients use it to ease themselves into the group environment and Nick and I use it to determine if a patient will respond better to the other doctor. Nick's and my approaches to therapy can be very different at times and watching a patient's reactions to our different methods, helps determine the treatment path we follow."

"Doesn't this break some confidentiality or HIPPA clauses?"

"Everyone in group is aware they may be watched and have signed a waiver." Watching through the mirror, Sam saw Elyse enter and move through the small group of patients, ending up at the coffee and donut table set up at the back of the room. Remarkably comfortable in her assignment to blend in, Elyse had already made a friend as she and a petite brunette made their way to the chairs arranged in a horseshoe with a wooden podium standing in the opening. The brunette, about Elyse's age was sporting at least ten piercings on her face alone, ears, nose, lip and brows. Entering the room, Nick took his place at the podium and began the session by asking any newcomers to stand and introduce themselves. Elyse glanced around the room, coming to the conclusion she was the only new person and stood to make her introduction.

"Most of these sessions are rated M for mature audiences," Edward said, taking Sam's attention from Elyse. "If someone gets too graphic, we stop them. The goal is to understand the obsession, what's causing it and finding ways to control it so the patient's comfortable in their day-to-day life."

"Your therapy attempts to control it, not stop it as with Sexaholics Anonymous?"

"We aren't affiliated in any way with that group," Edward responded with more venom than he would have liked, causing Sam to turn from the activities in the other room to look at him. "Neither Nick nor I believe in using the twelve steps and twelve traditions," Edward continued. "Success rates for both AA and SA prove that spiritualism doesn't work. It's unrealistic to expect a patient to stop a basic necessary instinct as you would no doubt agree sex is?"

"I agree it's instinctual, I don't agree with the idea anything goes."

"Neither do we. When sexual desires intrude into daily lives negatively, as with these patients, then it's time to learn to control those desires. Edward nodded toward the group, "For example, the gentleman seated next to the podium, that's James. He's a chronic masturbator, starting at the age of seven and progressing to the point that he felt and acted on the urges at least twenty times a day before he started treatment. How long do you think he'd stay in treatment if I told him he could never pleasure himself again? Not very long to answer my own question. But now, after a year in our program, he has that number down to an acceptable five times a week and he no longer acts on the urges in inappropriate places."

"Impressive," Sam said. "What about her?" pointing to the woman seated next to Elyse.

"That's Michelle and she's proven to be more difficult," Edward said, his disdain apparent.

"How's that?" "She's into needleplay, as you can probably guess by the piercings."

"Sticking needles into each other," Sam cringed at the thought. "I've heard of it, but it's considered mild in the hardcore BDSM community, right?"

"As with anything we talk about here, it isn't whether the activity is considered mild or edgeplay--things such as breathplay, knife play or gunplay to answer the question on your face. Every activity is subjective, depending on individual experience and preferences. Some people consider suspending themselves from hooks to be a mild form of piercing. Do you? I stick to the S.S.C. creed and preach it to my patients and my students."

"What's that?"

"Safe, Sane and Consensual. I can't stress enough that our program doesn't focus on stopping the behavior. Our goal is to help those who become controlled by their addiction to gain back their lives. Going back to Michelle, the majority of her needleplay is done to herself and so far in her treatment we haven't been able to curb her appetite for it, although of late she's showing some improvement. When she started the program, she was what we call a blue-piller."

"Blue-piller?"

"Many of our patients come to sessions expecting me to give them a little blue pill that'll magically fix whatever addiction they have. When they learn there isn't a quick cure, that their obsessions are something they'll have to battle each and every day for the rest of their lives, very few of them have the commitment it takes to stay. We also have patients that come to a few sessions, learn the strategies we use for containment of their various behaviors and quit. They think they can do it on their own, save themselves a little money. The ones that genuinely stick to our program are either required by law, or they are motivated by fear--fear of losing their job, spouse, power. James is required by his employer to attend sessions as part of his rehabilitation, otherwise he'll lose his job. The problem with sexual addictions is that there's little fear involved unless you're caught and very few are."

"Especially those that cross the line between legal and illegal."

"Those acting outside the law aren't in sessions. The majority of them consider their actions normal and therefore aren't seeking help. I have to take over for Nick now, detective. You're welcome to stay here for the remainder of the session if you wish."

"Thank you for your help," Sam said, shaking Holloway's hand as he left.

Watching Elyse through the observation window, Sam was glad he'd asked her to come. She'd been working for him for over a year now, handling all their clients with nothing but professionalism and concern, but he knew the death of Anna still weighed on her. Keeping to her part of the agreement, she limited the work on her one-woman crusade to find the bank robber to slow times at the office. She believed the suspect had been committing robberies all over the Chicagoland area for over two years, averaging one every two months. He rarely netted over five thousand dollars the highest haul only eighty-five hundred dollars. No one other than Anna had been injured in the robberies and he left no clues behind. Enlisting Sam in her search gave her someone to bounce ideas off of, but so far no real suspect. Hopefully getting her from behind the safety of her computer screen would get her back into the world again. As the session wound down, Sam watched as the two women gathered their things and headed out of the room together.

"Learning anything, detective?" Nick asked sarcastically from the doorway.

"Yes, and I have a few questions for you." Sam said, stepping back from the window.

"Such as?"

"What was your relationship with Jason like?" Sam asked.

"We tolerated each other, mostly for Maddy's sake. I don't have the patience for rich pretty boys who have everything handed to them and they continually screw up."

"Does that attitude work well for you with your patients?" Sam quipped. "Jason had his own business, which by everything I've seen so far was successful. Why do you consider him a screw up?"

"He's dead, isn't he. Doesn't get more screwed up than that."

"Maddy said he'd recently worked on a web page for you, that there was an argument? What was it about?"

"Maddy tends to exaggerate. I thought Jason was taking too long, he disagreed, stormed off in a huff. That was the extent of it."

"Dr. Holloway was treating Jason before his death. Do you know why?"

"You'll have to ask him yourself."

"Just from the short time I've known him, Dr. Holloway seems to take a highly personal interest in his patients. Wouldn't you agree?"

"We all have our faults, detective and I would agree that's one of his, but his methods work. As do mine."

"I'm sure they do. So, I can assume the clinic is doing fine financially?"

"It was rough for a while, but it's running on its own now."

"An audit of the books wouldn't show me you've been running in the red since the beginning and are still doing so?"

"Not making money isn't illegal."

"No, but lying to your investors is," Sam said, hoping to hit a nerve.

"I don't know how the hell you've gotten this idea, Bartell, but if you're accusing me of anything illegal, you'd better have proof."

"Do you do the accounting in house or do you have a service?"

"That's none of your business. You're here because Maddy can't accept the truth about Jason's death and that has nothing to do with my clinic."

"Your clinic? I thought you and Holloway were partners."

"You know what I meant."

"How's that working for you, Nick? The partnership? You and Holloway always see eye to eye on things?" "Keep your damn nose out of my clinic." Nick stormed out of the room.

CHAPTER 11

"I think summer is officially over." Elyse said to Michelle as they exited the clinic.

"I'm not looking forward to another Chicago winter." Zipping up her jacket, Michelle searched the parking lot. "I'm from Alabama where the temperature never goes below freezing."

"Did you forget where you parked?" Elyse asked. "What kind of car do you have?"

"No, Eric, my boyfriend is supposed to pick me up," pulling her phone from her jacket, Michelle called him.

"Maybe he got hung up in traffic," Elyse offered.

"He's gonna get hung up by his balls if he...no he'd probably like that," Michelle laughed, then spoke into her phone.

Elyse walked a few feet away, wondering what happened to Sam. She hadn't seen him before the session started and didn't spot him leaving. She grabbed her own phone just as Michelle was finishing her call with Eric.

"He's playing pool with his buddies, lost track of time. He's on his way."

"I'll just let my friend know where I'm at," Elyse said, typing a text to Sam, "and what do you say we go wait at that Starbucks across the street?"

Warming her hands on the Starbucks Caramel Macchiato cup, Michelle took a sip. "This is sooo good," Michelle said licking the cream from her lips. "Almost as erotic as a needle session," she said. "Can't wait 'til the pumpkin spice flavor comes back."

Grateful she had broached the subject for her, Elyse asked. "Is Eric into needles too?"

"Not really. He'll do it for me occasionally if he thinks he'll get sex out of it, but he doesn't have the hands for it. He pokes the needle in and out too quickly without letting me savor the experience. Kinda like the sex we end up having after." Her laugh was infectious, and Elyse laughed back.

"Preaching to the choir, girl. Why are they all in such a hurry? How did you get started with needles, if you don't mind my asking?"

"I had childhood asthma, spent a lot of time in and out of hospitals. Thank God I outgrew it, but most of my early memories are of Mom and Dad hovering around my hospital bed, giving me their undivided attention showering me with presents because they felt so bad about all the tests and treatments I had to go through. They would cringe every time a nurse came in to draw blood or give me a shot. Even then, needles didn't scare me, and the pain never bothered me. Dr. Holloway tells me I use needles now to get the same feelings of unconditional and unshared love I felt then. I don't know it that's true; I do know, for me there's nothing like the feeling I get when I pierce my skin with a needle and watch it come out the other side. I get this enormous endorphin rush, and the more needles I insert, the more rush." Michelle, caught up in her feelings, paused to catch her breath, "Before I realize it, I have a zipper."

"What's a zipper?" Elyse asked, fascinated.

"Exactly what it sounds like, except with needles. I usually insert them on both sides about half an inch apart from just under my breasts to the top of my vagina taking my time to enjoy each stick. When I get them all in, I connect them with a string, and pull them all out at once. Sometimes pulling them out like that will make me orgasm. It's phenomenal."

"Isn't it dangerous doing that stuff by yourself? Aren't you worried about getting an infection? What about the blood?" Elyse fired at Michelle.

"Hang on," Michelle laughed. "You're right, most people have a partner place the needles or go to a professional. You can make all sorts of things with needles: corsets, flowers, whatever you want. Then you can weave ribbons through the needles or add beads or feathers. Or you can just play with them- pull or twist them. I'm not into the whole BDSM scene-I don't want anyone telling me what to do and I'm not anyone's momma. As far as infection, when I got started with recreational needles, I was working for a tattoo artist. He was fanatical about cleanliness, taught me all about sterilization, diseases in the blood, disinfectants, and most importantly sharps containers. He was also my first boyfriend, our relationship didn't last long, but he taught me how to take care of myself. In more ways than one." Michelle winked. "As far as the blood, if you're doing it right, there shouldn't be much. The needles are very fine-I like twenty-four gauge with hubs because they have less of a tendency to bend and the hub gives me more leverage."

"You place it just under the skin." Reaching over the table, Michelle pinched the skin above Elyse's wrist. "Make sure the beveled side of the needle is facing up so it will go through the skin smoothly, then push it through. Easy peasy." Michelle chuckled as Elyse cringed.

"Sometimes," Michelle continued, "when Eric's in the mood, I'll let him weave a wire through the needles and use a vibrator to stimulate them. Truthfully, I think he likes playing with the vibrator more than the needles." Michelle laughed. "I could talk about needles all night, but your addiction to sex sounds intriguing. Tell me about it."

"Alright," Elyse said, taking Michelle's cup and hers. "But I think we're going to need a couple more of these." Elyse returned to the table with new drinks as Michelle was ending a call.

"Eric says he'll be here in ten," Michelle said, accepting her drink.

"Gives us time to drink these, then."

"And time for you to spill. Tell me all about the sex you're having," Michelle said.

"Sorry to disappoint, but I'm not having any right now," Elyse said, sticking as much as possible to the truth. "But the last few years have been a constant stream of meaningless sex. I like the chase, but once I've gotten them in bed, I don't want them anymore."

"Seems lonely," Michelle sympathized.

"Lonely and dangerous. The last guy I slept with wouldn't take no for an answer and began stalking me. I had to put a restraining order on him."

"Has he come back?"

"No, but it was the wake-up call I needed to get help. You know, from what I've read, doctors are still debating on whether or not sex addiction is a disease."

"Tell that to David Duchovny or Tiger Woods," Michelle giggled.

"I've gone to shrinks before, but I ended up sleeping with both of them and one of them was a woman. What a challenge that was," Elyse was getting into her story.

"I don't think that'll be an issue at the clinic. Dr. Maxwell is married and seems devoted to his wife and Dr. Holloway...I don't know what it is about him, but I don't think of him in a sexual way. Isn't that odd?"

"I hope I feel the same way," Elyse said.

"So, what's the deal with the guy you texted earlier?"

Elyse blushed, "He's my boss."

"A boss you'd like to be your boyfriend, from what I'm seeing."

"Sa...Steve doesn't think of me that way."

"Why not. Does he like boys?"

"No," laughing at the thought of Sam with another man. "He's definitely straight, but...it's complicated."

"Is he married?"

"No."

"Then I don't see the complication," Michelle declared. "If you like him, you should tell him--get it out in the open."

"He's still hung up on someone."

"Only one way to get over someone--get under another," Michelle said.

"Let's see how these sessions go first. Have they been helpful for you?"

"In the beginning, no. But that was because of me. I didn't really want to stop what I was doing, so I didn't attend sessions regularly and I didn't take them seriously. But now I'm motivated to quit."

"What changed?"

"I found something I'm more passionate about than the needles."

"Eric?"

"God, no. But he's the one who got me into it. He's in the Army Reserves and practically lives at the gym keeping in shape. I've started going with him and I love how it makes me feel. I want to become a trainer, but there's no way anyone will hire me with all the dermal piercings I have and I'm afraid if I don't stop with the zippers, the marks will be noticeable. There's no hiding them in the gym. So, I've been attending sessions every week for the past two months and I haven't even looked at a needle for over a month."

"That's fantastic. I hope you can stick with it." The women laughed. "I was hoping the guy who told me about the clinic would come to our session this evening."

"Who is he?"

"Jason Richards," Elyse replied. "I met him a few months ago when he did a website for my boss. He seemed nice and we talked a lot while he set up our site. I told him about my stalker, and my addiction. He suggested I go to a session or two."

"Jason Richards?" Michelle repeated, shocked. "He's dead. He died about three weeks ago."

"What? I'm so sorry. Did you know him?"

"I met him at the clinic. We talked a lot. He was a nice guy and if Eric wasn't in the picture…"

"How did he die?" Elyse asked.

"There wasn't much about it in the papers, but around the clinic, talk was that he accidentally hung himself."

"That's horrible."

"Yeah. He was the brother-in-law of Dr. Maxwell. What a mess that could've been. Especially with that other patient dying the day before Jason."

"What patient?"

"Lindsay Mathers."

Just then a horn honked outside, and Michelle waved at Eric through the window.

"There's my ride--such a gentleman." Michelle rolled her eyes. "Hey, if you want, you can stop by the gym sometime. I can get you a free pass and we can work out for an hour or so."

"How about Saturday morning?" Elyse asked, already cursing Sam for her impending sore muscles. "Let me put the address in my phone. What time?"

Elyse met Michelle at the reception desk just inside the doors to Planet Fitness early Saturday morning. The gym was huge, purple and yellow exercise equipment everywhere.

"Wow!" Elyse said. "That's a lot of treadmills."

"I've seen them all going at once and people waiting. This place gets hopping, usually around four and five o'clock when people get off work. Come on, let's get changed and get started."

Fifteen minutes of stretches later, Michelle lead Elyse over to the weight equipment. "We'll start out easy," Michelle said, demonstrating the proper way to do a chest press. "We'll work on the large muscle groups today and when you come back, I'll teach you how to finesse the smaller muscles."

"You're assuming I'll come back." Elyse laughed, taking the bar to begin her reps.

"You'll be back," Michelle said confidently.

Following Michelle's lead, Elyse found herself enjoying the workout, getting into each exercise and pushing herself with each circuit. Remembering her true purpose to find out the scoop on Jason, Elyse said, "I could really get myself into trouble here."

"You mean with all the hot bodies in here?" Michelle scoffed. "Take a look around, the closest one to hot is sitting on a weight bench, reading a newspaper propped up on his stomach."

"Isn't that the motto here?" Elyse laughed, pointing at the NO CRITICS in eight-foot block letters painted on the wall.

"No, it's Judgement Free Zone, and I totally agree with that, as an aspiring trainer. As a perspective notch for your belt---yuck. Come around later in the afternoon, then you'll see something worth the effort. Besides, I thought you were staying celibate."

"I am, but with what happened to Jason Richards and Lindsay Mathers, I'm not sure I want to begin sessions at the Hollowell Clinic."

"I don't know about Lindsay, but Jason and I talked a few days before he died and I still can't believe he hung himself."

"Why?"

"His girlfriend was into choking, not Jason. He broke up with her hoping she'd get the message, but he was finding it hard to stick to his guns. I told him he was doing the right thing, if he caved, she would control him for the rest of his life. Then I found out he died."

"Maybe he caved," Elyse said.

CHAPTER 12

About the same time Elyse was beginning her exercise class, Sam and Andy began their run at their second favorite running spot, Lyman Woods. Quickly picking up their pace as an overcast sky threatened an impending downpour, the two ran in silence for the first couple of miles. Then Andy couldn't help a discourse on the area.

"Have I ever told you the history of Lyman Woods?" Andy asked.

"Just that it got its name from a Presbyterian minister who moved here with his wife from Ohio in the early eighteen hundreds. I even remember his name because it was so odd...Orange Lyman."

"Their original home is still standing. It's the oldest home in Downers Grove and is believed to have been part of the Underground Railroad." Andy paused in his narrative as a pair of bicyclists passed them. "I've recently learned that pioneer spirit carried into the next generation. Orange's son Walter married a woman who was one of the earliest suffrage proponents in the Chicago area."

"You've been spending time at the library."

"No, I actually read the brochure the guard hands out at the entrance to the park. What I find the most interesting is that Walter, Orange's son was a beekeeper, an award winning one at that."

"I thought those were old honeybee boxes we pass on the trails."

"Those aren't old," Andy corrected. "Those are antiques. Let's pick up the pace before the rain gets here."

Easing his pace after a few miles, Andy broached the topic of Sam's investigation.

"I did some research into Glenn Arnold and Philip Hutchins at the station yesterday."

"Andy..." Sam said, panting.

"Before you get all motherly about getting myself into trouble, it's not a big deal," Andy cautioned. "I read the reports on their death and there's nothing in either one to indicate foul play. Glenn Arnold died at home alone in his swimming pool, Hutchins from a robbery gone wrong. You're going to poke around into their deaths, looking for a connection to Jason, but have you considered that his death was simply an accident. Tragic and senseless, but not murder. Maddy has gotten you fixated on finding a killer, and I know you'd like nothing more than to make her happy."

"That's not what I'm doing," Sam denied.

"Sam," Andy said, stopping on the trail. "I'm asking you to take the evidence you've found to the police. Walk away from the whole thing. There's no win for you in this. If Jason's death was an accident, then you're back at square one, with Maddy hating you. If he was murdered, your number one suspect is her husband. Do you really think she'll fall into your arms out of gratitude when they send him to jail and her name is smeared all over the papers?" Andy bent down to retie his shoe.

As it started to sprinkle, Sam ran on ahead, contemplating how much of what Andy said was true. Nick killing Jason because he'd found out about his second set of books didn't seem plausible, but if Nick thought Jason knew about his affair with Lindsey and suspected Nick had something to do with her death, that would put a different spin on things. But how did the other two deaths fit in? Andy was right about one thing, he needed to look deeper into the deaths of Arnold and Hutchins.

Allowing Andy to catch up, Sam said, "I don't believe Jason killed himself, not even accidentally. I think he was murdered, but I haven't any solid evidence to prove it, so until I do, I'm going to keep digging. If Nick's involved, I'll find out and whatever the fallout out for Maddy is, so be it. She's not my problem anymore."

"You keep telling yourself that, rookie," Andy said, as the skies opened up above their heads. "Come on," he yelled over a crash of thunder and broke into a full-out run. "I for one don't want to be struck by lightning."

Finding the door to his office unlocked, Sam wasn't surprised to see Elyse sitting behind his desk, typing on Jason's computer, a bagel and a Coke waiting for him. What he found surprising was the leggings and t-shirt she was dressed in.

"Thanks," biting into the bagel and opening the Coke. "What's with the Fabletics?" he asked, waving the bagel at her.

"Under Armor," she got up and twirled. "Michelle talked me into them. You think they're too tight, don't you?"

"Not on you," Sam said, thinking anything that tight didn't look good on anybody. "You and Michelle really hit it off, I guess."

"She invited me to her gym this morning. I had a fantastic time. I see what you and Andy get out of your running--all those endorphins."

"I don't think I have those," Sam said.

"I'm sure I'm going to regret it later. We started off with some Yoga stretches and I saw parts of me I haven't seen since I was three. But right now, I feel great. Thought I would stop by and let you know what Michelle told me about Jason.

"How did you know I'd be here?"

"How long have I known you, Sam?"

"That predictable, huh?"

"Let's call it consistent. Nothing wrong with that."

"I wanted to brush up on the Williams' case for my court appearance Monday morning."

"I've already pulled it for you," Elyse said, pointing to a thick manila folder laying on top of a pile of similar manila folders. "I was wondering if you remembered since the Richards case has been taking up all your attention the last few days," Elyse said reproachfully.

"True," Sam said, catching the admonishment, but choosing to let it go unchallenged. "Dr. Holloway says Michelle's into needles."

"Big time. She's been going to the clinic for a while, says it's helped. Also said she met Jason two months ago in a session."

"Did she say why he was there?"

"Pretty much what Dr. Holloway told you. He'd broken up with Ronnie because of her proclivity to strangulation, but he loved her and was missing her. He came to the sessions to remind himself how fucked up his life was going to be if he didn't stick to his guns. Either she gave up the choking or the relationship was over. Michelle told him he was doing the right thing and if Ronnie didn't agree with that, he was better off without her."

"This Michelle sounds pretty smart. Maybe she should lead the sessions."

Elyse laughed. "She reminds me of Anna before she was murdered." Sam moved behind her, placing his hands on her shoulders, massaging the tension there. She relaxed in her chair. "I've told you before, Sam you missed your calling. You should be a massage therapist. You have such gentle hands."

"No thanks, not a fan of touching people I don't know. But it's the least I can do since you spent the morning working a case, and money on whatever you call that sausage casing you have on."

"I knew you'd think that," Elyse slapped him on the arm. "But Michelle says these will help ease the soreness and that these sausage casings as you call them are all the rage. Everyone wears them."

"So, what else did she say about Jason?"

"That's pretty much it, except she thought he was cute." Elyse smiled. "And that she was hoping to see how things worked out at the next week's session, but he didn't show."

"Because he was dead, I'm sure Ronnie knows more about his death than she's telling. I think I'll stop by Playthings on my way home." Sam headed towards the door.

"On your way home after you refresh your memory on the Williams case, and you've called the clients I've been putting off for you the last few days."

"That's what I meant." Sam reversed his steps, picking up the file from his desk. "I'll make those calls in the other room."

"Don't bother, I'm on my way home while I can still move." Elyse laughed. "When the endorphins wear off, I'm going to be in a world of hurt."

Finishing his backlog of work, Sam decided to give Ronnie a call before he showed up at the store. Grateful he had after learning she was at home, Sam jotted down her address and was parked in her driveway thirty minutes later. Ronnie met him at the front door and ushered him into a spacious, modern designed living room overlooking a retention pond, augmented by a lighted vortex floating fountain.

"Nice view," Sam said, peering through the sliding doors leading to the patio beyond. "Peaceful. You could almost forget about all the traffic not a quarter mile down the road. I didn't realize your store produced such income for you."

"I get the feeling, Sam that you know exactly what my business earned last year. Don't play dumb."

"I do," Sam confessed. "But I didn't see any earnings from your sessions listed on your tax return."

"What's a few thousand among friends. You aren't going to report me to the IRS, are you?"

"Why don't you tell me a little more about those undeclared sessions and we'll go from there."

"Is your interest personal or professional--or both," Ronnie teased.

"You said Jason became jealous. Didn't he know about your sessions and the sex before he started dating you?"

"First off, I never have physical sex with any of my clients. That's understood from the beginning. I'm not a prostitute and there isn't an emotional connection, at least for me. Jason knew and understood that."

"Then why was he jealous?"

"I think it was more concern than jealousy. He thought I was pregnant."

"Why did he think that?" Sam asked, stunned by her announcement.

"Because I was late and I took a pregnancy test, one of those over-the-counter ones. It was positive. He got all upset and went on about how I couldn't be a dominatrix and be a mother. Then he started in on my choking habit. I told him I would do whatever the hell I wanted kid or no kid. We had a big blow-up and we decided to take a break."

"But the test was a false positive," Sam said.

"Obviously," Ronnie said, rubbing her flat stomach. "But we were broken up and I didn't tell Jason. I thought I would let him stew for a while."

"Is that why you went to see him the night he died? To tell him he wasn't going to be a father?"

"Partly, but mostly I wanted to get back with him. We talked for a while and had sex. Afterwards, I never got to tell him I wasn't pregnant and I'm glad I didn't. He died thinking he was going to be a father."

"He was looking forward to you having a baby?"

"Yes, he was shocked at first, as I was. I'm on the pill. But he would have been a fantastic father. I wasn't looking forward to telling his sister though."

"I thought you two had never met."

"I said we had never *formally* met. I was being nice, if you can believe that. If you want to know more, you'll have to follow me. I have a session in an hour, and I need to take a shower." Sam followed her up a circular flight of stairs to her bedroom loft.

"There's a vanity in the bathroom, you can have a seat and we can talk," Ronnie said, undressing.

Peering inside, Sam attention was immediately drawn to the tiled sunken tub. Big enough to accommodate two people and no doubt jetted. The rectangular vanity was a cosmopolitan gray matching the modern style of her home. A glass basin sat on top, a chrome faucet reaching over the basin. Mounted above was a lighted framed mirror. Underneath the vanity stood the padded stool Ronnie had mentioned. Sam didn't see a shower. Moving past him through the doorway, Ronnie reached for a panel mounted next to the door. Water cascaded from a rainforest ceiling panel across from the vanity, emptying into a linear drain Sam hadn't noticed.

Stepping under the stream, Ronnie slid aside a panel, revealing a recess holding her soaps and shampoos. "Have a seat," Ronnie said, provoking him with a smile.

"I'll wait out here," Sam said, stepping back into the bedroom.

"I'll have to take another one when the session is over," Ronnie said ten minutes later, returning to the bedroom wrapped in a towel. "I sweat like a bitch in leather. Where were we?"

"You were telling me about how you didn't formally meet Maddy."

"Right. I'd been dating Jason for about a month and she shows up at the store one day, asks if we could talk somewhere privately. We go to my office where she precedes to tell me she's Jason's sister and she didn't want me dating him anymore." Throwing her towel on the bed, Ronnie walked into her closet. Sam followed her. "I told her it was none of her business who her brother dated and I asked her to leave. She said she was only concerned for his mental health." Ronnie rolled her eyes. "She also told me Jason had issues and he didn't need me complicating his life." She picked a red crisscross bandage metal collared top and skirt from the bondage apparel section of her wardrobe. "I told her the only complication she was concerned about was the fact I owned an adult bookstore." She wrapped the skirt around her right hip, velcroing it across the top of the left one, tying it in a big bow on her thigh, leaving most of her hip and thigh exposed. "If she really cared about Jason, she would want him to be happy," she said as she slipped into the top and tucking her ample breasts under the taunt thin strips of leather.

"What did she say to that?"

"That Jason didn't know what he wanted and if I thought I was going to get any money from him, she would make sure he didn't get his trust fund for a long time. I didn't know what she was talking about. Then she threatened to get my business shut down if I continued seeing him."

"That doesn't sound like Maddy."

"Which is why I didn't tell you earlier. Everyone thinks she's a saint, especially Jason, but she isn't. She's a bitch and will do anything to get what she wants." She went to the dresser, wiped bold red lipstick on her lips and turned to face him. "What do you think?"

"Are you going out like that?"

"That's what this is for," she said, returning to the closet and coming back with a knee length leather coat.

"Did you tell Jason about your meeting with Maddy?"

"Seriously? No, I didn't. We hadn't been dating that long and I wasn't sure it would last anyway."

"It did. How did Maddy react to that?"

"How she said she would, tried to get my store closed down. But it didn't work, which probably made her furious. As you know, she doesn't take the word 'no' very well."

"I also know she doesn't give up easily when she has her mind set on something."

"She came to the store a few more times. Since intimidation didn't work, she tried bribery. Offered me money to stop seeing Jason. I refused it."

"Do you have any proof of this?" Sam asked.

"No, so it's her word against mine and we both know who you're going to believe."

"When was the last time you spoke to Maddy?"

"I didn't speak to her, but she stopped by Jason's apartment unexpectedly a few days before we split. Jason shooed me into the kitchen and got her out of there as soon as he could."

"Did you hear what they were talking about?"

"Not really, but I did hear something about a will. I think she wanted to get them updated or something. I really have to get on the road," Ronnie said, checking her watch. "The guy I'm seeing likes promptness."

"I thought you were the one in charge."

"There's never any doubt about that, but for what these clients pay me, I show up on time." She led him back downstairs to the front door, opening it for him. "Oh, and Sam please tell that old geezer to stop following me I know he belongs to you."

CHAPTER 13

S am spent most of the day Monday sitting in court, leaving Elyse at the office catching up on some bookkeeping and spending time on the ledgers Jason copied from the clinic. Finishing early, Elyse texted Michelle, hoping she was working at the gym. When she received an answering text, she headed to her car, thankful she'd thrown some exercise clothes in a duffle bag on her way to work this morning.

"We concentrated on your upper body on Saturday, today we're going to work on cardio," Michelle said, as she led Elyse toward the row of steppers and climbers. "You don't want to get top heavy."

"I don't think that could ever happen." Elyse laughed, adjusting the handles on the climber. "How do you get on this thing?"

Twenty minutes later, hot and sweaty, Elyse had reached her limit and stopped. "Whew," she said, toweling off the machine on wobbly legs. "That's intense."

"Are you Okay, Ellie?" Michelle asked, concerned with Elyse's shortness of breath. "You're in such good shape it's easy to forget you're a newbie."

Waving Michelle's concerns away, but unable to continue with the ruse Elyse said, "I need to tell you something. Can we go somewhere and talk?"

"Sure," Michelle said, puzzled. "But if this is your way of getting out of the rest of our workout, it won't work."

"Your name is Elyse, not Ellie?" Michelle said as they sat on the bench in front of their lockers. "That's your big secret? No offense, but considering you're a sexaholic with a stalker, I'm not shocked you're using a fake name."

"Well, I lied about having a stalker," Elyse confessed.

"You're a sexaholic though right?" Michelle laughed. "That's the best part."

"No, I made that up too," Elyse said.

"Why did you lie?" Michelle asked.

"I'm working undercover for my boss."

"Steve, the guy you have the hots for."

"His name's Sam."

"Of course, it is." Michelle laughed.

"Anyway, Sam's a private investigator looking into Jason's death."

Michelle sat back in her chair, digesting everything Elyse had just told her. "Why didn't you say that in the beginning?" Then it dawned on her, "You think I had something to do with it, don't you?"

"No! We don't, but Sam thinks someone at the clinic is involved and he didn't want anyone to know I worked for him."

"Damn girl, this is way more interesting than your sexaholic story anyway. But if you've ruled me out as a suspect...thank you very much...what are you hoping to get from me?"

Relieved Michelle had taken her deception so well and still wanted to be friends, Elyse asked, "Did you know Glenn Arnold or Philip Hutchins?"

"Those names don't ring a bell, but they could've been in different sessions than I attended, or they may have used aliases," Michelle replied, her subtle dig not lost on Elyse. "Do you have a picture of either one of them?"

"Not with me, but if you're coming to the meeting tomorrow night, I'll bring them."

"I'll be there," Michelle confirmed. "It'll be six weeks tomorrow, no needles, and Eric is out of town this week, so I have the car."

"Where did he go?"

"Phoenix. His two-week yearly training started this morning. That's the real reason he keeps himself in such good shape, wants to impress the other weekend warriors. C'mon let's go finish your workout."

Michelle was too tired to cook. Debbie had called in sick for her evening shift once again and she'd had to stay to cover her exercise class. The majority of the class was overworked, overfed, late Gen X'ers who came to the Monday evening class hoping to avoid the earlier muscle-bound crowd. They were an energetic and noisy bunch, which in turn pumped Michelle up, but by the end of class, her ass was dragging. She threw her gym bag and a tee shirt into the passenger seat of her car and pulled into early evening traffic for her drive home. She'd talked Ellie into buying a membership but had forgotten to give her the shirt new members received. Planning on giving it to her before tomorrow's session at the clinic, she'd grabbed one from under the reception desk on her way out. Ellie...Elyse she corrected herself and smiled. Ellie or

Elyse, they were going to be good friends and it was nice to have a friend. Michelle could have all the male friends she wanted, but other women viewed her as too pretty to be a girlfriend. Elyse was different. The cause behind their becoming friends had been on her mind all day. Thinking one of her fellow patients might be a killer was inconceivable, but do you ever really know what goes on in other people's minds?

Michelle didn't feel any guilt whatsoever pulling into the parking lot of Panda Express and ordering her orange chicken. Eric didn't like take-out, he was such a health nut, but what he didn't know wouldn't hurt him and Michelle certainly wasn't going to tell him.

As she entered her apartment building, she stopped by her mailbox on the way to the elevator. Her heart raced, recognizing the five by seven padded envelope crammed in the box: her needles came like this. Only she hadn't ordered any in months. Michelle stared at the package uncertain what to do with it, then finally stuffed it in her purse along with the electric bill and headed towards the elevator.

Placing her now cold food along with her purse on the kitchen table, Michelle opened the package after checking for a return address. Finding none, she examined the plastic bag of what she now knew for sure were needles, learning nothing about their origin. She shook the envelope and a card fell out onto the table. It was a black business card with the word 'Playthings' written in silver across the front and the address and phone number printed on the back.

"One mystery solved," she said to the silent room. "But who sent you?" Eric came immediately to mind, but she quickly dismissed the idea. Eric supported her decision to stop with the needles; and besides, he'd given her plenty of gifts, none of them needle related. She turned the package over in her hand, feeling the slender shafts and the hubs of the needles through the plastic. Unconsciously she licked her lips, her grip on the bag tightening as a junkie with a bag of coke. Why not...No one would know... Just one more time. The thoughts circled in her head.

Disgusted with herself for even considering throwing away the progress she'd made, she slammed the bag on the table, sending the business card fluttering to the floor. Turning from the needles, Michelle spooned her dinner onto a plate, warming it up in the microwave. Grabbing one of Eric's protein drinks from the refrigerator, she carried it and her meal into the living room, away from temptation. She'd eaten half of her dinner when the doorbell rang.

Setting the carton on the end table on her way to the door, Michelle peered through the peephole bewildered by who she saw on the other side. Opening the door, she said, "What are you doing here?"

"Did you get my present?"

"Your present? Why would you send me..." Michelle didn't see the taser until it was too late.

◆ ◆ ◆

Waking up from the stun, Michelle was hit with pain. Her body was paralyzed, her muscles useless. She was disoriented and confused. As she slowly regained control over her body, she discovered she was lying naked on her bed, her wrists tied to the bedposts above her. Her legs were spread agonizingly apart and tethered to the bottom of the bed. She felt the familiar sting of a needle piercing her skin. Praying this was a nightmare, she strained to get up, a horrific headache hitting her when she raised her head. She was pushed back down, told to be still. Determined, she raised up again, fear washing over her as the realization of her predicament brought her fully out of her stupor. She screamed for help using every ounce of breath in her lungs, her cries cut short when her attacker straddled her, roughly positioning a leather strap in her mouth, cinching it tightly, all the while pressing the needles excruciatingly into the flesh of her abdomen. Blackness began to overtake her as consciousness faded, but a voice full of hatred and anger brought her back.

"Be still. We're almost done."

Suddenly, the weight was gone from her chest and the piercing began again, methodically working down both sides of her toned abdomen. Michelle whimpered through the strap as the needles were pushed into her flesh, wincing when the soft skin surrounding her vagina was pierced. Then it stopped and Michelle prayed to every God she knew that it was over. She'd be left alone, she thought, tied and gagged and naked on the bed. She felt the weight again, pressing across her thighs. A wet ribbon was dragged across her face, leaving droplets across her cheeks. In earnest, her attacker began lacing the ribbon around the needles, pulling it taunt with each loop, keeping it straight and even.

"I'm not usually here for this part." Her vision was blurry now, she could only discern the shape of her attacker. "But you're a special case, Michelle. I couldn't take the chance that you'd truly given up on your little habit." The corset was complete, her captor assessing his work. "You're looking a little rough. This ribbon is poisoned, but I bet you've figured that out already. It won't be much longer, and I have to say it's been exhilarating." The seizures began, her body convulsed and rigid in successive waves. "But all good things must come to an end."

CHAPTER 14

It was Tuesday afternoon before Sam could get back to Maddy's case and he was grateful for the reprieve. Ronnie's accusations were disturbing, if there was any truth in them. Maddy denied ever meeting Ronnie, which Sam found unlikely. While they were together, Jason was away at school, but he was never far from Maddy's thoughts. The responsibility she felt towards him due to their parents' disinterest wasn't dampened by the miles between them. They called each other frequently and seemed to have no secrets between them. When Jason decided not to come home between his freshman and sophomore years, Sam and Maddy took their first vacation together in Los Angeles, at Maddy's suggestion. They had flown into LAX, Jason meeting them at gate. The next five days had been a whirlwind of sightseeing, Santa Monica Pier, Hollywood Walk of Fame, and Universal Studios-Sam's idea. Maddy insisted on The Broad Art Museum, Griffith Observatory, and the Museum of Jurassic Technology. Jason, for his part took them to Runyon Canyon Park, entering on Mulholland Drive, near various celebrity homes in Hollywood Hills.

During that visit, Sam hadn't noticed anything inappropriate between the siblings, nothing that would suggest Maddy possessed the controlling tendencies Ronnie professed she'd manifested. But looking back, he'd been so enamored of her, there could have been warning signs he'd missed. It was believable that Maddy was concerned that Jason's relationship with Ronnie would reflect badly on the clinic. Sam was truly convinced their relationship ended in some part because Maddy was concerned Sam's job would bring unwanted publicity.

As if she was reading his thoughts, Sam's phone buzzed, and he saw Maddy's name on the readout. He accepted the call.

"Sam. It's been days since I've heard from you. I know you've been busy, but

I was hoping for some sort of update."

"I wish I could give you some good news, but I was in court yesterday and I've other clients that need my attention." Sam tried to keep the harshness out of his voice, he failed.

"Is there anything I can do to help?" Maddy recognized the tone, Sam was irritated at her. She didn't know why.

"Not right now, but if that changes, I'll let you know." They said their goodbyes and Sam ended the call.

"That was short and sweet." Elyse said from the doorway.

"Nothing much to say," Sam said.

"Sam, I know it's none of my business, but what happened between you two?"

"I honestly don't know," Sam said with a huge sigh. "At first, I thought she broke up with me because her parents didn't approve of me--my background, my job--but I've come to the conclusion that if that was the case, then she never truly believed in us, what we could have been together. I loved her more than seems possible and I know she loved me...one day she just stopped. I don't know how that happens, and I think that was the hardest to accept, that you can love someone so deeply and then not."

"I don't think you can," Elyse said. Unless you're a cold-hearted bitch, she left unsaid. "You deserve better," she did say.

What Sam didn't tell Elyse was about the month he'd spent after he'd quit the force, driving by Maddy's house at all hours of the day and night, obsessed with the idea she would come to her senses, and want him back. That fantasy ended one rainy cold night when he drove by her house and saw her new boyfriend's car parked in the driveway. Sitting there, the realization finally sinking in that it was over, his pain turned to anger, which turned to rage, which turned to violence. He exited the car, the rain soaking him in seconds and had almost made it to the front porch before Andy tackled him to the ground. Andy punched him into submission and dragged him back to his car, where he threw him against the driver's side door. Sam had never seen him so angry.

"Get your ass out of here," Andy barked.

"Leave me the fuck alone," Sam responded in kind.

"I should throw your sorry ass in jail," Andy said. "I've seen you parked out here night after night. What the hell are you thinking? It's over, Sam. Forget about her, get on with your life. She's obviously gotten on with hers." Andy opened the car door and threw Sam in. "Look, I get off work in a few hours and then I'm going to run a couple of miles. I'll be at your house at six. You're coming with me."

What he never told Andy was what he did during those few hours. He'd driven home and drank two-thirds of a bottle of Scotch; he sat in the same chair Maddy had found him in the day he quit his job. He then loaded his revolver. He didn't want to die; he just wanted the pain to go away. He sat there, staring down the barrel of his gun and decided no one was worth killing himself over--no one. And he swore to himself then and there he would never let anyone hurt him again. Never.

"I don't know about deserving better," Sam said. "But I do know that this case won't solve itself. You've been pouring over those ledgers for days now, what have you found out?"

"To start with, there are two sets of ledgers here, covering the past six months. One of them shows the clinic making a small profit over the last two quarters, the other one shows them in the red."

"How much in the red?" Sam asked.

"About one hundred thousand dollars."

"Which one of the ledgers is accurate?"

"The one showing the loss is the correct one. It was done by the accounting firm the clinic uses. The false copy was done by Nick, but it wouldn't have fooled a professional auditor by any means."

"Maybe he was only trying to fool Maddy," Sam said. "That's why Nick got so bent out of shape when I asked about the clinic's finances. It was a shot in the dark, but it looks like I was right." Sam sat back in his chair, studying a spot on the ceiling.

"It's not unusual for a business to run in the red for a couple of years," Elyse said. "Looking at the past six months it's hard to tell, but I think things were turning around."

"Nick took a huge loan out to start the clinic. There may be contingencies attached to that loan stipulating the clinic be showing a profit after a specified period of time."

"Wasn't that loan from Maddy's parents and aren't they dead now?"

"The clinic would still have to pay back the loan, even if it was being paid to Maddy and Jason."

"Just Maddy now that Jason is dead," Elyse corrected.

"Yes, he is," Sam said, unconsciously pacing his office. "Nick might have been showing Maddy the false ledgers, hoping to stall any foreclosure."

"What I don't understand," Elyse said, "is why Jason didn't tell Maddy what he suspected Nick was doing. There was certainly no love lost between the two and Jason would've wanted Maddy to know."

"I don't think the ledgers are what put Jason in a frenzy the night he was killed. I think he suspected Nick of doing much more than just doctoring books. He was on his way over to Maddy's house to get her away from Nick before he told her what he suspected."

"Why didn't he go to the police if he thought either one of them was in danger?"

"We're missing something," Sam determined. "I'm going back to the clinic to talk to Nick again, see if I can get him riled up enough to give us another piece to this puzzle."

"I'm on my way there this evening, too. Andy was right when he said there wasn't anything suspicious on the Arnold or Hutchins' police reports, so I'm meeting Michelle at the clinic and I hope she'll introduce me to someone who remembers them. Maybe we'll get lucky and we'll find out more about their deaths."

"Couldn't hurt and since I have some time before I can talk to Nick, I'll go talk to Glenn Arnold's grieving widow."

Turning into what was an unquestionably affluent gated cul-de-sac in the heart of Naperville, Sam spotted the Arnold house at the apex of the circle. He pulled into the roundabout driveway, parking in front of an immense stairway leading to the arched front doorway. Waiting at the top was a thirtyish trim brunette woman he assumed correctly to be Mrs. Arnold. Sam had called earlier, asking to meet with her concerning her husband. She had been pleasant but unwelcoming on the phone.

"Mrs. Arnold?" Sam offered his hand as he reached the top.

"Yes," She replied, ignoring it. "Before we go any further, I want to know why you're here. My husband died three months ago."

Quickly deciding that anything but the truth would get him thrown down the stairs, Sam took a deep breath and stated. "My name's Sam Bartell and I work for Bartell Investigations. We're currently investigating a similar death and we're hoping you can clear up a few things for us."

"Mr. Bartell, he drowned after hitting his head and falling into our swimming pool. I don't see how I can make that any clearer for you."

"By similar I mean your husband was also a patient at the Hollowell Clinic," Sam said, stepping closer and lowering his voice to an almost whisper, "And I know he didn't die in a swimming pool." He added with enough conviction, he hoped, to make her believe his bluff. Sam waited as Mrs. Arnold sized him up, finally reaching a decision, and after glancing up and down the street, she turned toward the door and ushered him into the house.

Once inside, Sam soon realized his first assessment of Mrs. Arnold as standoffish and inhospitable was incorrect. She led him into a huge well-appointed living room and left him seated in one of two leather couches to get him an iced tea after declining her offer for something stronger. Waiting for her return, he performed his customary assessment of his surroundings, contemplating his approach to the subject of her and her husband's sexual activities. Elyse's background check into the couple said they'd married five years ago, they were childless. Glenn was an independent stockbroker; he had a small office not far from his home. Mrs. Arnold worked at Travel By Courtney. Mrs. Arnold returned with his tea, sitting down across from him in the matching couch after handing it to him. Insisting Sam call her Linda, she began talking about her husband, the sadness of her loss evident in her tone and the tears she absently brushed from her cheeks as they talked.

"We met in college. Both of us getting business degrees. Glenn started with Charles Schwab downtown, but after a couple of years, he wanted to start his own agency, so we moved back to Naperville. We both grew up in this area, our parents live nearby. I took a job part-time with my sister a couple of days a week at the travel agency she runs. I enjoy working there and the traveling I get to do," Linda said. "You probably know all this already, as you're an investigator."

"I don't mind. You two must have been very happy."

"We were, Mr. Bartell. Very, except for his," she paused, "activities that led to his going to the clinic."

"The client we're investigating died from choking." Was that what happened to your husband?"

"No, he was into bondage, not choking. I thought you knew that."

"I said your husband's death was similar, and it was. But to be completely honest with you, I didn't know that for sure until you let me in the door."

"You're very good at you job, Mr. Bartell, but I don't see the connection."

"At least four people that attended sessions at the clinic have died in the past six months. We don't believe this is a coincidence. Tell me what really happened. You may be stopping a murderer."

"I insisted Glenn go the that clinic," Linda said, dumbfounded. "But I don't see how anyone could have killed him. He was alone at the time of his death."

"Let's start at the beginning," Sam urged.

"When we met, Glenn was into mild bondage, sometimes he'd have me tie him up during sex. I really didn't think much about it; he wasn't hurting anyone, and he never got aggressive with me. Everybody experiments, right?"

"Sure," Sam said, sorry he hadn't been more specific when he asked her to start at the beginning.

"After we got married, he stopped asking me to tie him up and he started binding himself, first with Velcro restraints, tape, things he could easily get out of. Then he moved on to straitjackets, easy release ones at first, then ones with locks and chains. You can see where this is going, right?"

"Yes," Sam said.

"Over the past year, he'd gotten to where he didn't want me home when he did his bondage. He said he needed to feel completely helpless. That's when

I realized bondage wasn't a phase he was going through and if I didn't do something to stop him, he never would. I told him I wanted to have a baby and that I wasn't going to raise a child in that kind of environment. He argued with me, said he could keep his bondage separate, the child would never know. I told him I wasn't going to take that risk, that he needed help and if he didn't get it, I was going to file for a divorce. But it took me going to a lawyer for him to realize I was serious. He started going to the clinic after that."

"How did that go?" Sam prompted.

"He attended sessions regularly for two months and he stayed away from his man cave. That's where he did his bondage. I thought he was doing great. Then I came home early from what was supposed to be a long weekend reviewing a hotel for the agency and I found him," her voice hitched, and she held back a sob at the memory.

"Did he ever mention other patients at the clinic?" Sam asked.

"No, he didn't talk about them, said they were all perverts. I didn't tell him they probably thought he was a pervert, too." she smiled.

"I know your husband was Dr. Maxwell's patient. Did he ever mention him?"

She paused, giving his question some thought. "I don't think so. Sorry."

Disappointed, Sam decided to change his tactics. "I'm sorry to ask you this, Linda, but would you show me where you found your husband?"

She rose from the couch and indicating Sam should follow; Linda led Sam through the house, finally stopping at a locked door, which she opened with a key from a set she pulled from her pocket. Inside was everything Sam pictured his man cave would be one day: big screen TV, wet bar, pool table. Linda pointed to the far corner of the room. "That's where he would tie himself up. Sometimes for hours." Sam spotted three hooks extending from the ceiling he assumed Glenn used for his suspension equipment. "I never understood why he needed the bondage," Linda said. "Our sex life was always great, I was open to experimentation--to a point, mind you. He told me it was more about being helpless and caught between pleasure and pain. I guess I shouldn't have let it go on so long."

"Don't blame yourself," Sam consoled. "Can you tell me how you found him?"

"I can do better than that, I can show you. He always recorded his bondage scenarios so he could watch them later." Sam was both sorry and thankful Linda had a copy. "And you'll need to see it if you want to understand how he died."

She put a DVD in the player and turned it on. The camera was placed right in front of where Sam stood now. At first the screen was black, but then Glenn appeared in the shot, back to the camera, carrying ropes and other bondage equipment. He placed them on the floor and took off all his clothes, careful to fold them, placing them out of frame. He started by lacing a length of rope through each of the eye hooks mounted to the ceiling. He took the end of the middle one and put it through the center chain link of a pair of heavy-duty handcuffs with a built-in electronic timer. When the cuffs were closed the control buttons would be disabled and Glenn would be cuffed for whatever time he programmed into the mechanism. The second rope was attached to a set of nipple clamps. Adjusting the rope to chest high, he tied off the other end as he had the first, in what Sam recognized from his Boy Scout days as a taut-line-hitch. With two hands, you could slide the knot up and down for tightness of the rope, if you couldn't reach the knot, no matter how hard you pulled on the rope, the knot wouldn't slide, and the rope wouldn't loosen. With the third rope, Glenn made a loop on one end, tying it off so it wouldn't expand or contract under pressure; the other end, he tied off as he did the other two using a taut-line-hitch, making sure the knots would be out of reach once he was secured. Walking up to the recorder, Glenn made sure it was recording. Satisfied, he took a long drink from a water bottle and placed it a couple of feet from his setup. He placed a ball gag in his mouth, fastened it tight and reached for an ankle spreader. Attaching the padded leather restraints to his ankles, Glenn tested each lock. Next, he put on the nipple clamps, moaning both times as the clamp took its initial bite into his tender flesh. He grabbed the third rope placing it behind him and threading it through his ass cheeks. He placed the loop over his cock and balls and using the knot on the other end, he tightened the rope. As long as he had an erection, and that wasn't an issue now, the rope was not coming off. Glenn reached up on his tiptoes and tightened all three ropes. While in this position, his nipples and cock were uncomfortable; if he dropped down to rest his calves, the ropes would squeeze his cock and balls and pull his nipples. Finally, on his tiptoes, Glenn attached all three ropes to an ice lock slipping it over a hook also anchored to the ceiling and extending low enough for him to reach, barely. When it melted, the ropes would loosen, he would be able to lower his arms and calves without much discomfort and be able to move. He would still be handcuffed for the duration of whatever time he had set the electronic timer on the cuffs, but it would give him the freedom to masturbate. Satisfied, with his predicament, Glenn locked the handcuffs, Sam heard the click. For the next few minutes, Sam watched as Glenn's calves began to tire and he lowered his ankles to the floor only to moan as the pain in his nipples and genitals increased, his arousal never waning, in spite of the pain or because of it, increasing.

"How in the hell is he supposed to get out of that?" Sam asked.

Mrs. Arnold paused the DVD and pointed at the ice lock. "That was set for two hours but getting out isn't the point. He doesn't want to get out. Not really. He wants to enjoy the pain this is causing, and the longer he's tied up: the more the pain he experiences, the more the pleasure intensifies. That's how he explained it to me anyway. The timer on the handcuffs was set for four hours, but he didn't make it that long." She fast forwarded through several minutes of tape, stopping when Glenn began struggling against his ropes.

"What happened?" Sam asked, squinting at the screen.

"He vomited."

She was right. Sam could see the vomitus leaking around the ball gag. Within minutes Glenn strangled to death. Mrs. Arnold stopped the DVD. "I'm sorry," Sam said. "That was horrible, and you found him?"

"Yes, I'd left the night before and was planning on a long weekend as I said earlier, but I got sick, stomach flu, so I decided to come home early. You can see me on the DVD if you want, but by the time I got to him, he was gone. The handcuffs had opened by then and I found the key to unlock his feet. I didn't know what to do. I couldn't call the police and have them see him that way, but I couldn't leave him there. I couldn't think of anything else to do, so I put a pair of swimming trunks on him and dragged him to the pool. I threw him in, thinking the water would clean him up. Then I left and stayed at a hotel until the pool cleaners found him four days later."

"The police accepted your story?"

"After four days in the pool, they couldn't really prove anything else."

"What did you do with his restraining equipment?" Sam asked.

"The leather straightjackets and apparel he wore, I cut into pieces and threw away."

"What about the gag he had in his mouth?"

"I threw it out. It was disgusting."

"Did you notice anything strange about it?"

"I don't know what you mean strange. That he had the thing was strange. I had never seen it before."

"You were familiar with his equipment?"

"For the most part, I guess."

"Thank you for showing this to me," Sam said. "I know watching this again must've been hard for you. Do you mind if I borrow the DVD? You have my word you'll get it back."

"Take it," Linda said, pulling it from the player. "But you can have it. I don't want to remember him that way."

Leaving Linda at the door, Sam was halfway down the stairs, when he thought of another question and headed back up to the top.

"What is it?" Linda asked.

"The other client's name is Jason Richards. Does that name sound familiar to you?"

She thought for a moment. "I remember a Jason Richards, but not from the clinic, he worked on Glenn's web page when he first started his business. I'm sorry to hear of his death."

Rewinding the video for the tenth time, Sam watched as the spittle seeped out of the corners of Arnold's mouth. He tried to zoom the frame so he could see the area around the mouth, but instead the picture disappeared. "Damn it!" he said, frustrated. He had returned to the office after his visit with Mrs. Arnold, passing Elyse with a wave, who was engrossed at her desk. Putting the disc in his computer, he fast forwarded to the spot where earlier Arnold began to struggle in earnest against his bindings.

"Need some help?" Elyse asked from the doorway. She came around to the back of the desk, dragging a chair along with her. "Why do you have to be so stubborn, just ask for help."

"Because I need to learn how to do this on my own."

"Not right this minute," Elyse said, bringing the picture back up. "What were you trying to do?"

"I want to enlarge the area around Arnold's mouth. I think I see something." Elyse did what he asked and started the video. The screen was pulled in close to Arnold, the area below his knees no longer visible. They watched as he hung trussed to the ceiling for a couple of minutes; as he tired of standing on his tiptoes, he began to lower his body, the ropes cinching up against his groin and his nipples extended by the clamps. They heard his moans of pleasure and pain, watched as he bit into the gag.

"Do you see that?" Sam asked, pointing to the side of his mouth.

"See what?"

"Coming out of his mouth?" Sam said excited.

"I don't know what you're seeing, that's just spit."

"Spit isn't pink. But do you know what's pink? That stuff they give kids to make them throw up...you know... ippa..."

"Ipecac?" Elyse said, squinting at the picture. "Maybe he bit his lip and that's why it's pink."

"How did he bite his lip with that gag in his mouth?" Sam asked.

"I don't know, but it seems more plausible than ipecac in the ball gag."

"As plausible as your idea that Lindsay's estim box was intentionally amped up?" Sam said, getting up from the desk and pacing the room. "What if..."

"What is it, Sam?" Elyse asked, recognizing when pieces became a puzzle in Sam's mind.

"I think someone knew Lindsay and Arnold's sexual obsessions and provided them with exactly what he knew they couldn't refuse. And it killed them. Clever."

"And who would know more about their obsessions than their doctor?" Elyse asked. "But how do you prove that's what happened?"

"I can't," Sam replied. "But maybe we can find out how Lindsay got that estim box and when Arnold got that ball gag. Use that computer magic of

116

yours and see what you can find out for me. I'm betting you won't find any credit or debit card charges for them on their cards."

"Proving nothing then."

"But telling me someone else sent them. There's got to be a way to find out who."

CHAPTER 15

Passing by the group therapy room on his way to Nick's office, Sam noted the patients around the coffee and donut table, no sign of Michelle or Elyse. Uncertain whether Holloway or Nick were holding this evening's session, he headed towards Nick's office, running into Edward in the hallway.

"Here again, detective?" Holloway asked. "I don't have any time for questions, group starts in ten minutes."

"Actually, I was hoping to talk to Nick. Is he still here?"

"In his office. Are you two going to play nice this time?"

"I'll do my part," Sam said.

"I'm on my way home," Nick said, taking his jacket from the coat rack and walking towards Sam in the doorway. "You should've made an appointment."

"I won't keep you long," Sam said, stepping into the doorframe, stopping Nick from leaving. "I have a few questions about a couple of your patients."

"You know I can't discuss my patients with you without their consent."

"These patients are dead." "Then what do they have to do with Jason?"

"That's what I want to find out. Glenn Arnold and Philip Hutchins were both patients of the clinic, coming to sessions and individual appointments with you. Correct?"

"Yes, but from what I understand from speaking with Mrs. Arnold, Glenn's death was accidental, and Philip died when he surprised a burglar in his apartment," Nick attempted to go around Sam, who didn't move.

"I'm still looking into the circumstances of Hutchins' death, but I know for sure Arnold didn't die in a swimming pool. That makes at least four deaths with a connection to this clinic and at least three are directly connected to you."

"Are you insinuating I had something to do with their deaths? That's ridiculous," Nick said, his voice lowering as his anger rose. "Why would I kill my patients? I've worked too damn hard to get where I am to do any such thing."

"That's not really a denial."

"Fuck you," Nick said. "You're trying to get me mad enough so that I say something that incriminating but get it through your head: I didn't have anything to do with those deaths and you don't have any evidence that I did. You're blowing smoke."

"What I'm blowing is the whistle on your clinic's finances. I have seen evidence that you've worked up your own set of books showing a profit. We both know this clinic has been running in the red from the start. I think you're showing Maddy your rewritten version, so she'll continue funding this place. And, I know about your affair with Lindsay Mathers. Did she know too much? Is that why you killed her and Jason?"

Furious with Sam for the accusations, Nick punched him in the side of his face with a wicked right cross. Surprised by the blow and stunned, Sam fell to the floor, blood spewing from a cut on his temple. The sight of blood along with the pain in his hand brought Nick out of his rage. He helped Sam to his feet and into one of his office chairs leaving briefly to get a washcloth from the bathroom. When he returned, he handed it to Sam and sat down behind the desk.

"You have an irritating way of getting under my skin, detective. And despite the fact I know what you're doing, I can't help myself."

"Are there other things you can't help yourself from doing?" Sam asked, pressing the cloth against his temple.

"You're like a dog with a bone, aren't you?" Nick asked, shaking his head.

"I've been told that a few times," Sam said, wincing. "And between you and your wife, I'm going to end up with a concussion. But your attack only proves you're hiding something. Do you want to tell me or am I going to keep digging on my own?"

"My attack only proves how much you annoy me. I had nothing to do with any of those deaths. But, you're right about the books. I worked up a set showing the clinic is making a profit, but I only showed it to Maddy. I didn't want her to know the clinic isn't making money. She believed in me enough to convince her parents to lend me the money for the clinic and I don't want her thinking she was wrong in that belief. The terms of the loan require the clinic be making a profit by the end of our fourth year, which will be two months from now."

"As I've said before, Maddy needs to know the truth," Sam said. "Won't she find out anyway when the bank forecloses in a couple of months?"

"I'll never let that happen," Nick said, vehemently. "I've poured my heart and soul into this clinic, helping patients that most people consider perverts and not worthy of help. Our research has been extremely promising and the book we just published is going to put this clinic on the map. Money won't be an issue. I just need six more months and Maddy won't know the difference. You're here to find out what happened to Jason. Something we already know. The clinic and how I choose to run it is none of your business."

"If you're not involved, and I'm convinced you are, given that four of your patients are now dead, what do you think happened to them?"

Sitting back in his chair, Nick stared at Sam across the desk. Finally reaching a decision, he shrugged, and reaching into his top desk drawer, he shuffled through the files. Finding what he was looking for, he pulled out a file and handed it to Sam.

"Why don't you save me some time and tell me about..." Sam read the name on the file, "Dylan Taylor."

"Dylan is one of my patients, former patients now, I guess. He started coming to sessions on his own six months ago. He attended sessions regularly for a month and when I asked him to start individualized treatment with me, he began seeing me twice a week. Over the course of these individual sessions, he developed what we psychodynamic therapists call transference."

"I've heard the term on an episode of Criminal Minds. It's a real thing?"

"Very real. We all have it with everyone and everything. It's a part of how we choose our mate, our friends, our jobs. In therapy, it's based on the theory that everyone sees the world in a way that is unique to the individual and influenced by our unconscious and past experiences, usually with those who reared us. Sometimes what happens in therapy is the patient transfers feelings and attitudes from a person or situation in the past onto the therapist. This transference can be either positive or negative. If the patient had a supportive father, it's possible the patient will see me as such and be great to work with."

"I'm guessing Dylan's transference was negative."

"Dylan fears disapproval and rejection, stemming from an overbearing father who Dylan spent his childhood trying to impress. Those fears of rejection were transferred to me and he became angry when he felt I had also rejected him."

"What make him feel you had rejected him?"

"I delved into the reasons behind his fetish."

"Which is?" Sam asked.

"He's a furry. Are you familiar with the term?" Nick asked.

"Someone who dresses up as their favorite animal character."

"Yes, but it's more than that and there are many different types of furries. For our purposes, let's define a furry as someone who role plays as an animal, giving his character human personalities and abilities, such as talking or walking on two feet."

"Dylan came to you because of his furry fetish?"

"Yes, and as I got closer to the motivations behind the fetish, he became angry and hostile towards me. It happens. After a couple of sessions where his anger became increasingly uncontrollable, I told him I could no longer see him and suggested he go to another doctor. He took that as the ultimate rejection and for the past four months he's shown up unexpectedly, barging in and upsetting the patients, until I had to put a restraining order on him. He's not allowed near the clinic, but a few of my patients who recognize him from sessions have mentioned seeing him hanging around outside."

"I have a hard time taking someone who dresses up in a rabbit costume seriously as a murder suspect."

"Bear."

"What?"

"His fursona is a bear, not a rabbit. You have difficulty seeing a furry as dangerous because you aren't separating the two pathologies," Nick said. "The furry aspect is how he deals with his feelings of rejection."

"Why the fur?"

"Many reasons. Inclusion and belongingness are central themes in furry culture and Dylan craves those feelings. Many furries I've counseled, Dylan included, attest to a significant amount of their childhood spent watching cartoons, anime, science fiction and fantasy. And let's not forget The Teenage Mutant Ninja Turtles, one of the first comic books written about human animal characters. Coupled with the strong bond a real pet, such as a dog, can form with any child, the furry persona is entirely understandable."

"Where does transference fit in this picture?" Sam asked.

"Recently Dylan has become what is termed a lifestyler, his furry tendencies became extreme, to the point he became a 'barepaw'."

"'Barepaw'?'" Sam asked.

"It's common for some furries to not wear shoes whenever possible. Going barefoot, as you know toughens the soles of your feet to the point of developing paw like pads. Dylan refused to wear shoes; his boss had no choice but to fire him."

"I guess your therapy didn't work for him."

"Over the course of our therapy, my goal was to help Dylan realize the motivations behind the furry persona. Once he was aware of the unconscious reasons behind his behavior, I was hopeful he would find different coping mechanisms, be able to put his shoes back on. The goal with Dylan, as with all our patients, isn't to stop his furry activity, but to help him understand why he feels it necessary to dress as a bear. After that, if he wanted to continue to be a bear, as long as he isn't hurting himself or anyone else, my job is done. Unfortunately, Dylan took my probing into his motivations as a rejection of his actions. The rejection he always felt from his father he transferred to me, with the same negative results. The more questions I asked, the deeper we got into his psyche, the angrier he became."

"Then you kicking him out of the clinic sent him over the deep end. I don't buy it. Why is he killing patients and not you?"

"The death of his father four months ago caused his snap with reality, what sent him over the deep end as you say. For his entire life, Dylan feared rejection from his father and hated him for it, but he could never act on these emotions, he couldn't kill his father. The anger he feels from my perceived rejection I fear he is taking out on my patients."

"How is he picking which ones?"

"I don't know and there may not be a connection between them."

"That's not helpful and it's very convenient you are producing a scapegoat when I accuse you."

"He's not a scapegoat, he's dangerous and it's in no way convenient, I could lose my license for showing you that file, but if he's responsible for these deaths, I have no choice."

"Okay, Nick. I'll go off on your wild goose chase...bear chase, but don't think for a minute you're off the hook. Correct me if I'm wrong, but Dylan Taylor is between twenty-five to thirty, white, intelligent and highly functional."

"Spot on, detective. Are you profiling from a similar case?"

"No, I'm profiling furries in general."

Catching sight of Elyse in the group session room as they were finishing up, Sam motioned for her to meet him at the back of the room.

"What the hell happened to your face?" Elyse gasped as she got closer and saw the gash above his eyebrow. "Here, I've got something for that." Digging around in her oversized purse, she pulled out a Kleenex.

"It's nothing," Sam said, feeling the blood begin to drip again.

"Hold still," Elyse said, patting his forehead. "You may need a stitch or two. It's seeping through the Kleenex. I think I have some of that liquid bandage in here somewhere." She rooted through her bag some more, finally pulling out a small blue tube. She uncapped it and squeezed a thin line on the cut, patting it in place with her finger.

"Why do you have that in your purse?" Sam asked.

"This is great for when I break a nail." Elyse patted the cut. "I'm going to need a little more." Elyse put a dime-sized dot on her thumb and aimed it at Sam.

"Forget about the cut for a minute," Sam whispered, ducking. "Have you heard anything about a patient named Dylan Taylor? Did Michelle mention him?"

"No. Why?"

"Nick says he's been causing trouble around the clinic; says he may have something to do with the deaths we're looking into."

"Do you two know each other?" Edward surprised them both as he came up behind them.

"No," Sam said, stepping away from Elyse.

"Yes." Elyse replied. "We just met," Elyse said correcting herself, obviously lying.

"I see. How nice of you to assist a complete stranger," Edward said sarcastically.

"That's an amazing coat Dr. Holloway," Elyse said, hoping to distract him. "It's vicuna, isn't it?" Now herself distracted, she reached up, feeling the lapels and the mink fur collar.

"Yes, it is." Holloway moved away from her hand, obviously disturbed by her assault, and turned to Sam. "I guess you and Nick didn't play so nice."

"Not so much," Sam replied.

"You two clearly rub each other the wrong way. Did you give as well as you got?"

"No, he surprised me. I didn't know he even had it in him," Sam said. "Nick is full of surprises--especially where the clinic is involved. Well good evening detective. Ellie, I hope to see you at our next meeting," Edward said, addressing her by her alias. "

I'll be here, for sure Dr.," Elyse said, trying not to stare at the small liquid bandage spot she had left on his twenty-thousand-dollar coat. "By the way, Michelle said she was going to be here this evening, but I haven't seen her…"

"Michelle can be somewhat unpredictable."

"I don't like this," Elyse said to Sam, as they watched Edward exit the clinic. "Michelle told me she'd be here."

"When did you last speak to her?" Sam asked.

"She called me late yesterday morning to see how I was doing after our workout."

"Maybe she's sick."

"She would have answered my texts even if she's sick. I'm going to track down her boyfriend." Sam recognized the determined look that came into her eyes.

"Good idea," Sam said. "Did you find any patients who knew Arnold or Hutchins?"

"No, I'm sorry. I was too worried about Michelle to ask around."

"That's alright," Sam said. "But we shouldn't leave together. You go on ahead and I'll hang around for a bit."

"Okay," Elyse said, shaking her head as she put on her jacket. "But I think your idea of not letting anyone know I work for you is blown. Holloway certainly wasn't fooled, and the patients here have way more serious things to worry about than why a detective is poking around."

"No, he wasn't," Sam agreed. "Try not to worry too much about Michelle, I'm sure you'll hear from her soon. I'll see you in the morning."

Sam exited the clinic, watching as Elyse walked to her car in the dim glow cast by the sodium lights in the parking lot. To his left of the entryway puffing on cigarette stood a fiftyish looking bald man and a much younger man with a set of earphones blasting away his hearing while he waited on a cab. Taking a chance that one of them may have known the victims, he walked over to the older one. "May I have one of those?" he asked, pointing to the cigarette. "Sure," pulling one from his pack and handing it to Sam, he found his lighter and lit it for him. "I'm Frank," the stranger said sticking out his hand. "This is Mike," he added pointing to his companion, whose back was to them.

"Sam," he said, returning the handshake and fighting the urge to cough.

"I saw you talking to Dr. Holloway. Are you joining group?" Frank asked.

"No, I'm a private investigator."

"Who are you investigating?" Frank's curiosity was piqued.

"A couple of patients who died a few months ago. Glenn Arnold and Philip Hutchins. Did you know either of them?" Sam asked, letting the cigarette burn down.

"I never met Glenn Arnold, but I knew Phil from sessions. I couldn't relate to him. Can't understand anyone under thirty." He laughed. "My wife and I raised a son and daughter; their values and ideals are entirely different than what we taught them. Maybe I'm just getting old." He pushed the butt of his cigarette around in the decorative ashtray standing by the door. "Gotta get home." he said, walking toward the parking lot. "My wife worries. Good luck with your case. you should talk to Mike; he was a friend of Phil's."

Sam walked over to Mike, tapping him on the shoulder to get his attention. Startled, Mike whirled around on Sam who stepped back a pace, raising his arms to show he was harmless.

"Shouldn't do that," Mike said, turning his music off.

"Sorry," Sam replied. "Frank said you were friends with Philip Hutchins. Can I ask you a few questions about him?"

"Terrible what happened to him but can't say he didn't deserve it."

"Why do you say that? Wasn't he killed during a robbery?"

"More likely a hookup. Cybering was his thing, his virtual reality equipment was high-end and extensive. He showed it to me, and a game called Second Life he was hardcore into. But occasionally he'd hook up with another gamer, spend days holed up in his apartment having sex and playing games. Whoever this someone was, he probably saw all of Phil's equipment and decided to take it." A taxi pulled up to the curb. "My ride's here," plugging his earbuds back in, Mike headed off.

Adding his burnt-down cigarette to the tray, Sam pulled his collar up to deflect some of the chilly wind blowing across the parking lot and headed toward his car. Halfway across the lot, his phone chirped. It was Andy.

"Sam, I've got some info on Hutchins' death."

"What did you find out?"

"The detectives who caught the case first thought it was a burglary gone wrong and most likely it was. The victim had thousands of dollars in computer equipment," Andy said, confirming Mike's story. "Strange thing is, the burglar didn't take any of it."

"Maybe he got spooked after killing Hutchins and left in a panic."

"Possibly and what the detectives thought also. What it doesn't say is that after hacking into Hutchins computer, they found child pornography."

"I bet he didn't discuss that in group."

"What?" Andy asked.

"Nothing. But that doesn't rule out a robbery gone wrong." Sam stopped, taking in what Andy said. "Maybe whoever killed him discovered his porno stash and took matters in his own hands."

"Got what he deserved then," Andy proclaimed over the phone.

Sam didn't hear the car until it was right behind him. He turned toward the vehicle, the glare of the headlights the only thing he could see. His police training, always on the alert, he tried to spot the driver, only catching a silhouette before his fight or flight instinct kicked in. He jumped up and over, hoping if he was hit, it would be a glancing blow as the car passed. It wasn't.

CHAPTER 16

"How bad is it?" Maddy asked the attending emergency room doctor, hesitant to part the circular curtain around Sam's bed and see for herself.

"He's pretty lucky, considering he got hit by a car, no broken bones, but he's going to be very sore for the next week or so. We've given him some morphine for the pain, and I recommended he stay overnight for observation, but he refused. At the very least, he needs someone with him for the next twelve hours."

"I'll look after him," Maddy replied, relieved.

"Maddy?" Sam asked from behind the curtain.

Slipping into the cubicle, Maddy got a good look at Sam's injuries, tears welling in her eyes as she reached out to him, then stopped, unsure where to touch him. Sam had jumped up and out of the way of a direct hit from the car, but he'd landed on the hood, his momentum carrying him over the roof and across the trunk before slamming him onto the pavement. His body was a mass of cuts and contusions and Maddy was astounded that nothing was broken.

"It isn't as bad as it looks," Sam said grabbing the sheet to cover himself, the pain medication obviously affecting his coordination. He cringed when the cloth hit his abraded skin.

"Well it looks horrible." Maddy moved to his side, helping him with the sheet. "How's your pain?"

"Don't feel a thing right now," Sam said, a medicated grin crossing his face. "But I bet I will in the morning."

"The doctor said you refused to stay overnight. Do you think that's a good idea? What about that nasty cut above your eye?"

"That is courtesy of your husband, not the car."

"Nick...?"

Just then the nurse stepped into the cubicle, a tray of assorted bandages, antibiotic creams and tape in her hand. "I'll ask you to leave while I bandage Mr. Bartell," she said, not really asking and leaving no question as to who would win if Maddy argued with her.

Maddy went to the waiting room, finding Andy there. She sat down next to him, noting the surprise and disappointment vying for control of Andy's face. "I just got here and the nurse at the desk told me someone was already with him. I thought it was Elyse," not hiding his disappointment that it wasn't. "How is he?"

"Pretty beaten up, but he's going home tonight against his doctor's recommendation."

"Were you at the clinic when it happened?" Andy asked.

"No, Nick called me after the ambulance left the clinic. He said it was a hit and run, no eyewitnesses, but maybe the police can get a plate number from the security cameras."

"Does Sam remember anything?"

"We didn't get a chance to talk about it and he's on some strong pain meds, so I don't think he's going to be much help tonight." An awkward silence settled between them for several minutes before Maddy spoke again. "I know you didn't want Sam taking my case, but I had no idea this was going to happen."

"Being around you only causes him pain, one way or the other," Andy uttered. "And something is going on at that clinic. Maybe Jason knew about it, maybe he just stumbled into it. Either way, we both know Sam won't quit until he gets to the bottom of it."

"He's not getting to the bottom of anything tonight and as soon as they release him, I'm taking him home."

"No, you are not," Andy said fiercely. "You've done more than enough. I'll make sure he gets home and stays there; you go home to your husband."

"Alright, Andy," Maddy said. "But I'm going to check on him again before I leave."

As Sam was signing his release papers, Maddy came back into the cubicle and listened as the doctor gave Sam his discharge instructions. Finishing up, the doctor made one last futile attempt to convince Sam to stay.

"You're a very lucky man, Mr. Bartell. There's no doubt this could have been much worse. But I'd feel better if you'd reconsider and stay overnight."

"I appreciate the concern, but I'll be fine," Sam said. "I promise to take it easy for the next few days."

"A promise I'll make sure he keeps," Maddy added.

The doctor handed Sam a pair of scrubs. "We had to cut your clothes off when you were brought in." He handed Sam two prescriptions, then turned to Maddy with instructions. "You'll want to get those filled on you way home.

Get him started on the antibiotic right away and the pain medication is as needed. The pain medication he was given will be wearing off in about an hour, but we also gave him something to help him sleep and that'll be kicking in soon."

"You can go, too Maddy," Sam said as soon as the doctor left. "I asked the nurse to call Andy earlier, he should be here soon."

"You really think you can make it on your own from here?" Maddy asked, while Sam shifted to the edge of the bed and swallowed a cry of pain. "How do you think you're going to get these on by yourself?" Maddy asked, picking the scrubs up off the bed. "Let me help you, it's the least I can do, since this is all my fault."

"This isn't your fault and I can certainly get myself dressed," Sam said defiantly. "Someone doesn't like me digging into Jason's death, which only makes me want to dig deeper." Sliding his legs over the side of the bed, Sam used the bars to pull himself up, losing his sheet in the process.

"Stop being so stubborn, and you don't have anything I haven't seen before," Maddy said as he flailed around for the sheet. "Let me help you or you'll end up here all night. Andy is already waiting for you and he insisted on taking you home so be sure he gets those prescriptions filled on your way." Realizing Maddy was right, Sam let the sheet fall and Maddy dress him; silently thankful for the help.

Thirty minutes and one drug store stop later, Andy half-carried Sam into his house. After pausing on their way to the bedroom in the kitchen long enough for Andy to fish a Percocet out of the vial and grab a bottle of Gatorade from the frig, he laid Sam as gingerly as he could on the bed. Andy removed Sam's shoes and while Sam took off his shirt, Andy grabbed the pillow from the other side of the bed, sliding it behind his back. Leaning back and groaning from exhaustion, Sam said, "Thanks for bringing me home, Andy."

"How are you feeling?" Andy asked, shrugging off his gratitude.

"Like I was hit by a Mack truck instead of a car." Sam yawned, the sleeping medication kicking in.

"Are you hungry? I should have asked you that on the way home, but I can go get whatever you want or if you have something here…"

"No, thanks," Sam waved him off. "I'm not hungry. I think I'm just going to sleep for a while."

"Okay, but before you do let me ask you a few questions."

"Sure." Sam shook his head trying to clear his thoughts.

"Did you see the driver?" Andy asked.

"No, the car came up behind me and I only got a quick glimpse over the headlights before I jumped out of the way…well mostly out of the way. All I could see through the windshield was a dark shape wearing some sort of hat. I couldn't tell if it was a man or a woman."

"Who did you speak to at the clinic?"

"Nick and Edward briefly...and Elyse was there," Sam said through a yawn.

"Elyse? Why was she there?"

"Long story...maybe tomorrow." The phone rang in the living room.

Andy searched the bedroom for a handset, finding it empty on the table next to the bed. Surprised Sam even had a house phone, he went searching for it in the living room, grabbing it before the answering machine picked up.

"Andy...? How's Sam?" Andy heard the concern in Elyse's voice and the relief that it was Andy who was with him.

"He's fine, bruised and battered, but fine. I'll probably stay for a couple hours, make sure he's doing ok, but I need to be at work by five."

"I'll come over first thing in the morning, check on him and make sure he takes it easy."

"Sam tells me you were at the clinic too. Why?"

"He asked me to mingle with the patients, see if I could turn up anything new on the deaths that have been happening over the past few months."

"Have you?" Andy asked.

"Not really," Elyse said, hesitant to mention her concerns about Michelle until she'd spoken to Sam. "Do you think this was an accident or intentional?" "The only thing accidental about this was that Sam wasn't killed."

Returning to the bedroom, Andy found Sam dead to the world. Realizing he wouldn't be getting any more answers about the hit and run this evening, he covered Sam with a blanket and got the spare one from the closet. Heading into the living room, he gathered the throw pillows into a pile, kicked off his shoes and settled in for a few hours of sleep.

Two hours later, when his watch alarm chimed, Andy went into Sam's bedroom. He was sound asleep and appeared to be in little pain. Returning to the living room, he found a pad of paper and a pen, leaving Sam a note that Elyse would be stopping by soon and admonishing him to take it easy. Knowing his efforts were futile, Andy silently opened the front door and left through it.

Ten minutes after Andy had pulled out of the driveway, Maddy exited her car and walked to Sam's front door. Checking both sides of the concrete porch, she found what she was looking for, the spare key, hidden under a hollow rock. "You're so predictable," she said as she slid the key in the lock and let herself in.

She found him, much as Andy had left him, comatose from exhaustion and medication. She began taking her clothes off, "I'm going to stay in here with you for a while. Is that alright with you?" Maddy asked, not expecting a response and not getting one. She pulled back the covers, eliciting a grunt from Sam, and slid in next to him.

Sometime in the early morning hours, Sam woke to find Maddy curled up next to him sharing what she had once called the blast furnace of heat that came off him as he slept. He shifted to get a better view of her sleeping, the pain in his side quickly reminding him that wasn't a good idea. He silenced a groan, not wanting to wake her, then moved away from her. How she had gotten in, didn't take long to figure out, even in his clouded mind, but why was a different matter and something he fully intended to find out...Sam drifted off.

Waking to the sound of the phone ringing, Sam wondered why Maddy wasn't answering it. Then he heard the water from the shower and knew she wasn't getting it anytime soon. He sat up slowly, easing to the side of the bed and found the phone on his nightstand. Answering it on the fourth ring, he heard Elyse's voice on the other end.

"Sam, how are you? I wanted to come over earlier, but I came to the office first."

"I'm fine," Sam stifled a groan as he got out of bed. "Take your time."

"I've rescheduled your appointments for the next two days, so you can rest. Andy told me you were hit coming out of the clinic. You weren't that far behind me. What happened?"

"I stopped to talk to another patient who knew Philip Hutchins. I'll bring you up to speed later. Have you spoken to Michelle this morning?"

"I've phoned her a couple of times, but no answer."

"Have you tried the gym where she works?"

"Yes, but no answers there either. I'll keep at it, and I'll try the boyfriend again. You take it easy, Sam. I'll let you know if anything comes up here and I'll stop by soon to see how you're doing."

Sam heard the shower shut off and minutes later, Maddy walked into the bedroom, wrapped in a towel. She rummaged through his dresser, picking out a pair of sweatpants and a shirt from his running clothes drawer. Pulling the pants on, she drew the string on the pants as tight as it would go, and then slipped the shirt over her head. Looking comfortable and satisfied with her outfit she said. "I'm going to fix you some breakfast."

"That's not necessary, Maddy. You've done enough." More than you should have, Sam thought.

"Andy left a note that Elyse is going to be here to take care of you this morning and that he'll stop by later to get a statement. I'm getting the distinct feeling you don't want me here when she gets here."

"I don't want her thinking the wrong thing."

"If she does it's her problem. Nothing happened. Do you have a problem with my being here?"

"Why *are* you here?" Sam asked, scrutinizing her face. "If you thought something was going to happen, you're delusional and even if we did have sex, we both know it wouldn't mean anything."

"You've changed Sam. Sex always meant something to you..."

"I'm not the only one who's changed. I know about you and Ronnie. Your threats if she didn't stop dating Jason."

"That's what she told you?" Maddy laughed.

"She claims you tried to get her business shut down and when that didn't work you offered her money."

"Of course, she did, but it's not true," Maddy denied. "I'm hungry and I'm going to make us some breakfast. If you want to hear my side of the story, you can join me in the kitchen."

"I think I'll take a shower while you cook, work out some of this stiffness," Sam said, rubbing his neck.

"I can join you if you like." Maddy kissed him on the cheek and grinned. "No? Well, your loss."

Twenty minutes later with the smell of bacon wafting through the house, Sam sat down on one of the stools at the breakfast bar. "I almost feel human again," Sam said as Maddy stirred scrambled eggs and put a couple slices of bread into the toaster. "That bacon smells great, didn't realize how hungry I was."

"You may be feeling better, but the doctor said to take it easy."

"Elyse is way ahead of you, she's already cancelled my appointments for the next couple of days."

"She takes good care of you Sam. Don't let her get away." Maddy spooned the eggs into a bowl and placed them on the table. "I'm not referring to her assistant skills, if you didn't catch that," she said.

"Elyse has no interest in me that way and why do you care?" Sam asked bitterly.

"I want you to be happy and you can be so dense when it comes to women."

"Apparently, but I think you stopped caring about my happiness a long time ago."

"That's not true," Maddy denied, as she placed the butter on the table. "I know you're in some pain, Sam, but believe me when I say I only wish you the best."

"Like you only wished the best for Jason and Ronnie?"

"You're back to that, I guess." She sat down next to him on a stool, silently making plates of eggs, bacon and toast for herself and Sam as he waited. She poured them both orange juice, and began eating, leaving Sam to wonder if her silence was because he'd hurt her with his remark or if she was stalling for time, getting her story together about Ronnie. "When Jason started dating Ronnie," Maddy began, "he told me she ran an adult bookstore, but he never introduced us, and he was always secretive about their relationship. I was curious about her, so I stopped by her store. She tried talking me into a private session. She had no idea I was Jason's sister. I told her I wasn't interested, but that didn't stop her. She kept calling me and even showed up at my house a couple of times. Finally, I told her I was Jason's sister and if she didn't back off, I would tell him."

"And did she?" Sam asked.

"She stopped calling me and they broke up shortly after that..."

"Did Jason tell you she was pregnant?"

"Yes." Maddy paused. "I warned him that he needed to get a paternity test and he got mad at me for even suggesting it wasn't his child. He was so taken in by her, he would've raised it as his own even if it wasn't," Maddy said.

"She's not pregnant. It was false positive."

"She probably faked the whole thing," Maddy said.

"Why didn't you tell me about Ronnie?"

"Because it has nothing to do with Jason's death and I was hoping to forget the whole thing."

"You don't think someone you say is obsessed with you, but is dating your brother, is something I need to know? Have you considered she may have killed Jason as an act of retaliation?"

"No, I hadn't, and I didn't say she was obsessed. I just think she's a little confused."

"Withholding that information could lead me to believe you had a motive to kill your brother."

"Only if you think there's something between Ronnie and me. There isn't. If you truly believe I killed my brother, how can you just sit there and not turn me over to the police?"

"I don't believe you killed him," Sam said.

"You think Nick did. You said you'd keep an open mind about him when we started this investigation and yet all I see you doing is working to build a case against him."

"Because that's where the evidence is pointing. As I said in the beginning, you and Nick have the only motive for his murder."

"That motive being money? We don't need Jason's money."

"You might need it more than you think."

"What does that mean?"

"Nick has been doctoring the books from the clinic. It is hemorrhaging funds and if it doesn't start making money soon, the loan will go into default and the bank will foreclose on the clinic."

"I don't believe you."

"Why do you think he hit me?" Sam asked. "I confronted him about it last night. Then I almost got run over outside his clinic."

"It wasn't Nick behind the wheel, and I can stop any default action."

"Nick's pride won't let you do that."

"That clinic means everything to Nick. He'd do anything it took to keep it running."

"Including killing his brother-in-law in order for you to collect his inheritance?"

"I meant he'd swallow that damn pride of his and let me extend the loan if it kept the clinic open."

"You asked Jason to get a copy of the ledger, didn't you? That's why he was working on the website at the clinic and not from home and why Nick became suspicious of him. You knew about his bogus bookkeeping."

"No, I didn't, but I had an inkling something wasn't right. Nick has become so distracted and moody. I thought he was having an affair with one of his patients. That's why Jason was hanging around the clinic so much. I asked him to find out who the other woman was."

"Another reason to kill Jason. Nick was having an affair, but not with a patient, his accountant Lindsay Mathers; and Jason found out about it. That was what he was on his way to tell you the night he was murdered."

"No, it isn't. I already knew about the affair. Nick told me about it."

"Only because he knew Jason would tell you." The two stared at each other, then the doorbell rang. Maddy got up to answer it.

"Sam," Elyse said, spotting him at the table and passing by Maddy giving no indication she was aware the clothes she wore were Sam's. "How are you feeling? You look like hell."

"I'm fine. You didn't have to come over, I told you earlier, I'm fine."

"I need to talk to you." She looked at Maddy, indicating this was a private matter.

Taking the hint, Maddy said, "Why don't you two do your talking in the bedroom? Sam could use some rest and I can clean up in here."

"What's up?" Sam asked, settling on the bed and hearing Maddy running water in the kitchen.

"You asked me about Dylan Taylor last night, so I did some research. The ledgers go back six months and Dylan attended sessions and had individual sessions with Nick just as he said, then four months ago that all stopped."

"Because of the restraining order," Sam said.

"Yes, but in the two months before the restraining order, Dylan attended at least one session with each of the victims."

"He knew them, that's not surprising."

Elyse's phone buzzed. "It's Michelle's boyfriend Eric. I called the base and asked them to track him down."

"Hello." Sam could hear Eric yelling through the phone. "Who is this?"

"Eric, this is a friend of Michelle's from the clinic," not sure whether Michelle had told him of her alias. "I was with her at Starbucks the other night when you picked her up? I've been unable to reach her for a couple days now and she didn't show up for work this morning. Do you have any idea where she could be?"

"No, I've been calling her too…"

"When did you last speak to Michelle?" Elyse asked.

"Monday afternoon," Eric answered. "She was on her way home from the gym and said she would call me when she got there, but she never did."

"Sorry if you think this is personal, but did you two get into an argument?"

"No. Nothing like that."

"I work for a private investigator. His name's Sam Bartell. We're going over to her apartment and see what we can find there. Is there a code we need to get into her building?"

"Yes, and I'll give it to you as soon as I verify what you're telling me is the truth. I'll call you back in a few minutes."

Elyse picked up the pen and notepad Sam kept on his bedside table, waiting for Eric to call back. He did five minutes later, giving Elyse the security code to Michelle's apartment. "That will get you in the building," Eric said. "But I don't know how you're going to get in her apartment without contacting the super. I have the only spare key."

"That won't be a problem," Elyse assured Eric she would call him as soon as she knew anything and hung up the phone. "

You aren't going to Michelle's apartment," Sam said.

"Yes, I am, and you can't stop me."

"I need you to go back to the office and find out all you can on Dylan Taylor," Sam said, putting his arm around her. "That's going to be the most help to me if he's done something to Michelle." Realizing Sam was right, Elyse nodded, holding back tears of worry for her friend. "I'm glad you used an alias at the clinic." Sam got up off the bed, his body chastising him with pain for the effort.

"I told Michelle my real name," Elyse said, the possible repercussions suddenly dawning on her. "I'm sorry, but she was my friend. I couldn't keep lying to her."

"I'm sure we're worrying about nothing," Sam said, not sure at all. "I'll probably go over there and find Michelle sitting by the pool working on her tan." He winced as he pulled a pair of jeans from the closet to replace the sweats that he'd put on earlier. He went back to the bed and grabbed his bottle of Percocet, swallowing one dry and putting the vial in the pocket of his jeans.

"You can't go anywhere right now," Elyse said.

"I'll go with you, Sam," Maddy said from the open doorway. Elyse and Sam turned to stare at her. "Sorry for barging in, Elyse, but I told the ER doctor I would keep an eye on Sam for a while and I'm certainly not letting him drive. And as Sam's already said, you're more use to him being the whiz you are behind that computer of yours."

CHAPTER 17

Sitting in the passenger seat of Maddy's Lincoln, Sam was thankful his pain medication was also a sedative. She wove in and out of the bustling late morning traffic, seemingly heedless of her fellow travelers. Grabbing the handhold above the door as Maddy rounded the three hundred sixty degree on-ramp to the highway he said. "We're not in a hurry."

"I'm just going with the flow of traffic," Maddy replied, giving him a sideways glance, before craning her head in the opposite direction as she squeezed between a semi and a Prairie Farms milk truck before finally landing in the outer lane. "There's something I want to clear up, Sam."

"What's that?" Sam asked, grateful for the distraction from the road.

"Nick and I aren't like we were, Sam. It's not the same."

"I don't need to know this," Sam said.

"Nick married me because of my money and because of my dad's influence in the medical community, no surprises there and I'm fine with that. I married him because he was safe and would never have the ability to hurt me like you did."

"You're the one who walked away from me," Sam said.

"That doesn't mean I wasn't hurt by our breakup."

"So, hurt you married Nick less than a year later? Forgive me if I find that hard to believe. Did you ever love me Maddy, or was I just a curiosity to you, good enough until the newness wore off?"

"It was never like that," Maddy denied. "Our relationship was smothering, for both of us. That's not healthy."

"And what you have with Nick is healthier?"

"It may not meet your definition, but it works for us."

"Except when he cheats on you."

"Yes, Nick has cheated on me, probably more than once. But he was honest enough to tell me about Lindsay."

"You seem to think that makes it ok. That doesn't sound like the Maddy I know at all. And giving up teaching was something I thought you'd never do. What's happened to you?"

"I live in the real world, Sam. Not in the ideal world you have in your head." She exited off the highway, stopping at the light. "This Michelle we're hoping to find safe and sound at home," Maddy said, changing the subject, "tell me about her. Did she know Jason?"

"She met him when he began going to sessions and she also knew about Lindsay's death."

"Elyse isn't taking her disappearance well," Maddy noted.

"No…" Sam's phone buzzed.

"Sam, I'm at your place to get a statement. Where the hell are you? I thought you were supposed to be resting," Andy accused loudly over the phone.

"Sorry, Andy, I forgot you were stopping by, but there's nothing to report," Sam said, avoiding the question. "As I told you last night, I didn't get a look at the driver or get a license plate number. Come by the office later and I'll give you my statement."

"What's going on, Sam? Where are you?" Andy insisted.

"I'm going through a tunnel...I can't hear you Andy...talk to you later." Sam ended the call, conscience-stricken about his lie, but telling himself he was doing it to protect Andy, not because he wanted to play the hero for Maddy.

"There it is," Maddy said, pointing to a building in the midst of the apartment complex where Michelle lived. Parking in front of the building, Sam and Maddy approached the entryway, noting the call buttons alongside the door and the keypad.

Sam punched the numbers Elyse had gotten from Michelle's boyfriend, realizing as he did that the letters coinciding with each number spelled out the word 'needle'. "That's easy to remember." he muttered.

"What?" Maddy asked.

"Nothing," Sam said, pulling the door open for her. Passing a bank of numbered mailboxes, Sam and Maddy waited at the elevator doors as it came down from the upper levels. A couple of tenants disembarked, their leashed dogs at their sides, anxious to get to the dog park behind the building. The two rode in silence to the third floor, both of them apprehensive of what they were going to find. Pausing at door to Michelle's apartment, Sam scrutinized it and the jamb for signs of forced entry. Finding none, he was fairly certain that if any harm had come to Michelle, it was by the hands of someone she knew.

Knocking on Michelle's apartment door brought no response, but Sam easily opened it with the lockpicks he carried. Stepping inside, he was hit with the smell of stale food. He called out Michelle's name several times, getting no answer as Maddy stepped in behind him and closed the door.

"I don't think anyone's home," she whispered, coming to the same conclusion Sam had. "If there is, it's not good."

The apartment consisted of a small open living room, cluttered with mismatched furniture. Sitting on the coffee table was a two-thirds eaten plate of Chinese food, the source of the odor assaulting them when they entered. The kitchen was spartan, the only appliances a toaster and a blender for Michelle's assortment of smoothie recipes. Off of the kitchen was a small dining area. From the table, Sam had a view of a huge common area behind the apartments, where the dogs from earlier were getting their exercise. A good marketing strategy, Sam mused, opening a dog park behind a huge apartment complex brings a guaranteed customer base. On the table was a Panda Express take-out bag along with a purse and a couple pieces of mail. Stopping only long enough to confirm the purse hadn't been ransacked, Sam moved back into the living room, pulling a pair of latex gloves out of his pocket.

"Stay in here," Sam said. "I'm going to check the other rooms."

"I'm coming with you," Maddy said, holding out her hand. "So, you might as well give me a pair of those." Sam did as he was told, dubious of his decision. Two bedrooms and a bath were off the hallway past the living room. The first bedroom was mainly used for storage, unopened boxes on the floor and clothes strewn across an unmade twin bed against the far wall. The small bathroom was a cluster of sprays, soaps and various toiletries. Walking toward the master bedroom, the smell of stale food was replaced with what to Sam was the unmistakable odor or death. He motioned for Maddy to stay where she was, convinced she wouldn't. The bedroom door was halfway open, Sam pushed it all the way open with his gloved hand avoiding the doorknob.

Michelle lay naked on the bed, her beautiful body twisted in the pain and agony of her death. Vomit, dried and crusty framed her mouth, giving the room a sickeningly sweet, putrid smell.

"Oh," Maddy said, taking a step back, her hand covering her mouth and nose.

"I told you to wait in the living room," Sam said roughly, wishing he'd heeded his inner voice. "I don't have time to worry about you. I have to call Andy; but before the police get here, I need to figure out what happened and gather what clues the killer left behind."

"I'm fine, Sam," Maddy said. "I was shocked at first, but I'm fine now."

Pulling his phone from his pocket, Sam handed it to Maddy and hoping she was telling the truth, he said, "Take pictures of what I tell you to and if you feel like you're going to be sick, leave the room. And don't touch anything."

Returning his attention to Michelle's body, Sam examined her hands and feet.

Rigor had already passed. "She's been dead for at least twenty-four hours," Sam remarked, more to himself than Maddy. "Eric told Elyse he'd talked to Michelle late Monday afternoon, but didn't hear from her after that. That puts her death sometime Monday evening to Tuesday late morning. Stepping to the bottom of the bed, Sam examined the marks on Michelle's feet and ankles. "These are ligature marks," he said, showing Maddy the thin red band around Michelle's ankle so she could get a picture. She snapped a couple of both ankles. Moving upwards, he continued. "Her hands were also tied." The camera clicked several more times. "She was also gagged, see the marks on both sides of her mouth? But the gag was taken out before she died, the bindings on her hands and feet taken off after her death, otherwise there would be more signs of a struggle."

"Why would someone take them off after she died?" Maddy asked.

"To make it look like she poisoned herself."

"How do you know she was poisoned?"

Sam pointed to Michelle's chest, where needles ran down both sides of her abdomen, ending above her pubic bone. Laced between each needle was a purple lace string, tied in a neat bow between her breasts. "Look at those needles in the corset. If she'd inserted them, there's no way they'd be so perfectly placed. These were put in by someone else, while she was tied up. Then the lacing was put through, once again perfectly. My bet is that the string is laced with cyanide, see how the skin is blistered around each of the puncture marks? Cyanide can be absorbed through the skin, so each wrap around the needle put more in her system. It also causes the burning you see when it comes in contact with skin."

"That's horrible. No one is going to believe she did this to herself."

Sam took his phone from Maddy and took several pictures of the corset before saying, "I agree, which tells me our killer is losing it. The first three deaths were manipulated so the victims would kill themselves, Jason's death was hands on and this one." Sam looked at Michelle sprawled on the bed and shook his head. "He spent a lot of time with Michelle."

"Sam…" Maddy said, concern spreading across her face. "You could be right about Elyse being in danger if whoever is doing this saw them together at the clinic. Maybe you'd better get Andy over to your office to keep an eye on her."

"Already on it," Sam said, pressing Andy's number on his phone. "I'm calling Andy now, and then I'll make a call to the police."

Waiting for Andy to answer, Sam left the bedroom, taking another look into the other rooms, confirming his earlier conclusion that the intruder hadn't entered them. The call went to voicemail and Sam left a message. He dialed the police and headed to the kitchen, wanting to reexamine Michelle's purse. Approaching the table, he spotted a black card on the floor under the table.

"Thirty-fifth precinct station," he heard over the phone. "How may I direct your call?" bending down, Sam picked up the card, he recognized it. "Hello...Hello, may I help you?" Concern started to enter the operator's voice.

Sam pulled out a similar card from his wallet. "I need to report a death," he said, placing both cards in his pocket.

Returning to the office after forty-five minutes of explaining to the cops who arrived on the scene and then the detectives who came after, why the two of them were at Michelle's apartment, Sam and Maddy found Elyse engrossed in his computer as Andy kept a watchful eye over the street below them. Sam walked over to her and put his hand on her shoulder.

"How are you doing?" Sam asked Elyse, concerned she would carry the guilt of Michelle's death along with Anna's.

"I knew something was wrong," Elyse said, dabbing at her eyes with a Kleenex. "I've contacted her boyfriend; he should get home sometime this evening. The police have talked to her parents, so there's nothing more we can do except find the son of a bitch who killed her."

"We're going to do that," Sam said. "I promise you."

"You should be at home," Andy growled. "I'll take care of things here."

"Don't mind him," Elyse said. "He's just mad that you're out running around when you should clearly be in bed. Take a seat before you fall down." She pushed him towards the chair in front of the desk. "And as much as I love your charming personality, Andy, I don't know why Sam feels I need protecting."

"Just a precaution," Sam said, sitting down in the chair. "I can rest as well here as I can at home."

"I wanted to take him home, but he insisted on stopping here first," Maddy said, then addressed Sam. "I still don't know what you think you can accomplish here that you can't do from home."

"For starters, I can help Elyse hack into the cameras outside Michelle's apartment and see who went in and out over the last thirty-six hours."

"Sam, when have I ever needed your help to hack into a computer?" Elyse busted him. "I'm checking photos of residents against anyone who entered the building through the front door as we speak. So far, everyone going in lives there."

"What about the back door?" Sam asked.

"There's a camera there, but it doesn't work and hasn't worked for a couple of weeks according to the security footage I pulled up. I'm still looking for cameras in the area that catch the back door, but no luck yet. I will let you know if I find anything, so go home."

"You heard her," Maddy said. "I'll take you home. It's on my way."

"Haven't you done enough?" Andy asked no longer able to keep his hostility in check. "You almost got him killed last night and now Elyse may be in danger."

"Andy…" Sam stopped him. "I don't think this is the time…"

"When will be the time? When one of us gets killed because of her? You need to get your head out of your ass. You have enough evidence right now for the police to reopen Jason's case. Let them handle it."

"Like they did before?" Sam scoffed.

"Andy's right," Maddy said, looking between the two men. "We have enough to get the police involved, and I never meant to get anyone hurt." She turned to Elyse. "I'm sorry about Michelle and the position I've put all of you in." She walked to the door, turning to face them. "Thank you for your help, but I won't be needing your services anymore." She turned and left.

Sam followed after her, catching her at the top of the stairs and turning her to face him. "Forget what Andy said in there. He didn't mean any of it."

"Yes, he did. He's worried about you and Elyse and I'm the one causing it."

"Whoever killed Michelle isn't going to care whether or not we're working for you. If he's out to harm us, the only way to stop him is to catch him. Turning it over to the police isn't going to help."

"Then what do you want me to do?" Maddy asked exasperated. "Nothing we've done so far has gotten us any closer to the truth of Jason's death."

"You need to keep working on Jason's apartment. All you have left are personal items, right? Take another look through his things, maybe we missed something. I'll let you know if we find anything on this end."

"Okay…" Maddy turned to go down the stairs, turning back mid-way down to face him again. "I said it once and I'll say it again, I wish I'd never called you. Jason was right, if you aren't careful, and maybe even if you are, you're going to end up like that detective you like so much in your comic." Turning from him, she headed down the stairs.

Returning to his office, Sam was met with a still angry Andy who wasn't about to calm down. "Let her go, Sam. If you ask me, she's been gaslighting you from the beginning," Andy said. "Telling you one thing then changing her story every time you catch her in a lie."

"That may be true, but there's a serial killer out there."

"You don't know that for sure, unless there's something you're not telling me," he paused. "Is there something you're not telling me, Sam?" Andy stood in front of Sam, the silence palpable as the two stared at each other. Elyse cleared her throat, hoping Sam would tell Andy about his suspicions concerning Dylan Taylor. Sam turned from Andy and walked to the window. Andy shrugged, walked to the door and slammed it on his way out.

"Why didn't you tell him about Taylor?" Elyse admonished.

"You know why, I don't want him involved. When I...we," Sam corrected, "find the killer and the police have to answer for the way they've mishandled this case from the beginning, I don't want them accusing Andy of withholding anything. The less he knows the better."

"I hope you know what you're doing and that when this is all over, you and Andy are still friends," Elyse said, concerned.

Sam pulled the 'Playthings' card out of his pocket, showing it to Elyse. "I found this at Michelle's apartment, the needles the killer used were sent from Ronnie's store. I'm going over there to see who sent them, right after I make sure you get home."

"I don't think that's necessary," Elyse said, dismissing him.

"You're probably right, Taylor never met you at the clinic, but I don't want to take any chances."

CHAPTER 18

"People are going to talk, detective," Ronnie said, her eyes locked on the computer screen in front of her as she caught up on her bookkeeping.

"I need to know who ordered needles from your store," Sam said, skipping the banter.

She glanced up at him, got a look at his face and the determined look in his eyes and started again. "What the hell happened to you?"

"I was hit by a car outside of the Hollowell Clinic last night. I think someone was trying to kill me."

"Looks like they almost succeeded," Ronnie noted, sitting back in her chair. "What does that have to do with one of my customers buying needles?"

"Nothing. But it has everything to do with this murder." Sam placed his cell phone down on the desk in front of her. She picked it up, scrolling through the pictures and handed it back to him.

"Those needles could've been purchased any number of places," Ronne said, apparently unfazed by what she saw. "What makes you think they're from here?"

"Because of this," Sam flipped the black card on the desk. "I found it and the envelope the needles were delivered in at the scene. I don't think either of us want to get the police involved in this. That wouldn't be good for your business and I'm in no mood to explain why I took that card."

"Why did you take it, Sam?" She picked up the card, held it. "Are you trying to protect me? How sweet."

"Cut the shit and tell me who sent the needles," his patience was at an end.

"Calm down there, cowboy," Ronnie said, getting up from her desk and walking over to the file cabinet where she pulled out a bottle of Scotch and poured him a drink. "Take a load off while I do some research."

"Here it is," Ronnie said, "a fifty-piece order of needles placed last Thursday, delivered Monday." Ronnie turned the screen so Sam could see. "Dylan Taylor. That was the only order he's ever placed here, and the needles were the only thing purchased I don't recognize the name, do you?"

"He's a former patient at the Hollowell Clinic. Elyse is working on getting a picture of him. Nick has a restraining order against him, but that hasn't stopped him from harassing some of his patients. We haven't had any luck finding him."

"You think he's the one who killed Michelle and tried to run you over?" Ronnie asked.

"I'm not sure, but if he is, he's devolving and out of control. I need to find him."

"He paid with a credit card in his name. His home address is listed, as well as a cell number, but you probably already have those."

"Yes, but no one answers the door or the phone. I have someone there now, staking the place out. Let's get back to the needles, as you said, he could've bought them anywhere and this isn't the closest adult bookstore to his home. Why did he pick your store?" Sam asked.

"The police would've been all over this place if you hadn't taken this card," Ronnie said, twirling it in her hand. "Cops are never good for business; they scare the customers away. I guess I owe you a favor."

"And they might have found out about the sessions you hold if anyone around here has loose lips. Are you sure you don't know Dylan Taylor?" Sam asked again.

"I don't, but I do know someone who would like to cause me some problems with the police and lose my business in the process."

"Maddy?" Sam asked, "You're reaching. How would she pay with Dylan's credit card? I told her about the threats you're accusing her of, and she claims she's the one being harassed. Says you've had the hots for her for months. It could be argued you killed Jason because Maddy rejected you."

"So, it's her word against mine, and you believe her. Oh, of course you do, I can see it in your eyes. How long did it take for her to get back in your bed?" Ronnie didn't hide her disdain. "You should've learned your lesson the first time. Did she tell you that she came by the store checking me out about a month after I started dating Jason. Oh, I knew who she was; Jason has pictures of them together all over his apartment, or did you miss that? I thought I'd play with her a bit--I asked her if she wanted a private session. But it backfired, she said yes and insisted we have the session right away."

"She knew you knew she was Jason's sister. What did you do?"

"Well, I couldn't very well go on with the ruse. What if Jason and I got serious? I told her I knew she was there to see if I was good enough for her brother and that she could get the hell out of my store."

"What did she say to that?"

"She didn't say anything. Just turned around and left. Maddy would never make a scene, but as you know she has more subtle ways of getting what she wants. When those didn't work, she sent me this." Ronnie reached into the middle drawer of her desk pulling out an envelope. She handed it to Sam. "Open it."

Inside was a note offering Ronnie one hundred thousand dollars if she stopped dating Jason.

"Now who are you going to believe?"

"How did you get this? It wasn't mailed."

"She left it under my windshield. I locked up one night and went to my car. There it was. Funny thing is, we'd already broken up."

"This letter is typed and there's no date on it. You could have received it before the breakup and taken the money."

"That's not what happened. When are you going to accept she poisons everyone around her and we'll be lucky if we don't both end up like Michelle if you don't wise up?"

"You're afraid of her," Sam said, surprised to realize Ronnie was afraid of anyone and aware he hadn't given Michelle's name.

"You should be too. She's as crazy as this Dylan Taylor you're looking for."

"It's odd you use the word poison when that's how Michelle was murdered, and I never gave her name. How do you know her?"

"She was a regular here, but I haven't...hadn't seen her for a while. I wish there was more I could do to help you find this guy."

"Maybe you can, he's a furry. How familiar are you with that crowd? Do they have meetings, compare outfits..."

"You know that's offensive, right?" Ronnie said, quickly scanning the top of her-unlike Sam's-very orderly desk. "There's a huge furry convention held at the Rosemont every year, but not until December." Spotting what she was looking for, she picked a flyer from a stack of similar ones. "Here it is." she said, handing it to him. "There's going to be a furry extravaganza at the Congress Plaza running this Friday and Saturday. The organizer asked me to post a few of these last week. If he's a furry and he hasn't gone completely off the rails, he'll be there."

Reading over the flyer, Sam said, "All furries are encouraged to come dressed as their fursona. If he does show, he'll be dressed in a bear costume."

"If you'd done your research, you'd know not all furries dress in costumes, some only have an avatar online."

"According to Nick, he's recently became a lifestyler."

"That's the extreme end of the furry spectrum, so if he shows, there's a good chance he'll be in costume; but as I said earlier, he hasn't bought anything furry related here," Ronnie said. "Unless he used his fursona name. Do you know if he had one?"

"I don't know about any other names," Sam said, making a note to ask Nick.

"Well, we carry an extensive assortment of furry merchandise, that particular category of merchandise is exploding. You can look at what we have, get an idea of what he might be wearing if you think it'll help you find him."

"I will, but he shouldn't be that hard to find, a man dressed up like a bear, how many could there be?"

"You can't be serious," Ronnie rolled her eyes at him. "The organizer told me he's expecting a capacity crowd for the grand opening. There's going to be raffles every hour and the grand prize is a trip to Anime Los Angeles next year. It may not be as easy as you think."

"Grand Opening at six and goes until two in the morning," Sam said, reading the flyer. "Guess I know where I'll be tomorrow evening."

"Perhaps I should go with you," Ronnie suggested.

"Why?"

"Because you're way too vanilla. You'll scare them." She laughed.

Sam left Playthings and drove to Dylan Taylor's house, relieving the rent-a-cop he had to hire. Parking across the street within sight of the front door and a view of the side, he settled in, hoping to spot either movement in the house or Taylor arriving home. His efforts proved futile, and as the time neared midnight, he got out of his car and taking matters into his own hands, he headed toward the back of the house for a little B & E. Sam thought the better of it when a police cruiser rolled by, one of the patrolmen nodding in recognition. Sam left and headed home discouraged and crawled into bed shortly after one.

Waking in the early morning just before dawn, his sleep restless with scattered thoughts circling around in his head. Sam decided to take a short run around his neighborhood, the soreness from the accident making the first half mile painful. As the sun came up his stiffness eased, and his mind settled. Returning home, he stepped into the shower, his phone buzzing from the bedroom just as the water hit his head. Quickly stepping from under the spray, Sam grabbed a towel and retrieved his phone before it went to voicemail.

"Hope I haven't caught you at a bad time," Maddy said.

"What's up?" Sam asked, toweling the water from his hair.

"I've been going through some papers as you suggested and I think I've found something, but I don't want to get into it over the phone."

"I'm stopping by the office briefly then going over to Taylor's house to see if I can catch him at home and ask him some questions. You can come by the office this afternoon, unless you think what you've found points in another direction."

"No, you do what you need to do. I'll see you later." Sam ended the call and returned to the shower, perplexed as to what Maddy could have found.

"I know there's something bothering you, Elyse." Sam hadn't been in his office for five minutes before he called her out. "You might as well get it off your chest."

"I don't think it's a good idea not telling Andy that you suspect Dylan Taylor in Michelle's murder."

"We've been over this. If I tell him that now, he's going to ask why I didn't tell him earlier and I don't appreciate the lack of confidence you have in me."

"It's not that. It's just that you've never kept Andy in the dark about a case before. It's because of Maddy, isn't it?"

"No. I'm just not convinced Taylor had anything to do with Michelle's death, and I'd like to have some evidence before I tell the police. Have you found anything on the videos outside the apartment building?"

"I'm working on a photo taken around nine o'clock. The picture is fuzzy and whoever it is has a hat on, but I'm almost certain it isn't a resident."

"Why?"

"Because he's looking at a piece of paper while he punches in the code. I've been running it through a program to get a clearer picture, but it takes a while. Should have something in a few minutes."

"Did you get a picture of Dylan Taylor?"

"Got it from his driver's license. It's three years old, and I have a blown-up copy for you," Elyse said, handing him a five by seven picture of Taylor. "From what I've found out about him, it's no wonder he prefers being a bear."

"How so?"

"His mother died when he was ten, his father is a long-term alcoholic, several domestic violence charges filed and then dropped before his mom died.

Things got worse after her death. He lost several jobs, all janitorial and they moved ten times in the next seven years. Dylan did graduate high school at eighteen and moved out of the house, but moved back five years later when his father lost his leg to diabetes. Dylan is a member of Freelance Comic Artists Association and has published several of his works, but he lost his job at Variety Publishing four months ago about the same time his father died. Talk about a double whammy."

"Nick thinks Dylan is killing patients to get back at him, some kind of transferred daddy issues."

"Why Arnold and Hutchins?" she asked. "We haven't found any connection between the two of them, they don't share the same obsession and neither one of them could be father figures to Dylan."

"There may not be any connection, but I don't think Lindsay's or Jason's death are random. I don't believe in coincidences."

"I'll say it again, Sam, I think you need Andy." Her computer pinged as the program finished on the photo.

Placing the driver's license photo alongside the console as Dylan's picture filled the screen, Sam said, "We need to talk to Taylor. Find out what he was doing at Michelle's apartment. I'm going back to his house and look inside this time. I'll let you know what I find."

"I know you haven't forgotten this," Elyse said, stopping him at the door, an envelope in her hand.

"No, I haven't."

"We both know you've already read it. Why haven't you given it to Maddy?"

"Because it was opened before I found it and I need to find out if Maddy is the one who did it."

"If she did...then everything she's told you has been a lie."

"Pretty much, but she hasn't mentioned anything about it yet." Sam took the letter, slipping it into his jacket pocket. "Maddy may get here before I get back. She thinks she's found something. Call me if she shows."

There was no sign of life outside the Taylor residence when Sam parked across the street from the small saltbox-style home. A home not surprisingly in disrepair from what Elyse had told him. Pulling his binoculars from the storage space between the seats, Sam peered through the lenses, checking for movement in or around the house, careful to watch for pedestrians who wandered up or down the street; he didn't need the police stopping by again. Sam called Taylor's cell phone number, got no response, left no message. Lowering the windows as the sun started to heat up the car, Sam eased his seat back a few notches to stretch his legs, settling in for the long haul.

Reaching the end of his patience two hours later, he exited his car and walked to the front door. Knocking elicited no response, which came as no surprise. What was surprising was that the door was unlocked when he turned the knob. Pulling his gun, he quickly stepped inside and closed the door silently behind him. The house was hot, a ceiling fan in the living room slowing pushing the stale air around. Momentarily pausing at the kitchen, he saw stacks of unwashed dishes next to the sink, a box of Lucky Charms and a bowl on the table, curdled milk pooled at the bottom.

Leaving the kitchen, Sam opened the door onto the master bedroom. It must have belonged to Taylor's father, a walker stood next to the bed, the dust thick on the nightstand and the smell of disuse in the air. Moving to the back of the house, Sam found two more bedrooms, one of them outfitted with a hasp and lock, which was open. Opening the door to the other bedroom, Sam found it furnished with a bed and dresser, the bed was neatly made, the dresser mostly empty. Sam quickly rummaged through the drawers, finding nothing out of the ordinary, then went to the bed and slid his hand between the mattress, not even finding an adult magazine, or a furry one. Bending down and checking underneath the bed also turned up nothing.

He went back to the hallway, and removing the lock from the hasp, he went into the third bedroom. The room held a desk and a printer stand, the desk held an assortment of computer accessories including a bear shaped mouse pad, although the laptop Sam assumed them to be for was gone. The all-in-one printer sat empty on the stand. Lifting the top, Sam was not surprised to find it bare. Stepping over to the closed closet doors, Sam opened them to find a few dozen empty hangers. Reaching above his head, he ran his hand along the shelf above the closet bar, stopping and yanking his hand back when he felt something furry run across the top of his hand. He reached up again, finding a cheap bear mask, the fur worn off in places. He threw it back on the shelf and pulled out his phone.

"He's gone," he told Elyse.

"What do you mean gone? Where did he go?"

"I don't know, but he took his laptop and his furry stuff. He's not coming back anytime soon."

"Now what?" Elyse asked.

"See if you can find any relatives he may have gone to, or some friend he may have crashed with." Leaving the house and returning to his car, Sam took his jacket off and threw it on the passenger seat, as much from the heat as the frustration of not finding Taylor. The envelope Elyse had given him earlier fell to the floorboard. Sam reached to pick it up, placed it on top of his jacket, then picked it up again. He pulled on the flap, trying not to tear it, unsuccessfully. "Screw it," he said, ripping it open and taking out a one-page letter obviously written in haste.

Maddy,

If you're reading this, then I'm dead, and you may be next. The flash drive has evidence against Nick, get away from him and take it to Sam, he'll know what to do. I know about you and Ronnie. I understand how difficult this has been for you, but she's having our baby and I trust you to do the right thing. I love you.

Jason

Rereading the letter brought Sam no closer to understanding what it meant. Was Jason pleading with Maddy to get over her hatred of Ronnie or did he know about Ronnie's obsession with his sister? Sam folded the letter, placing it on the dashboard. Unconsciously glancing into the rearview mirror, Sam saw Maddy pull up and park behind him, watched as she got out and approached his car. She came to the passenger side, Sam unlocked and opened it for her, throwing his jacket into the back seat. She slid in, closing the door behind her.

"What are you doing here?" Sam asked too surprised to be angry.

"You told me you would be staking out Taylor's house. It wasn't that hard to find you."

"Ok, maybe the better question is why are you here?"

"You may be watching the wrong man," Maddy said, pulling out a folded piece of paper. "I wanted to see for myself that Nick was fixing the books he's been showing me, so I did some research on my own. I found this in his desk at home." She handed him a manila envelope.

Sam poured the contents in his lap. The envelope contained a wallet and several online order receipts. He opened the wallet to a picture of Nick, but the name of Dylan Taylor printed under his image. In the pocket were several credit cards, all of them in Taylor's name. The receipts were for various items, all from different adult bookstores. Sam flipped through the pages, noting the purchase of a ball gag send to Glenn's Arnold's home, a package of fifty count needles sent to Michelle, and an electric stimulation box sent to the Hollowell Clinic.

"What going on, Sam? Why does Nick have these?"

"Let's not jump to conclusions just yet."

"Let's confront him then," Maddy demanded. "I'll know if he's lying."

"Maddy, that isn't a good idea. Let me do my job. If Nick's guilty, I'll prove it. But right now, you need to go home keep quiet about this," Sam said, stuffing everything back in the envelope. "I'll talk to you in the morning."

"What are you going to do?"

"I'm going to the Congress Plaza for the furry convention opening this evening and hoping Dylan Taylor shows up."

CHAPTER 19

"Where's Sam and why the hell isn't he answering his phone?" Andy asked, storming into Sam's office and demanding answers from Elyse.

Surprised, and unsure what to say, Elyse stammered. "Ah...he's on a stakeout."

Realizing Elyse wasn't the one he should be taking his frustrations out on, Andy calmed down. "I know who he's staking out, so you don't have to cover for him."

"Good." Elyse breathed a huge sigh of relief. "How did you find out?"

"One of my patrolman buddies mentioned passing him outside the Taylor house last night. It didn't take me long to figure out why."

"I'm glad you know about Taylor because I think Sam could use your help. He went over to his house earlier and probably silenced his phone."

"Because he broke into Taylor's home and didn't want it going off while he was in there, right? I'm going over there."

"Andy, wait." Elyse stopped him. "He called about forty-five minutes ago. He said it looked like Taylor wasn't coming home for a while, packed his clothes and took his computer. I've been looking for anyone he may be staying with, but so far, nothing. You know Sam, he probably forgot to turn his phone back on. I'm sure he'll be calling you any minute."

"Well, when he does, he's going to get an earful, and an ass kicking as soon as I see him. What the hell is he thinking?"

Elyse knew Andy was more hurt by Sam's exclusion than angry and tried to assuage his feelings. "He's only trying to protect you, you know that, right?"

"I know that if Dylan Taylor is a serial killer, then Sam could use some help finding him and keeping me in the dark about what he's doing may end up getting him killed."

"He's going to be at the Congress Plaza and Convention Center in about an hour," Elyse said, checking her watch. "Ronnie's going with him. They're hoping Taylor shows up for the grand opening."

"Why didn't you say that in the first place. Let's go." Andy headed towards the door.

"I need to make a quick stop on the way," Elyse said, "And do you have an extra walkie talkie in your trunk?"

A troop of parking attendants with red flashing batons and whistles directed the flow of traffic outside the hotel. One of the attendants waved them toward Wabash Avenue where the nearest parking lot was quickly filling up. Ronnie handed the attendant twenty dollars and followed another one as he pointed Ronnie into the next open spot with an exuberant display of whistle blowing.

"It's not even five o'clock," Sam said, getting out of the car and checking to make sure Ronnie was centered in the laughably narrow yellow lines.

"Again...I told you it would be big." Ronnie grabbed a bag from the back seat. "Wait a minute, I have something for you," she said, pulling two fox masks and two huge foxtails from the bag. "They're Columbina-style masks so your mouth won't be covered."

"You're kidding me, right?" Sam said, backing away from the mask as if it was alive.

"No, I'm not. I picked the gray for you and the rust is for me. It accentuates my eyes, don't you think?" Ronnie placed the half-mask on her face and grinned at him. "Now put yours on, you need the disguise more than me."

Shrugging his shoulders, Sam put the mask on, surprised at the comfortably snug fit and the cushiony micro suede that covered the interior side of the mask. He took a look at the leather ears, velveteen face and nose of a gray fox in the passenger-side mirror and was fascinated at the detail.

"Hey handsome, we can't stand here preening all night," Ronnie laughed. "Clip this on the back of your belt." She said handing him the tail.

"It's a bit long," Sam said, petting the thirty-five-inch baby soft white-tipped gray fur tail."

"Just put the damn thing on and let's go."

Following the signs, but mostly the crowd into the immense atrium of the hotel, Sam glanced above his head at the open floors of the hotel rising above him. Curious hotel patrons were lined along the railings, enjoying the view. Directly in front of them, a wide ostentatious staircase led to the second floor, where a huge placard directed the crowd to the Windsor Room, the largest of the four ballrooms in the hotel, with three thousand square feet of space. "We're never going to spot him in here," Ronnie shouted over the crowd once they had made their way through the security posted at every set of double doors. They were standing at the front of a maze of vendors who were selling all things anthropomorphic. Past the vendors, they found small tables were scattered around an open dance floor, and a small l-shaped portable bar with two costumed bartenders trying, unsuccessfully to keep up with the hot, thirsty crowd. The walls were covered in mirror tile, providing the furries ample face time with themselves and giving Sam and Ronnie twice the crowd to scan. Techno music blared from every wall, TVs hung from the ceiling every fifty feet, their screens filled with scenes of the crowd, screams of recognition following each pixel.

"I know," Sam agreed. "We'll have to find a place to watch the crowd and hope we don't miss him."

"I have a better idea, I'll work my way to the back, see if I spot him. If I do, I'll text you. You go back to the front doors, see if you catch him coming in." Ronnie propelled her way through the crowd expertly twisting out of the way of inadvertent elbows or protruding costume accessories. Sam watched until she disappeared in the crowd, then turned back towards the front door, winding his way through the dealers. He was greeted at the front by the sight of Andy and Elyse, just passing through security and acclimating as he had done earlier to the noise and flashing lights. He headed towards them.

"What the hell are you two doing here?" Sam asked, not realizing that with his mask, they had no idea who he was. "And what do you have on?" he directed at Elyse, who was dressed in a thigh length bear costume complete with paws, bear ear headband and knee-high fur covered boots.

"Sam...?" Elyse asked, taking a closer look at him. "Sam is that you?" a grin blooming across her face. "I didn't recognize you. That's a fantastic mask. I wanted a Panda outfit, but the shop was sold out. Go figure." Elyse laughed as she twirled.

"It wasn't my idea," Andy said, shaking his head.

"Taylor is into bears, makes sense to me that he'd be attracted to another bear," Elyse said.

"I'll give you props for initiative, but you're going to roast in here," Sam said, then turning to Andy, "I guess she's told you everything?"

"She didn't have to, I found out on my own," Andy said. "And I'm pissed you didn't tell me yourself."

"Have you said anything to your boss?" Sam asked.

"No, Elyse tells me you aren't convinced Taylor murdered anyone yet. I figure if we catch this guy, I'm taking him in for questioning and you're turning your investigation over to the police."

Sam knew there wasn't any changing Andy's mind and decided not to argue with him. "Ronnie's working her way to the back. I'm going to catch up to her, you two stay at the front in the vendor area, watch the doors and text if you see him enter or leave."

"This will be quicker." Andy handed Sam a walkie talkie and an earpiece. Sam turned and headed off into the crowd.

"Nice ass," Elyse whistled at his tail as he walked away. Sam ignored her.

Finding Ronnie in the crowd proved to be difficult, fox costumes were by far the most common fursona. Finally spotting her on the dance floor with a man in a bear costume, he approached the two, trying to ascertain if she was dancing with Taylor. She spotted him, shaking her head slightly to answer the question she knew was on his mind. Disengaging from her partner and leaving him to dance solo, which he didn't seem to mind, Ronnie danced seductively in front of Sam, holding out her hands for him to take. Sam took them, with the intention of leading her to a table where they could talk, but she wouldn't be led. Instead she turned and backed into him, rubbing against him as she danced.

"No sign of him," she said, running her hands down his sides as she danced. "Let's have some fun."

"We're here to find Taylor." Backing away from her proved ineffectual, as the undulate crowd surged to the music.

"Who says we can't do both?" Ronnie asked, taking the lead and guiding them to the middle of the floor. Working through the crowd, they slowed unobtrusively near every bear-costumed furry they passed, eliminating possible suspects. Dylan's picture and description were of little use to them as there was a surprisingly, at least to Sam, large number of bears in the crowd.

Thirty minutes of searching proved fruitless, no sign of him on the dance floor; Elyse and Andy coming up empty plying the vendor booths. Sam couldn't be sure they hadn't missed him, or that he would even show. He was beginning to think their search was a waste of time and said as much to Ronnie.

"Let's grab a seat," Ronnie said, winded, and led them off the dance floor. Finding one of the few empty tables left in the very back of the ballroom, they plopped down on the fur padded seats. Seconds later, a waiter in a pony costume greeted them as he placed glasses of water and appetizer menus in front of them. "I'll be right back," he said before prancing off.

Sam asked, "Is he a brony?"

"Please don't go there," Ronnie said, rolling her eyes. "You have no idea how complicated that subject can get." She laughed. "Anything from Elyse or Andy?"

Clicking the walkie talkie off and on again, Sam replied, "No, and I'm beginning to think he's not going to show." Sam checked his watch.

"It's early yet; give it some time," Ronnie said.

◆◆◆

Elyse was beginning to worry. Andy had left her to get a couple of drinks thirty minutes earlier. She wandered up to an accessory hut full of jewelry, scarves and hats. Her attention was drawn to a spinner rack of fur covered ties, and a collection of bear tie clips.

"You look amazing," a man wearing fur-covered pants and tunic said, coming up next to her, a bear head atop his own, a mask covering his eyes.

"Thanks," Elyse replied, straightening her ears, and noting the resemblance to the picture of Taylor in her purse even with the mask he wore. "I'm Elyse."

"No names here," the man replied, taking her hand in his clawed ones and keeping it for an uncomfortable amount of time.

Elyse pulled it back, looking around for Andy. "I like your costume. Bears are amazing, aren't they?" Noting the type and color of fur on his costume, she continued, "Grizzlies are my absolute favorite."

"It's not a costume," he snapped, causing Elyse to jump. "I'm sorry," the stranger said. "Sometimes I get a little carried away, but it's more than just a costume to me."

"I'm getting that," Elyse replied, almost convinced the man was Dylan but needing more in the way of confirmation, she dropped her purse to the floor, getting a closer view of his weather worn, calloused bare feet. Certain it was the man they were searching for; she stood back up, taking a calming breath, and searched the immediate crowd for signs of Andy.

"Did you know males are called boars and females are called sows, just like with pigs, although they aren't in any way related?" Dylan asked, searching for conversation. "I would never call you a sow. You're a she-bear." Dylan grinned at her and Elyse began to feel sorry for him: his awkwardness, his dependence on the bear persona, the childhood she knew he'd had.

Suddenly, Andy appeared in the crowd, directly behind Dylan, a beer in each hand. Quickly, she raised her hand to Dylan's hood, petting the fur and waving behind his head, trying to get Andy's attention.

"Wow, this fur is so soft. Is this homemade?" Elyse asked, keeping Dylan from turning his head.

"Yes," Dylan said proudly. "The ones at the store looked so fake. I have a full fur skin too, but I thought it'd be too hot to wear. Would you like to see it?" He asked hopefully.

Andy stopped in his tracks, spotting Elyse's waving hand, the drafts sloshing over his fingers. He could only see the back of the bear hood, but knew she was with Taylor. Realizing he couldn't do anything with the drinks in his hands, he stepped up to the vendor table and set the beers down. Turning to Elyse and her friend, his jacket opened, exposing his badge clipped to his belt. Taylor spotted it...and bolted.

Sam heard Andy's voice in his ear. "He's heading your way." Andy yelled. "He saw my badge and took off. I'm about twenty feet behind him."

"What's he wearing?" Sam asked, getting up from the table.

"Brown fur covered pants and shirt," Andy said.

"He left his bear head hood here," Sam heard Elyse yell in the background. "And he's barefoot."

"Half the people in here are barefoot," Sam yelled back. "Andy, keep on his tail and I'll find you. Elyse you stay up front in case he heads back that way. I'm sending Ronnie up to you. If either of you spot him, do not try to stop him."

"I'd rather stay where the action is," Ronnie countered, as they scanned the heaving throng of people.

"In this crowd, who knows where that will be," Sam said, stepping up on his chair to get a better view. "But if he heads back up front, Elyse could use your help." Ronnie shrugged and disappeared.

Sam turned his attention back to the dance floor, spotting Andy a few seconds later, heading toward him, but on the other side of the room. Looking ahead of Andy, Sam saw Taylor, shoving his way through the crowd and glancing back at Andy every few seconds. Sam jumped down off the chair and joined the chase, hoping to catch up to Taylor before he got to the fire exit door at the back of the ballroom. He didn't.

◆◆◆

Reaching the exit door, Taylor flung his inconsequential weight against it, banging it open and setting off the fire alarm. The exit opened to the back of the building, where a couple of overflowing dumpsters waited for tomorrow's pickup. Sprinting to his right, he hoped to reach the edge of the building and around it before the cop spotted him, but he didn't see the watering hose in time to avoid it. He hit the pavement hard, the air knocked out of him.

"Stay down!" Andy yelled. Taylor didn't, he got to his feet and took off around the building. "I hate it when they don't stay down," Andy said, disgusted. "Now what?"

"I'm going to keep chasing him," Sam said. "He's probably trying to get to his car. But you need to get back into the hotel. Let the security guys know this is a false alarm before all hell breaks loose in there and make sure Elyse and Ronnie are okay."

Sam followed after Taylor, spotting him halfway to the front of the hotel.

Out of shape and out of breath, Taylor began to slow, and Sam quickly closed the gap. Sam yelled at him. "Dylan! Just stop! I only want to talk to you." Taylor leaned against the wall capable of going no further. Suddenly another exit door opened five feet from where Taylor stood, panicked furries spewing out. Capitalizing on his, luck, Taylor pushed through the outward flow and disappeared into the hotel.

Quickly radioing Andy, Sam yelled, "He's in the building! Went in through the side door. Should be somewhere in the middle of the room. I'm coming in now. Where are you?"

"Got him," Andy's voice crackled in Sam's ear. "He's heading toward the front exits."

Catching sight of Taylor, Sam chased after him, pushing through the crowd as the speakers overhead beseeched the crowd to remain calm.

Taylor plowed through the vendor area, leaving overturned tables and stunned furries in his wake. Sam spotted Andy, approaching Taylor perpendicularly, they would cross at the front doors.

"Where are the security guards?" Sam yelled to no one as he neared the front, finally spotting one standing outside the doors with his back to the crowd, keeping people from entering the ballroom. The guard didn't see Taylor running up behind him and was slammed to the floor when he barreled into him. Snatching the gun from the guard's holster, Taylor turned and waved it in an arc towards Andy, spewing bullets.

Sam drew his gun and fired, hitting Taylor in the shoulder, his weapon clanging to the floor. He bolted from the ballroom, Sam chased after him, noting the droplets of blood getting bigger as he followed him up two flights of stairs. Finally catching him at the exit door onto the fourth floor, Sam grabbed him halfway through the doorway, Taylor's blood-soaked furry shirt ripping in his hands. Pulling against Sam's grip, Taylor broke free, a momentary smile of triumph crossing his face, then replaced with fear as he fell backward against the railing, his reverse momentum driving him over the side. Sam reached to grab him. Too late, he heard the thud of Taylor's body as it hit the staircase below.

Racing back down the stairs, Sam pushed his way through the horde of people being held back by arriving police and security guards. Quickly checking the crowd for Elyse or Andy, he spotted Maddy among the throng instead. Pushing through to Taylor's mangled body, Sam leaned down to check for a pulse he knew he wouldn't find.

Turning from Taylor, Sam found Maddy at his side. "What are you doing here?" Sam asked.

"Andy was shot and I don't know if the ambulance is going to get here in time."

◆ ◆ ◆

"You haven't changed at all, have you Bartell?" Sergeant Billings growled. "You still think you can do whatever you want and talk your way out of it. Didn't work so well for you last time, did it?"

"You know damn well I did nothing wrong while I wore my badge and you still don't have the balls to defend the men who work for you. You're still sitting at the same ol' desk, kissing the same ol' asses. Why don't you tell me again which one of us hasn't changed?" Sam seethed. He was sitting in interrogation room number two, across from his former boss, who'd dragged him in before he could get to the hospital and check on Andy. Elyse told him over the phone Andy needed surgery on his leg, but they were waiting for another surgeon to get there. Another busy night in the ER.

"Why don't you tell me again, why a man is dead and one of my officers is in surgery?"

"I've already told you. Andy was helping me on a case--on his own time. We only wanted to ask Taylor a couple of questions. He bolted and ran. You know the rest."

"Your questions had to do with the death of Michelle Obermann, am I right? As I recall you made no mention of Dylan Taylor when we questioned you at the scene."

"I was trying to make a connection between the two."

"We already have. We found a shitload of pictures he'd taken of Michelle and those of your other three victims in a shoebox under his bed along with surveillance logs." Sam knew there wasn't a box under Taylor's bed when he'd broken in. "What I don't know is what I'm going to do about your impeding an investigation. Did you even once consider that if you had voiced your suspicions about Taylor, he'd still be alive and one of my best officers wouldn't have been shot? Furthermore, your hot-headed shooting into a crowd of people could have gotten more people killed. Did you ever consider you could have missed his arrogant ass?"

"I didn't miss, did I?" Sam said, wanting to tell him they both knew who the ass was in the room, but also wanting to get to the hospital, he let it go. "How did you find out about Taylor?"

"Doing our job, his fingerprints were on one of the needles he used to kill Michelle. Sloppy."

"I'm sorry he got killed," Sam said, genuinely remorseful, "But I can tell you that evidence in his house was planted and your serial killer is still out there."

"And I think you're full of shit. Now get out of here, but the next time you interfere with a police investigation, I'm going to throw your ass in jail and lose the key."

◆◆◆

Finding Elyse and Maddy in the surgery waiting room, Sam hugged them both. "How's he doing?" he asked.

"They just took him back. The doctor said the bullet barely missed his femoral artery. He would have bled out in minutes if it had, but it didn't, so he should be fine," Elyse said.

"The surgery may take a couple of hours, Sam," Maddy said. "Elyse and I will stay until he's out of recovery. Why don't you go home--get some rest, you're still recovering from your accident. I'll call as soon as he's out of surgery, and we won't be able to see him tonight anyway."

"I'm not going anywhere, it's my fault he's here in the first place," Sam said.

"No, it isn't," Elyse said. "It's mine. If I hadn't told him you were at the Congress, he never would have been there."

"There's no sense blaming each other," Maddy said. "What's done is done."

"She's right," Sam said.

"Why don't I get us something to eat? I bet neither one of you has eaten since this morning," Maddy offered.

"You two go," Elyse said. "I won't be able to eat anything anyway and I'll be here if there's any news about Andy."

Unable to convince Elyse to leave, Sam and Maddy found a Steak and Shake near the hospital and ordered food neither one of them wanted to eat. Sitting in the corner of the empty restaurant, Maddy pushed around her food, while Sam, finding his appetite, ate his hamburger and fries.

"Why did they take you to station?" Maddy asked.

"To bust my balls about withholding the fact I considered Taylor a suspect in Michelle's murder."

"What would they have done if you had voiced your suspicion?"

"My thoughts exactly, but I didn't want to spend the night, so I kept my mouth shut." "For once," Maddy laughed.

"Why were you at the hotel?" Sam asked, taking a drink of soda.

"Earlier in the car, you told me you were going. I thought I'd give you a hand finding Taylor. I didn't know Veronica would be with you," Maddy said, an air of coldness in her voice. "I was going to confront her, but Elyse stopped me, and when we saw Andy running towards the front of the building, we followed him, then he got shot. We got to him, tried to stop the bleeding and while Elyse called for an ambulance, I went to the front hoping to find someone who could help and to direct the EMTs when they arrived. That's when I saw Taylor fall and hit the stairway." She shivered.

"What about Ronnie?"

"What about her?" Maddy asked.

"I didn't see her after I ran out after Taylor. Where did she go?"

"I lost her in the crowd," Maddy said. "I guess she went home."

Returning to the waiting room, Sam and Maddy saw Elyse talking to the surgeon. They waited as the two finished and Elyse came over to fill them in. "The doctor said the surgery went well," Elyse said, as they all breathed a sigh of relief. "He's going to be in intensive care overnight and then they'll move him to a room sometime tomorrow."

"What about his leg? Will it completely heal?" Maddy asked.

"He'll need some physical therapy," Elyse answered.

"The only physical therapy Andy believes in is running," Sam said, "And if I know Andy, he'll be up and running before the stitches come out."

CHAPTER 20

Walking into his office after spending the morning in court and visiting with Andy at the hospital, Sam handed Elyse a Subway Chicken Teriyaki sandwich and an iced tea.

"My turn to treat," he said.

"Thanks," Elyse said, digging into the sandwich. "You're in a good mood. I guess Andy's doing well."

"Yes. He's already asking when he can come home," Sam answered, unwrapping his roast beef.

"Does he need anything? I can stop by his house on my way to the hospital after work if he does."

"Why don't you give him a call," Sam said, looking at her computer screen. "What're you working on?"

"I went through the bills this morning and paid what was due. The last two days have been so chaotic with Andy getting shot, and the Richards case has been taking up so much of our time...but now that the case is over, we can get back to being a detective agency again." She stopped mid-bite. "Sam...it's over, right?"

"Well..."

"I know," Elyse said, not letting him finish. "You're not convinced Dylan was the killer. What will it take to convince you? Let it go, for your sake and mine. After lunch, I'm going to attack that pile of mail sitting there," Elyse said, pointing to the tray stamped 'in-box' that was sitting on the corner of her desk.

"I have more," Sam said, pulling an envelope and a small package from his pocket and dropping them on the pile. "I stopped by the box on the way in."

"Thanks," Elyse said caustically. "Feel free to give me a hand."

Picking up the tray and heading to his office, Sam stopped at the doorway and turned back to Elyse. "Something's nagging me about Jason's death and until I figure out what it is, I'm not going to be able to let it go." Going into his office and sitting in his chair he turned the tray over, picking up the letter on top. "First in, first out," he said, grabbing his letter opener.

Reaching the bottom of the pile and the small package he'd picked up from the mailbox today, he could tell through the envelope it was a flash drive. He didn't recognize the return address, but he did catch the Attn: Elyse Carter he'd missed earlier. Needing to stretch his legs, he left his office just as Elyse was asking the hospital operator to put her through to Andy's room. As she waited on hold, Sam pulled the drive from the envelope and waved it in front of her. Elyse motioned for him to wait as she listened to the nurse on the other end of the connection.

"I'll wait," she said into the phone. "Andy's getting his blood pressure checked, it'll be a minute," she said to Sam. "That's the video I asked for from the dog park surveillance camera behind Michelle's apartment building. Guess we don't need it now."

Just then, Andy came on the line. Sam went back into his office, letting them talk, hearing Elyse's laughter as he sat back down. After a few minutes he heard her repeat the list of things Andy asked her to bring to the hospital for him. Taking the drive out of the case, he slid it into his computer, watching as the grainy videotape started up. The camera was mounted on a pole across from the back of Michelle's apartment building, but it was aimed to videotape activity in the park, catching the hotel's exit was accidental. Residents could be seen entering and exiting, but only on a small portion of the screen. Determined to do it on his own, Sam navigated the photo options until he had the doorway centered on the screen and a grainy, but passable picture of the people coming and going.

Working off the coroner's estimated time of death, Sam skipped to nine o'clock and skimmed through hours of footage, slowing down every time the door opened, mostly as employees came out back for smoking breaks. As one-thirty came up on the clock, Sam saw a figure exit the building. He rewound, watched again tinkering with the focus. He paused the frame, blew it up.

"Gotcha." Sam pushed the print button and waited as the printer slowly slid out a full-page picture of Nick.

Coming into Sam's office, Elyse spotted the picture and look in his eyes. "You don't need to do this. You're not going Sam!" Elyse cried, blocking the door with her body. "Call the police, or I will."

"No, you won't," Sam said, stepping back. "I've been trying to get hold of Nick on his cell, but he isn't answering, so I'm going to the clinic. If you don't hear from me in an hour, then you can call the police."

"Let me go with you! I'll wait outside, but at least I'll be able to help."

"You're more helpful here. Go through the tapes of the front and back doors again. I didn't see Nick go in, so he must've gone through the front. Find out when." Sam put his arms on her shoulders. "Don't worry, I'll be fine."

Pulling into the empty parking lot at the clinic, Sam's training took control over his emotional impulse to go running half-cocked into the building. He drove around to the back and found two cars there, one of which was Nick's. He went up to the back entrance where a sign declaring FOR EMPLOYEES ONLY was posted on the door. Expecting to need his lockpicks, Sam was surprised to find the door unlocked. Hoping he still had the element of surprise, he opened the door onto the hallway leading to both Holloway's and Nick's offices. Quietly stepping inside, he headed towards Nick's office, his footsteps seeming to thunder in the silence.

Reaching Nick's office door, he found it half-open. He kicked it all the way, making sure no one was behind it. Satisfied, he stepped into the room, a quick scan showing it was empty, a second look revealing a hand on the floor sticking out from behind the desk. Rushing to Nick's side, Sam spotted blood on his temple, and checked for a pulse. He found one, weak but steady. He reached for his phone but sensing movement from behind him, he turned. Sam saw the taser aimed at him but couldn't get out of the way fast enough.

◆◆◆

Checking the clock for the hundredth time, Elyse wasn't surprised only two minutes had passed since the last time she'd glanced at it. Resisting the urge to call Sam, she turned her attention back to the apartment footage on her computer, not expecting to find anything new--she had watched it thirty times. No sign of Nick in the hour before Dylan showed up around nine or in the intervening hours before he exited shortly after midnight. Watching Dylan as he slowly walked toward his car and out of the frame, the same thought crossed her mind that had crossed it every time before. She rewound and watched again as Dylan shook his head and rubbed the back of his neck as if he'd just woke up from a nap and had slept wrong, had a crick. Sam had noticed it too and she knew it was part of what had been nagging him. These were more the actions of someone who'd been hit on the head and stuffed in a closet in order to take the fall for the murder that was happening three floors above.

Thirty minutes later and several times through the footage, Elyse hadn't seen Nick enter the front. Thinking Sam had missed him enter from the back, she went into his office where the screen was still filled with the picture of Nick. She scanned back through four hours of footage, never seeing Nick. "If you didn't enter by the front or the back, how the hell did you get in?" She started over, going all the way back, stopping at someone entering at eight forty-five, fifteen minutes before Dylan. All she could see was his back, a man dressed in an overcoat with a hat. Nothing useful there. She forwarded, finding the spot where Nick came out, no hat now, but he still wore the overcoat. Then she saw the sharper edges around Nick's face and neck, barely noticeable, especially with the poor quality of the picture, but she caught it...it was edited. Praying she could get the picture underneath, she began working her magic. Minutes later, she had it. "Oh my God!" she screamed at the screen, grabbing her phone from the desk to warn Sam, dropping it in her panic. His phone went straight to voicemail. She ran out of the office, grabbing the only weapon she could find--the pry bar from the storage closet.

The first thing Sam became aware of as he woke up was that he was naked from the waist up and barefooted. His head was pounding, and his hands were numb, tied behind his back. Sam felt a noose around his neck, the rope looped on a steel hook screwed into the ceiling. It was slack, but tight enough to rub his neck raw as he twisted and turned to find out where he was. The end of the rope was wrapped around a hook in the wall to his left. A spotlight was directed on him, he couldn't see past the light, but he could sense someone moving in the shadows. He struggled against the ropes tying his hands, but his efforts were rewarded with the tightening of his bindings and the skin chaffed from his wrists. He heard the scuffling of a chair being dragged to the edge of the circle of light.

"The more you struggle, the tighter it gets," Edward said.

Sam screamed. "HELP! Someone help me!"

"Also, futile, detective," Edward said, sitting down in the chair and placing the gun he'd found in Sam's jacket on his lap. "This room is soundproof."

"Where am I?" Sam asked.

"My office. To be more specific, a room behind the bookcase in my office. No one knows about this room--not even Nick--so don't get the idea he'll save you, even if he does wake up from the drug and the love tap I gave him." Edward rose from the chair and grabbing the rope from the wall he pulled it, yanking Sam into a standing position, the noose cutting off his air. "Since you have such an interest in autoerotic asphyxiation, I thought you should experience it for yourself. Of course, you won't get the sexual gratification, but you can't have everything."

"Why..." was all Sam could get out as the room began to go black around the edges.

Edward let the rope go slack, stepped back into the darkness and turned off the spotlight. Behind him was a desk with three TV screens and a keyboard in front of them. The middle screen showed Holloway's office, the one to the right was split into four smaller screens, each showing a different aspect of the clinic, inside and out. On the third screen, Sam saw himself, as the camera set up directly in front of him was catching every moment.

"You tell me why, detective. Why did you come here alone when you could have called the police?"

"Who said I'm alone?"

"Your secretary or that has-been cop is going to save you?" Edward scoffed. "I don't think so."

"She knows I'm here. And the police know all about you," Sam lied, as he spotted Elyse's car on the security camera behind Holloway pulling into the parking lot. He watched as she came to the front door. Then his view of the camera was blocked as Edward pounced on him.

"They don't know shit!" Edward screamed. He grabbed the rope again, strangling Sam. He looped it back over the hook, keeping it taut and Sam gasping for every breath. For the next twenty minutes, Edward pounded Sam, in a rage he obviously couldn't control. Sam, barely able to draw breath, twisted as best he could out of range, but couldn't get far, then desperately curling inward taking the blows on his sides and back. Finally, spent, Edward stepped back, his hands dripping with Sam's blood. He looked at them, his breaths as labored as Sam's. He let the rope go slack, enough to ease the burning in Sam's chest, then sat back down in the chair, staring at his captive.

Banging on the front door to the clinic, Elyse screamed for help, her cries unanswered. Running around to the back she saw Sam's car and desperately pounded on the back door. Suddenly the door swung open and Nick stood before her, his hand cupped to his head.

"Ellie?" recognizing her from the therapy session. "What are you doing here?" Nick's speech was slurred as he staggered on his feet and fell into the doorframe.

"Elyse. I'm Sam's assistant. What happened to you?" Elyse asked, helping him stand.

"I don't know. The last thing I remember was sitting at my desk," Nick said trying to shake the cobwebs from his mind. "Then I heard you banging on the back door."

"Sam's here somewhere," Elyse said, rushing past him into the hallway. "And if we don't find him, Holloway is going to kill him. Where's his office?"

"Last door on the left," Nick replied, following, using the wall as support. The door to Holloway's office was closed but unlocked. Elyse entered, automatically reaching for the light switch, then realized the light was already on. The room was empty, the open laptop sitting on the desk drawing her attention.

"He's not here," Nick said behind her. "He must've already left for the day."

"His car is still here," Elyse said, walking over to the desk. Praying Holloway had left it on, she hit the enter key, the screen saver disappeared, and Holloway's computer jumped to life.

"I don't think you should be doing that," Nick said, coming closer to the desk.

"Where is this room?" Elyse asked, panic in her voice as she turned the computer so Nick could see.

"What are you talking..." Nick stopped, staring at the screen. "There's no room like that here."

"It has to be here!" Elyse cried, watching as Edward beat Sam. She looked around the room, desperation and panic starting to crawl up her spine. Then she spotted it, a camera above the bookcase. Checking the screen, she realized it must be wired so Holloway could see into his office, make sure it was clear for him to come in from behind the bookcase. "The bookcase!" she screamed at Nick. "It has to behind the bookcase."

"You know why you came alone, Sam, may I call you Sam?" Edward asked, his outburst seemingly forgotten. "You came because you couldn't stop yourself. Just like everyone else you think I killed. I simply provided them the opportunity to choose their own fate. If Arnold hadn't used that gag I sent him, he wouldn't have died. If Lindsay hadn't stuck those electrodes on herself and turned the juice on, she wouldn't have either. So, if you think about it, it's their own fault. I was just saving them a lot of time and money, not to mention the heartache to their families. I wish someone had been so kind to me. Hutchins was going to be arrested for child pornography, he was right where you are now and told me so. Yes, I use this room for extreme punishment, but they ask for it, it's their choice. And when it doesn't work, what choice do I have."

Spotting Elyse and Nick on the screen, Sam knew he had to keep Holloway from turning around and seeing them for himself. "What about Michelle or Jason? It wasn't their choice..."

"Jason? You're so fucked-up you can't see what's in front of you. Michelle gave up the needles. A contingency I hadn't planned on, but watching her die was exhilarating and I must confess I got a rager." Sam pulled on his ropes again, his blood making the ropes slippery. He felt the rope slide toward his thumbs and stop. He knew one more hard tug would free them. Holloway got up from the chair, started for the desk.

"What did you mean you wished someone had been so kind to you?" Sam was desperate to keep him from turning around. "Are you talking about your mother?" Hitting a nerve, Holloway turned back to Sam.

"My mother was an alcoholic whore who put my father in an early grave and then replaced him with anyone who would pay for it and so many more who didn't. When I was twelve, she added me to the menu."

"She died in a fire when you were fifteen, right? I'm guessing you had something to do with that?"

"I see you've done your homework, but I've had enough reminiscing." Using both hands, he pulled the rope, hoisting Sam an inch off the floor. "No more games."

Outside the room, Nick had given up trying to find the opening to the bookcase with the pry bar Elyse had brought and was on the phone to the police. Elyse was certain the bookcase had an electronic opener somewhere on the keyboard and was doing her best to concentrate on finding it and not watch what was happening to Sam fifty feet from where she sat. Finally, hitting the right key, the bookcase slid open. She grabbed the only weapons she could find, a letter opener and a heavy round paperweight.

His time and breath running out, Sam used his last burst of air and strength to pull his hands free of the ropes holding them, tearing off skin as he pulled. He flailed at the rope around his neck, hooking his thumb under the noose and loosening it enough for a trickle of air to get through. He saw Elyse enter the room and throw a heavy round sphere at Edward's head. It hit him above the ear, drawing blood. He turned, surprise and pain crossing his face. Grabbing Sam's gun from the chair, he fired. Elyse screamed and fell to the floor. Sam unwound the rope from the wall and now free, he jumped Edward, hitting him with everything he had left and as he caught a glimpse of Elyse's lifeless body, he put his hands around Edward's neck and squeezed as hard as he could.

"Stop! You're killing him, Sam," he heard Nick faintly as he Nick pull him off Edward.

He fell away, scooting to Elyse's side. Then the police and EMTs arrived and darkness overcame him.

CHAPTER 21

"The bullet wound on her arm needed a couple stitches," the same
ER doctor who'd treated him three nights earlier told Sam. "But
when she fell, she hit her head and she has an impressive goose
egg. I'm going to admit her for observation, and if all goes well, we'll release
her in the morning. You can see her, but only for a few minutes."

"Thank you Dr...I'm sorry, I don't remember your name," Sam apologized.

"Douglas," the doctor said, laughing. "and I'm not surprised. You were in a
lot of pain when you came in and then on some pretty strong meds. I see you
ignored my instructions to take a few days off and rest." He pointed at Sam's
neck. "Those neck wounds are fresh and they could become infected. Would
you like to tell me what happened? Elyse is claiming she can't remember
anything."

"My memory's kinda vague on the whole thing, too," Sam said. "I'm going
to check in on Elyse and then go home, get that rest you suggested."

"Somehow I don't believe that's going to happen. I'll bring you some salve,
and make sure you keep taking the antibiotic I prescribed until it's gone."

"Sure thing," Sam said, trying to remember the last time he'd taken a dose.

"Oh, and detective," Dr. Douglas said on his way out of the waiting room,
"You might want to consider getting into a different line of work."

"At this point, I tend to agree with you."

◆ ◆ ◆

Entering the room, Sam watched Elyse silently for a few moments as she
napped, blaming himself for her injuries and thankful they weren't more
serious. As he approached, she woke and looking up at him she said, "You're
okay." She smiled and reaching out from under the covers, she took his hand

168

to confirm for herself he was there. "I thought Holloway was going to kill you."

"He would've if it wasn't for you," Sam said, bending down and hugging her. "I didn't do anything but get myself shot and a headache. Tell me what happened after I was knocked out."

"He can fill you in tomorrow," Andy said from the doorway. "You need to get some rest and Sam needs to get home to his own bed." He hobbled to Elyse's bedside on a pair of crutches and inspected the dressing on her arm. "Sam tells me you throw a wicked fastball. You're full of surprises." Andy sat down with a grunt in the chair next to the bed. Sam watched them, two of the people he cared about the most in the world hurting because of him.

Catching sight of his expression, Elyse reached out her hand to him and waited until he took it in his. "I know that look. You think this is all your fault, and it isn't. Blame Holloway and be glad you caught the crazy bastard before he killed anyone else."

"She's right, Sam," Andy chimed in. "We're both going to be fine. We'll be released tomorrow and then we can stamp closed on this whole damn case."

"And there'll be one more ghost haunting the halls of The Congress," Elyse chimed in.

"I hate to break this up," Douglas was back. "But if you stay much longer Sam, I'm going to throw you into that empty bed over there. Here's something for your neck," he said, handing Sam an ointment. "Now you two gentlemen get out of here."

Standing in front of the mirror above his bathroom sink the next morning, Sam stared at his reflection in the mirror, the deep red rope marks around his neck now blooming with dark blues as the bruising appeared. His wrists were skinned, his hands tender and the rest of his body sore from the beating he had endured during Holloway's tantrum. He opened the medicine cabinet and fished out three Percocet from the bottle, washing them down with a handful of water from the tap. Walking to his closet, telling himself he'd feel better if he got moving, he pulled a pair of jeans and a shirt from their hangers, throwing them on the bed. Planning on working a half day so he could pick Elyse and Andy up from the hospital, he pulled his jeans on and sat down on the bed. Four hours later he woke up.

Waking up from his unplanned nap, Sam called Andy, surprised to learn he was still at the hospital.

"The nurse said she'd be right back with my release papers," Andy said, disgusted. "That was an hour ago."

"Is Elyse there too?"

"Yes, but she's just waiting around to take me home. One of the guys from the precinct brought my car over a couple days ago, but the doctor doesn't want me driving yet. I told Elyse I'm fully capable of getting myself home, but you know how she is."

"Yes, I do," Sam replied, visualizing Elyse shaking her head at Andy and smiling to himself at the two of them. Then he heard shuffling noises as the phone changed hands.

"How are you feeling?" Elyse asked.

"Good enough to come get you two."

"No, I've got it covered here. If that nurse doesn't show up in the next five minutes, there's going to be hell to pay. You stay home."

Sam fully intended to do just that, until after a quick bite of lunch, he began feeling guilty about the mess Elyse, with her wounded wing would be walking into, and decided to spend the afternoon at the office catching up things for her.

Arriving twenty minutes later to his uncharacteristically silent office, Sam sat down at his desk, deciding where to start. Jason's laptop was in front of him, open and running as Elyse had left it in her rush to get to the clinic, to him. Shutting the lid, he set the laptop aside and pulled the lockbox over. The lid, skewed from his prying it open, wouldn't close. He picked it up emptying the contents onto the desk and tapped the side of the box on the desk, hoping to square it up. He heard a ping as something tiny and metal hit the floor. Hoping he hadn't busted the hinge, he bent down under the desk and picked it up, rubbing it against his thumb and forefinger. His phone rang.

"Ronnie. How nice of you to call," Sam said sarcastically.

"Don't be rude. There wasn't anything I could do for Andy at the hotel and I thought it was in everyone's best interest for me to disappear."

"Including yours. Why are you calling now?" Sam asked.

"To tell you congrats on catching Holloway. I heard you had your own experience into the deep dark world of kink. I hope it didn't dissuade you from the practice."

"Not any more than I was before."

"You know, Sam, I could show you the better side of kink."

"I know that you left the hotel to avoid a confrontation with Maddy, and that your dominatrix persona is all an act."

"Let that be our little secret, Sam." Ronnie ended the call.

"We knew you'd be here," Elyse said from the doorway and as she came around the desk to give him a gentle hug, Sam slipped the metal into his pocket and hugged her back.

"What are you two doing here?" Sam asked.

"Keeping you from staying her too long and overdoing it."

"I haven't even been here an hour," Sam said, gathering Jason's things.

"There's a couple questions that have been bothering me about Holloway," Elyse said.

"What things?" Sam asked.

"Why did Holloway drug Nick and how did he know you'd figure out he was the killer?"

"He drugged Nick because he was going to torch the clinic and kill him in the fire. I showed up before he could. He planted that evidence at Taylor's house and was hoping the police would blame Nick when Maddy found the fake I.D. and credit cards in his desk."

"He got away with killing his mother in a fire. I guess you use what works," Elyse said.

"You went over to the clinic to protect Nick?" Andy asked.

"Yes, I tried to call to warn him several times, but he wasn't picking up his phone. When I finally got the picture from the dog park to focus, I recognized Holloway's jacket Elyse was so excited about the other night at the clinic, even without the liquid bandage spot you put on it," grinning at Elyse. "I realized he must have been setting Nick up, but by the time I got to the clinic, Holloway had already drugged Nick and you know the rest."

"Now that we've cleared that up, let me take you home and then drag my own sorry ass home," Andy said.

"You should go home, too," Elyse said to Sam.

"I will, after I stop over at Maddy's and officially close this case," Sam said, with a note of finality. "But before you go home Elyse, would you do something for me?"

"Sure," Elyse said. "What do you need me to do?"

"I was hoping you'd take the day off after what happened to you yesterday," Maddy said as she opened her front door for him. "I hope you feel better than you look, because you look like hell." She stepped aside to let him pass.

"I wanted to return Jason's things," Sam said, placing Jason's laptop and lockbox down next to her purse on the table in the foyer. "I still have his phone, but I'll mail it back to you."

"Come sit in the living room and I'll get us something to drink." Maddy went behind the bar.

"Are you going somewhere?" Sam asked, sitting down on the couch and watching her mix their drinks. "I saw some tickets next to your purse."

"Nick and I have decided to go on a cruise. Get away for a week or so.

Hopefully things will have settled down some by the time we get back."
Maddy came around the bar, walked over to Sam and handed him his drink.
"How about the affair he had with Lindsay?" Sam asked.

"We've both done some things," she gave him a long stare. "I'm hoping we
can get past them." Maddy sat across from him, sipping her own drink. "I
don't know how to thank you for all you've done," she said, detached. "I
know you won't let me pay you, but at the very least, I can pay the medical
expenses I've caused. How are Elyse and Andy?"

"They're going to be fine," Sam replied. Maddy nodded her response and the
conversation lagged as she sipped her drink and Sam searched for something
to say.

Finishing her drink, Maddy got up and said, "I don't mean to rush you, but I
do have some packing to do and you should probably be home in bed."

Placing his glass on the coffee table, Sam fished into his front pants pocket
and pulled out a small key designed to fit onto a bracelet. "This belongs to
you," he said, holding it up to her.

"That isn't mine," Maddy denied, skirting around the bar and pouring herself
another drink, not asking Sam if he wanted another.

"It's from a bracelet I bought for you when we went to the Titanic exhibit,
years ago? I'm sure you remember it. It has five charms; a boarding pass,
captain's hat, ship's steering wheel, the heart of the ocean jewel, and this," he
rubbed the key, "a miniature room key."

"I remember you giving me the bracelet, but I lost that charm months ago,"
Maddy said, nonplussed.

"No, I don't think you did. I found it in Jason's lockbox."

"It must've fallen off at his apartment. No offense, Sam, but it was a cheap
bracelet. Jason probably found it, put it in his lockbox and forgot to tell me
he'd found it," walking over to him, she took the key from his hand. "Thank
you for returning it, but you'd better get going. Nick will be home soon."

Sam's phone buzzed. It was Elyse. "I've checked the phone," Elyse's voice
was barely a whisper. "You were right." Sam held the phone away from his
ear, watching Maddy as she paced the room. "Sam...what do you want me to
do now?"

"Go home and get some rest." Sam put his phone away.

"You'd better leave, Sam, you're looking pale," Maddy said, coming to his
side and taking his arm.

"I know you killed him," Sam said, removing her hand.

"What are you talking about?"

"Jason. I know you killed him. Something Sargent Billings said when he was
telling me about the pictures that were planted at Taylor's house. It just kept
nagging at the back of my brain. He said there were pictures of all four
victims. Four victims. But there were five...Lindsey, Arnold, Hutchins,
Michelle, and your brother. Why wasn't Jason's picture in that box, Maddy?"

"That's crazy! You're basing this insane accusation on that. Why would I kill my brother?"

"Because you didn't want Jason marrying Ronnie and you knew he would if she was pregnant. You can't let a woman like Ronnie join the family. What would it do to your father's good name, a dominatrix raising his grandchild? You thought it was over between them when they broke up and Ronnie took the money, but you stopped by Jason's apartment that night and saw her car parked out front. When you thought they were back together, you lost it, didn't you? You went into Jason's apartment, found him putting the lockbox under the floorboards and tased him. I'd like to believe what happened next was an accident, that you wanted him to wake up with a noose around his neck, hands tied behind his back and not remember how he'd gotten that way. Maybe blame Ronnie and tell her it was over. I'd like to believe you had the taser set that high by accident and didn't mean to put the noose on so tight. I'd like to believe it, but I don't. I know too much about obsessions and what horrible things they can lead you to do if you let them," Sam spat the words at her.

Maddy walked over to the couch, sat down and leaned back into the cushions. She looked up at him all trace of the Maddy he once knew gone. "Prove it," she said. She met his gaze and held it, challenging him.

"The phone message," Sam stared back at her. "Elyse traced the time and place you erased it. You erased it at six the morning of Jason's death, right here in this house. How could you erase that message hours before you found the body? I think you picked up Jason's phone just like you said, but it was after you killed him, not when you reported his death."

"What are you going to do?" Maddy asked, the faintest bit of concern only Sam could've picked up in her voice.

"Nothing. You were wearing the bracelet when you went in Jason's apartment, for the kids you visited at the hospital earlier. That charm fell off when you opened the lockbox. I wondered why you weren't interested in what was inside it when I found it; it's because you already knew what was inside. But I can't prove that, and a good lawyer would get any phone evidence thrown out," Sam said, kneeling in front of her and taking her hands. "I know that Jason was the last person on this earth you would ever harm and the fact that you killed him tells me how truly messed up you are. You need help and when you accept what you've done and are still doing to protect your dead father's name, you'll realize that you killed Jason for nothing."

"I did what I had to do," a lone tear sliding down her face. "But it doesn't have to end this way. I can leave Nick; we can be together. I know you still love me."

"God help me, I do, but not like before. We were never good for each other, Maddy and I've found someone who is, if I can ever give her the chance. No, you stay here with Nick, you two deserve each other. There'll be some publicity around the clinic for a while and I know how much you hate that, but this too will pass. Knowing Nick, the publicity will probably triple his business."

"Are you going to tell him?"

"No, all I ask is that you leave me and the agency alone." Sam headed towards the foyer, then stopped and turned back to her. "The case was closed, Maddy, you got away with Jason's murder. Why call me at all?" Sam paused, letting the final pieces of the puzzle fall into place. "Andy was right, you wanted me to get the police to reopen the case with Nick as their number one suspect. You would have Jason and Nick out of the way. Sorry to disappoint." Sam turned to leave, meeting Nick at the door. Sam nodded at Nick and shut the door behind him on his way out.

Backing out of Maddy's driveway, Sam's cell phone buzzed. Stopping at the end of the long drive, he answered, "Elyse, I thought you were going home to rest."

"I was, but on my way out, my computer pinged. You know what that means."

"That another robbery has been committed with the same MO as the one at your bank. I'll look at it in the morning." He reached to turn the phone off.

"Sam, the robbery is still going on and it's just two blocks from you."

"On it," Sam said.